FRIEND. FOLLOW. TEXT.

Friend. *Follow*. Text.

#storiesFromLivingOnline

Edited by **Shawn Syms**

ENFIELD
&WIZENTY

Enfield & Wizenty
(An imprint of Great Plains Publications)
345-955 Portage Avenue
Winnipeg, MB R3G 0P9
www.greatplains.mb.ca

Great Plains Publications gratefully acknowledges the financial support provided
for its publishing program by the Government of Canada through the Canada Book
Fund; the Canada Council for the Arts; the Province of Manitoba through the Book
Publishing Tax Credit and the Book Publisher Marketing Assistance Program; and the
Manitoba Arts Council.

Design & Typography by Relish New Brand Experience
Printed in Canada by Friesens

Library and Archives Canada Cataloguing in Publication
        Friend.follow.text : #storiesFromLivingOnline / edited by Shawn Syms.

Short stories.
Issued in print and electronic formats.
ISBN 978-1-926531-80-9 (pbk.).--ISBN 978-1-926531-81-6 (epub).--
ISBN 97-8-1926531-82-3 (mobi)

    1. Short stories, Canadian (English). 2. Canadian fiction (English)--21st
century. 3. Social media--Fiction. I. Syms, Shawn, 1970-, editor of compilation

PS8323.S53F75 2013   C813'.0108356   C2013-904466-3

                                                    C2013-904467-1

Contents

Introduction

One of the first pieces of short fiction to explore the usage of online communication was E.M. Forster's "The Machine Stops." In this story, Vashti and her son Kuno speak to one another face-to-face from across a vast distance. The device Vashti holds in her hand is not dissimilar to an iPad, and the conversation she and Kuno have resembles the sort that might take place using an app like FaceTime or Skype.

To focus on their chat, Vashti touches her isolation knob so others can't reach her, not unlike the Invisible setting in a program such as Yahoo Messenger. Vashti rarely travels; she stays in her room and the information she needs is drawn to her at her command over a vast interconnected system called the Machine. Sound like the Internet? But the Machine isn't perfect; it generally fails to "transmit nuances of expression" – a potential pitfall familiar to anyone who's ever used e-mail. "The Machine Stops" was first published in 1909.

The ways we live online are no longer simply fodder for science-fiction tales – and we've come a long way since the early days of text-based web browsers and rudimentary chat programs like ICQ. Today people use smartphones and tablets and apps to buy their furniture, reschedule flights en route to the airport, read and exchange views about the verdicts of murder trials in real time while sitting on public transportation, share information on political uprisings in faraway nations, meet their mates, keep tabs on their kids. Technology, social media and online communication have changed the way we live our lives – and the way we write about them.

More and more authors are incorporating Twitter and Facebook and eBay and Pinterest into their fictional explorations of the worlds they live in. Recognizing the role of social media in our lives has opened up exciting options for fiction in terms of both content and formal innovation. The twenty-seven pieces of writing brought together in *Friend. Follow. Text.* offer a panoramic view of these possibilities. You'll read award-winning, long-time authors and fantastic folks being published for the first time in these pages. Whether you're holding a book in your hand or sampling these stories on your device of choice, you'll enjoy a blend of traditional narratives with some truly experimental pieces. And most of all, I hope you'll see something of your own world reflected in these stories from living online. And enjoy some laughs – and maybe even shed a tear or two – along the way.

Is the digital realm a technology-driven paradise? Perhaps not. All the time, I hear about rude or facile conduct exhibited on Facebook, for example. I usually read about it on Facebook, in fact. The authors of *Friend. Follow. Text.* steer their craft toward all kinds of behaviours facilitated by online modes of communication – the good, the bad and the ugly.

Forster's "The Machine Stops" was a dystopian, cautionary tale about a world in which people become alienated and withdrawn, languishing in their personal chambers, anxious about direct contact with others. Is this really what we have to look forward to as our use of social media continues to evolve? I hope not. And I don't think so. After all, similar concerns were once raised about the potential antisocial impact of the widespread availability of the telephone. As you'll see in the stories that follow in these pages, ultimately social media are tools for bringing people together – in all of our complicated beauty as well as our glorious imperfections.

We friend. We follow. We text. Above all, we connect.

Shawn Syms
July 2013

IMHO
by Marcy Rogers

Although Jude had never met Scott he knew everything there was to know about him. He knew that Scott was a twenty-five-year-old model/actor who grew up in the Midwest but was now working and living the dream in Los Angeles.

Scott was single because he was looking for a real man, real as in keeping it, not as in working on the Alaska Pipeline.

He was spiritual. His status updates were usually quotes from Kahlil Gibran, Rumi or a plethora of people with eight-syllable names.

Scott loved animals and joined every Stop Animal Cruelty site he could find. And he had a chocolate brown Chihuahua called Baby Snoots that he dressed from head to toe in replicas of vintage Bob Mackie.

Scott also loved Gaga, The Cure, Helen Reddy, dim sum, Kir Royales, morning dew, skeet shooting, Fred Astaire, Clive Owen, his grandmother and Mother Teresa. Scott disliked h8ters, corduroy, Rob Zombie, Kid Rock, Kanye West, oxtail, domestic beer, lacrosse, fog, the Pope and his mother.

Scott read whenever he had the time.

Jude knew Scott inside and out and he loathed him. So much so in fact that he had decided to unfriend him with a bullet to the head.

The decision to kill Scott was not an impulsive one. It had evolved over time from a feeling of irritation to the embarkation of a heroic quest. A quest in which Jude would slay the... sometimes he wished that Scott would take up drag so he could say he was off to slay the drag queen. But while some of his best friends wore dresses, Scott himself preferred tight jeans.

Jude liked to imagine Scott's jeans getting tighter and tighter until he was squeezed right out of them like ground-beef toothpaste from a tube.

Just seeing Scott's head-shot profile pic was enough to make Jude's blood boil. Reading his comments only made it worse.

He had considered unfriending him in the traditional way but it was far too late for that now. He should have taken that option when Scott had belittled his love of Maugham.

But he hadn't of course because while he couldn't understand it, he knew that Somerset Maugham was not everyone's cup of tea. Neither was Haydn's *Seven Last Words of Christ* sung with a *basso profondo* choir or Japanese punk bands or Lenny Bruce, Doris Day, Fritz Lang, Beany and Cecil or Habitant pea soup...

It had taken Jude almost a year before he realized that Scott was a flaming asshole. It had taken him another to realize that he detested Scott and finally a third to conclude that until that evil son of a prick was dead he would be completely unable to enjoy his social network.

The thought of shooting Scott in the head did not bother Jude at all. It bothered him far more to think that he had ever liked him in the first place. But then that was before the thing that finally pushed Jude over the edge, the proverbial final straw.

It is hard to know what will finally break a person. The switch that shuts off the electric fence that keeps his Tyrannosaurus Rex locked in. For Jude it was James Dean.

Looking back he should have known he was tempting fate by posting the milk-bottle clip from *Rebel Without a Cause*, the one where Dean rubs the milk bottle across his forehead, with the comment that James Dean's performances are so real, because in less than two seconds Scott posted that IHO Dean was about as real as Tom Cruise's marriage to Katie Holmes. And to make it even worse the comment started with "Are you fucking kidding me?!!!!"

Jude should have known, but he had forgotten. He'd been in a good mood and just wanted to share something he loved and then Scott came along and pissed all over it.

From that moment on every time Jude read or saw a comment of Scott's he imagined himself putting the cold steel muzzle against Scott's lips and pulling the trigger.

But it was all good now, in just ten minutes Jude would no longer have to imagine and neither would his friends – because he was going to film it with his iPhone and post it on YouTube. He could hardly wait to read the comments.

And Also Sharks
by Jessica Westhead

Oh my God Janet, you are so brave. Your bravery astounds me. Because you lay yourself bare for the world when you put your feelings out there to be known. But just basically because your words touch so many people, and there are so many of us who are suffering from the self-esteem issues that affect our very lives. So I guess what I'm saying here is that you are doing something extremely BRAVE.

Plus that recipe you shared on your last post for the ham casserole with white sauce is AMAZING! I made it the other day and it was so easy, exactly like you said it would be, and I was supposed to have my brother and his wife over for dinner and that was what I was going to serve, and they were going to bring a salad which I think was going to be a macaroni salad. But then they called at the last minute and said they couldn't make it because her pregnancy was acting up, which I guess you have to understand, pregnancies being the way they are.

But anyway, the casserole. You said it would nourish the soul, the making part and the eating part, and like you always are, you were right. Last week I did the exercise you suggested where you cut out pictures from magazines that appeal to you, and paste them onto a piece of paper to make a collage which represents how you want your life to be, but all I had at home were a bunch of *Reader's Digests* and an old copy of *National*

Geographic which was the Shark Issue, so my collage ended up being about this family that got trapped by an avalanche and also sharks.

So after I got that very disappointing call from my brother, I reframed the situation like you say to do, like how you can make an ugly painting look beautiful with a beautiful frame, and I thought about how extremely lucky I was that I was going to have so many leftovers. Even though I was really looking forward to that macaroni salad.

I lit some candles in my strength corners and I sat down at the table with the casserole, and I inhaled deeply and closed my eyes to savour the first bite, and do you know what was weird? It was so weird but the first thing that came to my mind was my mother. She looked like an angel. So I thought, There's my mother, I guess I should give her a call. So I called her up and said to her, "Hey, I've got this ham casserole with white sauce and it serves four, do you want some? I'm all alone over here with this ham casserole." And she said, "I'd love to honey, really, but I've got this comedy show buffet. It's a comedy show with a buffet? And then your stepdad and I are going to the Polish Combatants Hall." So I said, "Fine, Mom, do what you want, you always do." And she said, "What is that supposed to mean?" and I said, "Nothing. I have to go, my casserole is getting cold."

Anyway, Janet, what I really want to tell you is that I really respect your opinion and what you have to say, but most of all your bravery. You are not afraid to state your opinions, even when some people put comments like Kate P. did last week, though in a very small way I have to say I agree a little bit with what she put about your post that talked about adding a dash of joy to your daily routine, which is not so easy for everyone although you made it sound easy.

But my main message here is that I wanted you to know that there are those of us who read Planet Janet that believe what you say is TRUE and BRAVE. You keep putting yourself and your opinions – and your recipes for white-sauce casseroles and two-step stews and sinfully gooey desserts! – out there. And Janet if we all had your guts then I am proud to say that this world would be a better place. But we don't and basically the world is a harsh reality for those people who choose to live in it.

The photo of the avalanche family, it was taken after the fact. So it was all staged because of course a professional photographer wasn't with them when the avalanche happened. They're all hugging each other and at the same time sort of hugging themselves, to give the impression they need to for warmth, is I guess the idea. And then there's the photo of an avalanche actually happening, but it wouldn't have been THEIR avalanche, just an avalanche wherever. With the purpose being to show all that snow cascading down, which apparently that's all an avalanche is – just unstable layers of snow letting go.

I would hate to be trapped in an avalanche, wouldn't you? God, that would be awful. All that pressure, all that snow pushing down on you. Apparently the sheer weight of dense snow makes it very difficult to breathe, and it takes only three minutes for a person to die from suffocation. I did some Internet research on this stuff, that's how I know, in case you were wondering. And this family SURVIVED! The daughter lost a toe to frostbite, but that's pretty much it for lasting damage. And I'm sure all of them will have terrifying nightmares forever. But everybody gets nightmares, don't they?

The way the family survived was they created air pockets for themselves. There was so little air for four people, and yet nobody hogged it. They shared their body warmth too – they huddled very close together, protecting each other. And do you know what this family said in the interview? "We remained calm, and we waited." How could they do that? Who ARE these people? But who knows if they were telling the truth, since nobody wants to look like a jerk in a *Reader's Digest* interview.

My mother's voice does this thing where you can always tell when she's lying. Kind of a gulping noise that you can detect at the end of her sentences. And I heard it when I called her about the ham casserole, so I don't know, maybe she wasn't actually going to the comedy show buffet and then the Polish Combatants Hall with my stepdad, who is not the most reliable person either, but that's another story.

Then there's the shark, which is a Great White, and he's got his mouth wide open so you see these rows and rows of deadly sharp teeth. And so smooth, like the white sauce – it had lumps in it at first, but I used a fork to stir it, like you said to, and eventually the lumps went away, and I found that whole process very rewarding. I guess that's why they call it comfort food.

So there was this husband, and he heard his wife screaming and that's when he saw the fin and he ran down the beach, and he dove into the ocean and he was yelling at her to "Swim! Swim away!" And she did and do you know that it was actually HIM that got bitten? The shark was after her but the husband put himself between this truly fearsome predator and his wife, and the shark grabbed him by the torso – that's how large this shark's jaws were, they could go around a man's TORSO! – and isn't that amazing, I mean that a person would save another person from a shark, I mean a SHARK! Isn't that one of the number-one fears in the world? It must be way up there anyway, and this man put himself in that shark's path to save his wife. And now he has this long scar from it, which his wife probably kisses all the time, gets down on her knees and kisses that scar all over, at least I hope she does – I would if I was her, I would be so grateful. It's something else, Janet, I'm telling you. This man was in a shark's MOUTH and he SURVIVED! It's an awe-striking fact when you take the time to think about it.

I guess what I'm trying to get at here is that nobody else says the things you say, Janet. You have a way with words, that's for sure. Myself, it takes me a lot longer to get my point across. But what do I have to say? I've never been trapped in an avalanche or bitten by a shark or anything like that. I live a pretty ordinary life. Though I wonder how brave YOU would be in the face of a Great White Shark. I like to think you would save all of us, that you would throw yourself in the path of the Great White Shark that is all of our self-esteem problems. But somehow I doubt it. You are wrestling with your own demons and I can accept that.

But it is so HARD, Janet, and you know what it's like, I can tell. I know that you know how we all feel. I try my utmost to stay on track, every day. I get up and I have my routine and at the end of the day I go to bed. And I understand, like you tell us, that it's all a process. But sometimes I just lie there and imagine what it would be like to be trapped by an avalanche or bitten in half by a Great White Shark. But then think, I can avoid both of those things. Easily. A) Don't go on mountains. B) Don't go in oceans.

I do try to be good to myself, Janet. I try to take comfort from the everyday and eat comfort foods and say comforting things to myself, reassuring and self-affirming things. And yet it's very hard to stay positive, as you well know. Or do you, Janet? You can read all of our comments here and know that you're not alone in this cold world. You are not alone on Planet Janet, because we are all there with you.

Apparently with some shark attacks, you can hear your own bones snap in the shark's mouth. Now that is SOMETHING. And the thing is, a shark may bite a human out of hunger, but just as often, it'll bite out of simple curiosity. Just to see what we taste like.

And the thing about my brother is, is that I have doubts, and I mean serious doubts, that he would ever save his wife, pregnant or not, from a shark. He loves her, sure, we all love her. She's very personable. Which is why I was additionally surprised and saddened when they called and cancelled on our dinner plans at the last minute. But I guess with babies involved there's no telling. And my brother adores this woman, there's no getting around that. Still, if he saw a fin in the same water she was in, would he dive in and swim towards it, or would he run the other way? You tell me.

Maybe on Planet Janet there are no sharks, and maybe there are no avalanches, but some day there might be. Some day it will snow on your mountains and your oceans will fill up with fins. Something that shark-attack victims often say is: "It came out of nowhere." Actually, that's what avalanche victims say too. It makes you think, doesn't it?

But really overall there are so many of us who support you, Janet, and your daily struggles with self-esteem. And I am here to say, for once and for all, that your life will get better. It will get better, Janet, I promise you. It has to.

This Just Isn't Working Out
by Zoe Whittall

Dear Katie,

I woke up with a lingering vision of my Aunt Agnes's swollen feet propped on her filthy coffee table. They looked like two puff pastries stuffed into once pastel blue slippers, now the colour of a greying robin's egg. Aunt Agnes smoked like a tire yard on fire. When I was a child it seemed she ate nothing but bridge mix. She drank sherry from a highball glass. We kids were offered warm tap water in Styrofoam cups that she rewashed and used only when we came around, the rims worried with eight-year-old teeth. This was my introduction to single living.

I left Tom a few hours ago. I've been thinking of you and your apartment in the city. I know you say it's too expensive and your neighbours are always yelling obscenities through the floor, but I've been dreaming of moving in with you. Going to the market to buy an apple, just for myself. When I'm standing at the Fiesta Farms with a bag of apples – because Tom eats one a day, every day, cut into quarters – I dream about that single apple. I rip into the plastic bag with a finger and isolate one, hold it like a bowling ball, and lift my curled hand above all the other groceries in the cart. I see it as clearly as I saw my Aunt Agnes's feet this morning. At first, I couldn't picture anything but her feet, not until I willed my eyes up to see her face, the lines gathering around her lips like a tightly pulled seam. Cigarette held in her puckered lips.

Yesterday at work, I was holding a white ceramic bowl hot from the microwave. It was balanced in both of my hands like I was holding somebody's head still and with love. I was staring at my computer screen, at an Excel file stacked heavily with numbers and letters. I didn't want to look down into the warm bowl because I feared that it might be filled with blood. I glanced down at it. I knew there would be no blood in it, and I was right. Lentil soup. But every time I lifted the spoon, I had that thought. The soup even changed in flavour. Like metal, similar to the taste that erupts when you pull the tip of your tongue from away from a frozen, metal surface.

I threw the soup away and shrugged it off. I had a deadline to meet. You know how Sherry gets, sucking in her teeth and orbiting around your cubicle in those ugly black turtlenecks, pretending to look distracted, eyes burrowing holes into your head. She still talks about you, like you're friends or something. Asks how you're doing all by yourself in the big city. I say you've gone off with a biker. She always believes me for a second, cause she doesn't really get sarcasm. I say you're great, starring in a play, etc. All those things that you do. It's amazing, Katie. I'm so proud of you. Sherry smiles, but I can tell she's jealous of you, and jealous of me for being your friend, and staying in touch even after you quit.

There's a new girl at work whose entire family was killed. I do not think suffering ennobles. But I watch her when she smiles. It's like she knows something I can't. She spends all day looking at the horoscopes.

Last night I slept at the office. I stayed behind to work on something and told Sherry I'd lock up and I just never left. I slept on the scratchy paisley couch in the break room and ate everyone's leftover lunches for dinner. I snooped in Sherry's desk drawers. You won't believe what I found in them. I'll tell you when I get to your place. I hope it's okay to stay with you. I just can't go home, you know. Not even to get my things. My things weigh me down. Do you know what I bought last week? Stuff off the TV. Tom will be so mad when he gets the Visa bill.

I called Tom from the office and said I was staying over. He thought I'd gone mad or that I was lying, that I was really having an affair – but I took a photo on my phone and it showed him where I was. He said I must be going really crazy this time and that he was on his way to get me. I told him not to. I wasn't surprised when I saw his face on the intercom video screen, his time-delayed voice of concern begging me to buzz him in. I had no choice really, I had to tell him it was over. IT'S JUST NOT WORKING OUT, I said, pressing the talk button on the intercom. GO HOME. He just kept saying LET ME IN, over and over, until I turned away, went back to the break room and turned up the volume on the TV. I watched the cooking channel and fell asleep. When I woke up, a half hour ago, he was gone. It's dawn now and the sun is coming up over the industrial park. I can see the early bird cars on the highway curling around the overpass. I'm going to have to hide under my desk soon when the cleaners come. That, or act like nothing is weird. I just came in really early. I'm a keener. You know.

Love, Mary

Dear Katie,

Remember when we were 12, and we used to read all the dirty parts from Judy Blume's *Forever...* into a tape recorder so we could listen to them later in bed? How did we even come up with that? Then you'd talk about wanting to be a star on Broadway in New York City, and I was going to be the next Judy Blume. Seems ridiculous now, doesn't it?

This Just Isn't Working Out

There's still that sign above the photocopier that Tom made when we all worked together. The one that reads, "Flaubert never wasted a word. Why waste a sheet of paper?" Underneath it I scrawled "Oh, and no need to talk down to us, either," I added a smiley face too. It was funny when I wrote it. I can't even tell you how much that sign bugs me now. It's a daily reminder that I once graduated with an English degree. That I was the first one in my family to graduate from college, and that 13 years later it still doesn't mean shit. My brothers make $85,000 a year in jobs they only needed trade school for. I make $27,000 a year take-home. That sign reminds me that Tom started out as my employee, and then got promoted, and promoted and then headhunted out of here. And I'm still here. Middle-management Mary. Sherry got drunk at the Christmas party and said I won't ever get promoted because James thinks I'm just going to end up getting pregnant again soon. Jesus, Katie, sometimes those family photographs up in everyone's cubicle are enough to make me want to weep.

I had to fire a girl in customer service a few weeks ago. I could tell she thought she was so much better than me, than this whole office. She had a streak of blue in her blonde hair. She wore Fluevog shoes, so I know she has rich parents, right? She published a book of poetry on the internet. An ebook. Whatever. We logged her internet hours and you wouldn't believe how little work she did. I said, we don't pay you to chat. I'm sure they'll hire her back as our Social Media Manager or some bullshit in a few months, especially since she has great tits, but until then, I got to fire her and I tell you something, firing people used to make me cry. I cried every time. Not this time. I felt energized. Take your smug little scarf you wear in 30 degree weather, your third generation granny boots, your pop culture blah blah blog, and go back to your mother's basement suite in Brantford, little one.

I didn't say that, of course.

It's almost noon, and I just bought my train ticket. Thanks for the invitation to your opening night. I will definitely be there. I'm just waiting for pay day.

Love, M

Dear Katie,

I'm so glad we connected on Facebook. Your photos are so awesome: I love the one with you smoking under the bridge wearing that evening gown. I gave up smoking years ago when I was pregnant with Maggie. I started again when she died, but I only smoked until the funeral. I just didn't enjoy it anymore anyway. Or anything else, really. Has it been three years already? It still seems like yesterday. That week you let me sleep on your couch was so important to me. I know you know that. I remember how glad I was when Tom came to get me, though. Back when I still loved him. I know you say you're lonely sometimes, and you're tired of never finding the right guy, but you have no idea how lucky you are. I'd rather have a gay best friend and a book club and three-day benders (great photo of you singing shirtless karaoke!) than the same night every night, that thick silence of two people who have given in to growing old. Tom started playing golf. Do I even need to expand?

Love, M

Dear Katie,

Thanks for letting me stay for at least a little while. I totally understand that it's not a great time for me to move in. I get it. Maybe I can get a place in your building? And don't worry, you know how clean I am. I won't leave a trace! We can run your lines together. I can help you with your costumes. Really,

I can't wait to just sit still in a café and watch people. I used to love doing that when I went to U of T. Remember that place in Kensington Market? I still dream I'm there sometimes. Is it still there, Moon-something? I can't believe my two most incessant daydreams involve buying myself an apple, and watching people while drinking a cup of really good coffee. I am so sick of Tim Hortons I could cry some mornings.

Love, M

Dear Katie,

I'm not sure what to tell you. I came in to work this morning, after a terrible sleep at the Comfort Inn across the highway the office and security was waiting to greet me at the door. Apparently Sherry caught on to my expense account scheme. I may have skimmed a few dollars here and there, but seriously, no promotions ever? I only took what I was worth. It's bullshit. I can't even tell you how mad I am. I'm slamming on the keys here in the Comfort Inn business centre. I'll be out of here today, Katie. I hope you don't mind that I arrive a bit early. Tom wants me to come home, I know. Lena told him where I am and he's been sitting in the van in the parking lot for an hour now. I can see him from across the little window, he's been going to my room and knocking, I suppose. I guess that's love, right? Or craziness. I'm not sure how I'll get my stuff. Maybe I'll just show up with nothing? I'm afraid to see him.

When I see Tom in person, I know I won't stand my guard. He's just so safe. I'll walk towards him because I'll have no control over my body. Bodies crave security. It's like when you're freezing to death and you just go on autopilot doing things to get warm, like shivering. Your body tricks you. My body will open the van door, and slide into the front seat, and he'll say, "How about a pizza, my best girl?" and then I'll be 68, in a matching recliner next to his, and we'll be watching some awards show. You'll be getting a lifetime achievement award, and I'll be getting him a beer from the cooler between us. And that will be my whole life.

Love, M

Our Warm Peach
by Charles Lowe

The plan is foolproof enough. I buy a virus. Those things are easy enough to catch. My best friend has a girl off campus. She has a nice skin and an uncle from Beijing who has access to the latest software. Then, I wait patiently. My Dean says patience is my most outstanding virtue. My professor neglects at last to log off. The matter is simple after that. I stick my USB in the hard drive inside a wooden lectern shaped like a slumped boat and check afterwards at my leisure my professor's account.

Nothing interesting: a couple of e-mails from students with questions on the final exam. I delete that garbage. A note from the Division Secretary with the agenda of a department meeting: in the trash. Then, a message from AR in big red letters, the grades for Marxist Ethics posted. Displaying the virtue the Dean has gently noted at my expulsion hearing, I wait until three in the morning when certainly my professor will have shut his glassy eyes; then change my grade: a C in Marxist Ethics (I smile) becomes an A for Táo Xiěng. I'm not done though. The Dean remarks approvingly at my expulsion hearing that I have a greater knowledge of regulations than many of his faculty. Indeed, I download the entire regulation handbook, all 199 pages: taking note of AR 1.1.3 which reads as follows: "in order to maintain academic standards and the College's increasingly high minded reputation with foreign and Hong Kong experts,

15 percent at most of each class shall be permitted to receive a B+ or higher; further no more than 40 percent shall be permitted to receive an honours grade or above."

Translation for those of you with clay pots for skulls, if Táo gets an A, a suitable candidate has to be found for Táo. Hóng Měi takes his place. Hóng Měi has an A average as well as long and very attractive curls protecting a shoulder stained like a peach. Hóng Měi has also rejected the generous offer of a certain very patient second-year student to take her to the two-story KFC. The restaurant has excellent chicken wings. It affords well-scrubbed windows that provide a scenic vista of a mud-stained Hěi River. My friend, the seller of viruses, says the view is very romantic.

Of course, I don't just change her grade. What if the professor double-checks his Excel sheet, he is a thorough bastard. So in addition I alter the grades of four other classmates: one from B to C, another from C+ to B, enough so that the whole mess balances itself out. Then, I'm done except I'm not. Here's the thing; some of those grade-hungry bastards start to complain. I can't believe it. There's one kid who complains that he's not worth a B. Really, that guy ought to be shot. So, you guessed it, the Dean starts an investigation and pretty soon his people latch onto a certain set of entries at three in the morning and trace those entries to an apartment on the fourth floor above a certain set of milk cartons. Then, the Dean calls Mom to his office and constructs his fingers so as to give a likeness of a tent with an open flap. After that, he starts a carefully balanced lecture, noting my industry in discovering an advanced Trojan virus at an economic price (less than a couple hundred bucks), but commenting (quite fairly I may add) on the overall sloppiness of my approach. After all, if I had traveled to the basement of the library, I could have (from the safety of a warm cubicle) altered the grades without ever having to fear being known. Instead, here I am on a weekday afternoon, watching a studio audience full of moms with their clay-brained children receiving a lecture on how "we Chinese don't pay attention to our kids' insides."

The advice does seem sensible. Just this early morning, I am listening to the diamond-shaped kitchen window catch the cinder from Race Course Avenue. During March, the wind comes from the Mongolian desert in the Northwest and sweeps up plenty of cinder from the unfinished roads. We have plenty of unfinished roads in our District when I begin to count the number of specks hitting the small diamond-shaped window above Mommy's wok. If you find the habit odd, you're most likely correct, but then you've never been evicted from school or had a bout of unemployment – Dad did a few years ago, or else you'd understand. First your waking time tends to be spent in darkness like you're a vampire. When it's about daylight, you shut the door of your room whose right wall is occupied by a poster of three revolutionary heroes, knee deep in the snows of *Yán'ān*.

Second, your ears develop a sensitivity to sound as your brain empties of responsibility, which is why I hear my dad say Táo. You have to understand my surprise. Dad hasn't directed three words to me in the last five years. No hatred there. It's not that at all: well, you understand.

He's a computer programmer. Dad programs supermarket registers throughout China, you know, bling, bling, and when he comes home, he's got no time for me and mom. He's busy in the garden. Dad's developing magnificent bok choy flowers, purple and green that Mom mixes together with tomatoes and eggs. What a sweet supper, so I don't mind his silence. It's kind of pleasant to see the mirror image of yourself, a fat guy with a big butt, knee deep in shit, totally uncaring about the world.

It's a comforting sight. But still I am discomforted to hear my name over my father's cell at four in the morning until I realize he's not saying my name. He is repeating peach, my warm peach. How do I know this? While happening to be beneath an end table shortly after Dad receives another morning call, I spot the scrawl running across the screen of Dad's cell. Now a fact: the word, peaches, sounds the same as my name but its picture is vastly different. Here is how a picture of a peach appears on a cellphone screen, 桃. Now my name means pottery and here is what a piece of clay pottery looks like, 匋. Different, right, but if I am not such a thorough bastard, I won't have needed to crawl soundlessly on a richly textured carpet in order to reach my favourite crawl space. I would have only had to listen to the tender sound of my dad's voice, his lips looking like they're about to blow a bubble into a plastic screen.

I don't jump to the obvious conclusion. He is after all my father, not someone easily mistaken for a player. Mom has to remind him to wear a belt every day; otherwise, when he bends down, you know you'd see well, not a pleasant sight. Still when watching the woman with lots of make-up dispensing advice to a bunch of bored housewives and their clay-brained offspring, I start considering, well maybe Daddy's making reference to his garden. Now I know: what peach would have a chance in our northern soil; it's littered with glass, a neighbour using our backyard as a dump. But still I wait until four in the morning, listening to the specks of cinder catching our small kitchen window when I hear him say in a deep voice, Táo.

The sound of my name causes a shiver to travel down my spine even though I know he is speaking to his sweet peach, not a stiff piece of clay, and I grow all the more curious. Well, getting your dad's cellphone is sure a lot less challenging than plugging a Trojan into the school-wide grading system; nevertheless, I remain cautious. That is my, and, if I may say so, Dad's most promising trait. Then, I spot him sticking his cell in the front pocket of his striped shirt. It's Tuesday morning. Suddenly I run at him. I am sure he is surprised. We are hardly the affectionate couple, and I grab him hard, saying in as loud a voice as possible D-ad-dy. Mom, Dad, we are all surprised; I am even surprised to hear my voice. I hardly talk and when I talk, it is usually like I'm a dummy who has not bothered to memorize his lines. Well, the plan works. The cell pops out of his shirt pocket, almost ending up inside Dad's pants. He's forgotten his belt. Mom has to remind him. I hide the phone. Mom starts, making tomatoes, eggs and bok choy; she's taken to adding in a smidge of ginger, a delightful addition. Then, the two of us sit on the couch and watch this soap on time travel, waiting for the start of our favourite talk show when our host is scheduled to work on the confidence of her overweight bookworm daughter. What a loser.

At two when Mom goes out to have a fire-cup treatment on her shoulder muscles that have been tightening lately: I have the chance to take out Daddy's cell and start skimming through his messages. Most are from one supermarket chain about a program Daddy installed which its junior accountant is worried may be leaving a very narrow trail though certainly wide enough to be caught by a diligent official from the District tax office when I come to the first note.

"Your Warm Peach wants an updated version of Windows. Can you bring the software over, ha, ha": then, a few hearts plus a picture of a peach?

Next message, "yes, your warm peach wants a chicken wing. Ha, ha: then a few more hearts and a peach."

Well, you can imagine the discovery provokes mixed feelings on my part. I want to say way to go, Dad. I mean up till now Dad has been this guy who forgets his belt regularly and bends down when planting bok choy, thereby presenting uncomfortable shots of his crack. Suddenly, he's a player receiving a few hearts from his warm peach. But there's Mom to consider. I don't think she knows. After all, she does continue to add a smidge of ginger for Dad as well as making sure the top of my bed sheet is folded so that the blue green fabric fits like an envelope over my frilled pillowcase. But still, I start to ponder the interesting observation committed by the talk-show host whose skin is caked with tissues of white paint: Chinese parents do not listen to their children's hearts. But isn't it as true Chinese children do not have their ears to their parents' hearts unless of course the clay-brained offspring can gain access to their father's cellphone – which I do.

So I make sure to leave the cell beneath an end table. Then, wait for Dad to notice his loss. He does. Then, I indicate with my left forefinger the location of a dark-framed phone on a thickly carpeted floor. Mom smiles, I do also, while Dad's complexion gradually acquires an off-coloured gleam. I wait, demonstrating again what the Dean has properly identified to be my most outstanding feature. Sure enough, Dad says he has a late meeting with a customer and gets on a plaid jacket and this time, is wearing a belt with a shiny bronze buckle. Dad leaves right after dinner: does not spend time even watering the tomatoes behind our apartment house. They do look hungry planted between two glassy remnants of a recently disposed bottle of Qingdao beer.

Dad bikes to the Agriculture Bank of China and stands in line with a bunch of customers waiting in front of a machine with a greenish white overhang. I must admit he is better dressed than the other customers. One guy isn't wearing any footwear but is standing in front of the machine for a while, taking lots of cash. Then, Dad waits in front of the two-floor KFC for his warm peach. Meanwhile, I travel downward to a stone passage that starts from the Liberation drawbridge. I do worry that I will stand out and move closer to a fisherman who I have the sudden inspiration is my father, though giving off a body odour, nothing like the smell of bok choy filling my parents' apartment. I wait. Dad does also, cinder catching the edges of his bronze buckle. Dad leaves shortly after the fisherman drops his steel net into the mud and cinder lining Hǎi River.

When I get home, Dad has already slipped beneath a sheet and is asleep. Mom is folding his pants and cleaning the cinder from his bronze buckle, mom's lower shoulder blades covered with brownish-sparked scars. The scars look like mountains, and the mountains look newly grown. Mom opens her mouth and falls asleep. I wait another half hour for the diamond-shaped kitchen window to catch enough clay and cinder. I sneak then into my parents' room and check our messages for any sign of our warm peach.

Sure enough, our warm peach has written: "Sorry honey: got nervous. My membership runs out tomorrow, could really use some help with my computer which is slowing down for no apparent reason, what is your thinking.

"Ha, ha," a couple of hearts: then a couple more "ha," then a few more hearts.

You can imagine how upset I am. Here I have wasted my whole evening waiting beside a fisherman wearing an odour nothing like the aroma of bok choy and ginger, so let me tell you, I do feel the right to write back telling her that calling her a warm peach means she has grown to occupy a very special place in my heart, and though we may have never met in the physical sense, we do have responsibilities to our virtual community. We do and then, I am about to press the send button when it occurs to me how foolish I must sound.

Why give this peach the feeling that she's hurt me? So I delete her apology. Let her have the pain of silence I say, and that's what Dad and I do. From that day onward, the two of us grow silent. He in his tomato and bok choy garden and me playing games on my computer, and it all works out in the end.

My uncle who's with a Watch Committee in my District gets my expulsion washed out, and the girl who has well-pressed

curls guarding her off-coloured shoulders reconsiders my offer
and unlike the peach, shows up at the KFC and the two of us sit
in front of a well-scrubbed window, waiting for a fisherman to
lift his steel-meshed net from an envelope of mud and cinder.

Oniomania in the Empty Days
by Beverly Lucey

Mavis couldn't say that buying the tapestry on eBay was the most intelligent thing she'd ever done. She didn't know anything about tapestries in the first place. And in the second place Darnell had told her that if she bought one more thing for the new house before they sold the old house, he'd have to dig out his combat boots, rejoin the Reserves, and he'd likely be sent to some godforsaken sandy place, lose the new job that brought them to Missouri in the first place, and then they'd have *two* houses they couldn't afford.

So she didn't bring up the lamp she'd bought either. At the time, a lamp base with a monkey, a coconut palm, and a hula lady who looked like a belly dancer seemed just funny enough not to be tacky.

Cruising eBay between unpacking boxes couldn't quite be called a full day's work. Except she was hooked. Darnell had always given her the paperwork to keep and rarely saw the bills. In fact, in the old house, he'd never even noticed when she'd gone shopping. Everything looked familiar. A new candle holder, a map of Napoleon's campaign into Russia, a factory-reconditioned bright green MixMaster. He just assumed Mavis had moved something. Or she'd brought it with her from that other life she lived and just got around to putting it up. They'd only been married five years. Both had grown kids living along various coastlines. She'd left a few good jobs behind as well so Darnell had encouraged her take it easy for a while, but clearly he was tense.

This last move he started keeping a sharp eye out. Couple of times he'd come up behind her when she was online and scared the hell out of her before she could hit the Buy button. She lost out on a Krazy Kat clock with moveable eyes.

Lost goods, stuff that Mavis thought belonged to her, or should belong to her, nagged at her. Moving so much made her feel incomplete. If only she could have picked up that wrought-iron étagère, if only she hadn't chickened out on the self-cleaning litter box – with a timer, a motor and a sensor – she might just feel a bit more settled.

They didn't have a cat. But when she was bidding, she was sure they did have one. Its name was Boojums. Of course, Darnell would notice a cat they never had before. Good thing she wimped out on the litter-box contraption.

Then again, Mavis got a super deal on a bread-making machine. You wouldn't catch Darnell complaining about fresh dill bread. Or pumpernickel.

Tonight Darnell was taking her to The Pig Out BBQ for a kick-back Friday. His work team had made goal this last month, so the plant manager reserved the back function room for his supervisors. Mavis hadn't met anyone in their neighborhood yet and she was hungry for company. And ribs. Even though she'd probably be outbid on the Bulgari perfume and a cookie tin.

By the time they got to The Pig Out, almost all the tables were full. Only one of the other workers had brought a spouse. Otherwise it seemed as though all the men and women were from the plant. They were laughing about all kinds of in-jokes and references to things she didn't get.

"Shorty, said oh, yeah? Well, you can kiss my…"

"Well what about when Taco took a hold…"

"So I said to her, fine. Turn me in. You know what'll happen next?"

Then people would rear back their heads, laughing, and pound the table at the memories of tiny things on their way to becoming worklore.

Mavis sat down next to another dazed-looking woman. Shouldn't they be sitting boy, girl, boy, girl? But Darnell grabbed the seat next to some guy and launched into a story she'd heard three times already. The man next to the quiet woman had his back turned away talking to someone at another table.

Mavis said, "Hey. I'm Mavis."

The woman nodded and shredded a napkin. Sauce collected in the corners of her mouth. The buffet was all you could eat.

Mavis started looking around to see where the ribs were. The line extended quite a ways. She'd wait.

The woman took a big breath and said, "I'm Theresa."

"You know many of these people, Theresa?"

"Uh uh. We just moved. About two months ago. We move a lot. I don't get to know people much."

"I hear ya."

"Yeah?"

"Yeah. You got kids?"

Theresa shook her head.

"So what do you do?"

Theresa leaned over close, after checking to be sure her husband couldn't hear. She whispered, "eBay."

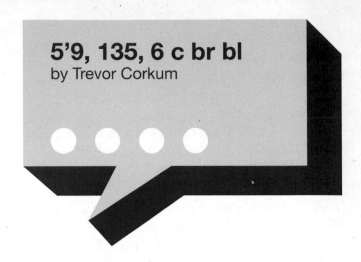

5'9, 135, 6 c br bl
by Trevor Corkum

10

It was clearing that night, the earlier clouds of grey disappearing like a freak mist behind the forlorn rocky slope of the North Shore Mountains. While I walked over the water the music that played in my head was soothing like an orchestra, soft brutal strings and beautiful big brass instruments arranged by a guest conductor in the sky. The cars made their way in a tiny parade over the aging Burrard Street Bridge, heading toward downtown and the sleek towers of glass where so many lives were lived, and so much love was squandered.

It was nearly perfect. I was high as a kite. The moon was cut rough into the sky like some school kid's weekend project, a yellow crude felt, jagged on one edge, pinned onto a black fuzzy backdrop by a shaky hand. I was admiring this powdery moon and the stars that rarely seem so gifted to Vancouver as the way they were that night. Also the dive-bombing seagulls, God's little helpers, climbing up to these twinkling stars before spiralling down into the muddy bowels of False Creek, splashing into that icy gut like dark mechanical props on a second-rate Hollywood set.

I was God's little man in my own right. I knew without a doubt that I could fly if I wanted. So I didn't think anything of it, hopping onto the ledge that bordered the old bridge. It was a high stone ledge, with pillars and columns and lots of fancy millwork. I'd done it a million times, sometimes with a friend, usually alone. The Burrard Street Bridge is the oldest in Vancouver, built on a blanket of land stolen from the Squamish. It's because of this I think it's haunted.

I was thinking about all of this. About the stolen land.

Also about my date.

I could taste him still on my lips. Not love. Just the crude salty resin of whatever trace was left of him; his elemental essence, lust, the residual forensic evidence.

The edge of a bridge so high up, it's like God whispering lullabies in your ear.

goodnight do it do it do it goodnight goodnight goodnight

When I was a little kid, my favourite book was *Jonathan Livingston Seagull.*

I didn't jump. I want that in the record. When they fish me from the Creek, trawling at first light for my slowly swelling body; when the students of art and sculpture lumber onto the ferry heading for Granville Island, and the soupy Vancouver rains erase any nocturnal memory of this beautiful cut-out moon, all remnants of desire.

I fell.

Okay?

It's simple.

9

At the door to his well-kept condo, in the building on West 14th, Guy leaned over.

Goodbye, he said, still horny.

I had fun. I hope I see you again.

And he kissed me.

Surprise. Usually there's no kiss, and definitely no kiss at the door, no goodnight kiss, the romance and deferred promises like the commercials or in a film.

He smelled nice. Sweaty, ripe, deodorant fresh, pine soap underneath. I wanted to fold myself back into him, fall asleep like a baby on his shoulder.

At the same time I was buoyant, giddy, a teenager resurrected. It was always this way, leaving some guy's place at such an early hour, ready for another beer, more dope and time to be by myself to consider whether the night had been a success, whether I felt closer to God or any religion, lonelier or less lonely, evil or more pure.

8

Earlier I'd been crying. Although I don't think he noticed.

We'd been naked a long time. I'd let him suck me off and then I did him too and now he was coming inside me. He had me face down on the bed, in his navy-blue, 400-thread-count sheets, on the solid teak bed frame in the guest room of the condo on West 14th. I was crouched into a ball. My face was crushed like a catalogue page into his expensive pillow. But he was gentle. So gentle and then rough it rocked and cajoled the liquid emotion right out of me.

He moved quickly, with some urgency, as if his wife were going to be home at any minute and he didn't, under any circumstance, want to be caught in the bed of the guest room shoving his marital payload into another man.

7

Feel this, he said, when we were finishing our beer.

We were together on his leather couch in the den. It typically starts this way, very casual, all very civil. Paintings from Zimbabwe hung around the room. Photos of grandkids, or who I assumed might be grandkids, smiling and gregarious, rested in strict rows on a stately cedar bookcase beside the plasma TV. The lights were dim. There were candles. He'd put in some soft

music, Billie Holiday or one of her friends, something bluesy
and very melancholy from a long time ago.

Like this?

I let my fingers run lightly over the knee of his jeans, strok-
ing the creases of denim, moving stealthily and slowly up to the
inner thigh. I rested the hand there a while, innocently, liking
the sound of the breath catching in his throat, the surprise and
surrender, like it was his first time all over again.

He moaned.

Here, he said, spreading his legs, leaning back his head.

Right here.

I want you to touch your Daddy here.

6

He lived in a building fancier than I had expected. It was new,
maybe a year old, a glass tower with fourteen floors, edgy art
in the lobby, complicated security codes, a doorman.

The doorman eyed me suspiciously when I told him the code.
His blue beady eyes could barely conceal his judgment. He was
maybe 65 and looked like one of my uncles: grey-looking face,
peaked security cap, a concave, hollow chest beneath his navy
uniform. I could tell he knew I was high.

Who do you want?

Eggleston. Guy Eggleston. He lives on the seventh.

Is Mr Eggleston expecting you?

Yes sir. Yes sir he is.

5

On the way, I stopped on the steps of the Art Gallery to buy
some more weed.

I knew the dealer. He was just some scrawny white kid who
had been kicked out of his house in Coquitlam. I think he was
maybe queer. Once he told me a story about how two muscled-up

jock boys from Texas asked him back to their hotel so they could undress him and take photos. They gave him a hundred bucks and then posted it on XTube. He shrugged it off. Said it was cool.

Thanks, I said, when he handed me the baggie.

A homeless woman with a doily on her head was slapping a circle of jingle bells against her thigh and pretending to sing into a microphone she'd attached to a city garbage can. All that came out in her high-pitched voice was *gahhlastopabalabala-bala*. I imagined her in front of a Christmas tree with a dozen cheerful elves. We clapped when she was done and Luke, my dealer, gave her five bucks and told her she was amazing. I was suddenly in love with him.

It was almost dusk. The air was cooling off and everything was beautiful. Pigeons the size of cats were fluttering around us like the world was coming to an end. I threw my last bit of pizza a couple of feet away and a chorus of squawking erupted, a fierce battle broke out like in some forgotten Shakespearean tragedy, the winning pigeon gobbling it down whole. You could see it stuck in its mouth, this giant blob, so big you thought he should choke, maybe even die, but the pigeon stood defiantly right on the edge of the parapet watching the cool sunset like nothing of real interest had occurred.

4

Slipping through the dark, along the empty beach near English Bay toward the towering Art Deco bridge, I pulled out my phone and rang up my mom.

I don't know why. There was nothing in particular I wanted to tell her. I certainly wasn't about to say I was on my way to sleep with a perverted father figure I'd met a few hours ago online. And that I was hoping for a good time.

The phone jingled. Again. And again. But no one picked up.

Hi mom. It's me. Just wanted to say I was thinking of you.

I shut the phone, stopping on the rocky beach to listen to the crashing waves ride up again and again against the shore. The air smelled salty, also of cedar from the clump of tall trees behind the Aquatic Centre. I lit another joint and watched a kayaker glide by across the shaky water.

So serene.

I wanted so bad to be that kayak, moving softly and swiftly and perfectly through that dark and gentle night.

3

In my apartment, I wasn't sure what to wear. I rested out on the balcony for a while, rolling a joint, then lighting it, sucking in the sweetness slowly, then exhaling, all the while studying the tiny slice of mountain and the little bit of ocean I could see between the nexus of high-rises. I live on the twelfth. On my balcony I own a row of tropical plants, purchased at IKEA, and an orange hammock stretched in one corner. I sat on the edge of the hammock considering my date. I was excited to have a date. It had been a long time since I'd been with someone or had any sort of human contact. It had been a long time since I'd touched another dude. It was a little bit like Christmas.

In the end I wore what I always wore. A pair of cut-off cargo pants, green, vaguely military; a faded grey retro Boy Scout T-shirt (Pack 192, Bloomington, Indiana); and my favourite Expos ballcap. I showered, stuck on some deodorant, practiced my boyish smile in the three-way bathroom mirror, then practiced looking sullen and bored, practically uninterested, in case the occasion called for it.

2

I've had other dates like this. You can't really call them dates, but I do, because if I didn't then I would have no dates, no real dates I mean, where a dude picks up you up in a car or on the back of his Yamaha motorbike and brings you to a funky restaurant and foots the whole bill and tells you how great you look, how wonderful you are, how even your small insecurities are attractive, your tiny compulsions are charming, even the truly minor ones, and how much he wishes he could meet someone just like you to move into his fancy mansion in West Vancouver and be his monogamous boyfriend and live together quietly forever and ever.

1

In the report, if there are reports filed in the Afterlife, I could say that one thing leads to another, nothing happens by chance, you can follow the past thread by thread or clue by clue back to the first catalyst. Like I could say that if it weren't for factor *x*, action *y* would never have happened. It's algorithmic; it's all a matter of the *scientific method*.

If that's the case, I could argue that my death was nothing more than a chemical reaction. An excess of testosterone, a buildup of hormones in the system, caused me in the middle of my workday temping at some unethical law firm to sneak a peek on a website where other men, some married, some not, some ugly, some not, all faced the same scientifically documented condition of an excess chemical in the system.

Horny white dude needing to get off.

Need to get off RIGHT NOW!

Fill me up with your man juice...need it real bad.

God help us, Allah help us, Buddha help us all. We're lonely. We're bored. And we're human. At least for a few years, until we rot and decompose and generally help sustain the planetary ecosystem with our plentiful nutrient by-products.

It all started then when I updated my profile, recorded my earthly stats, left my own invitation on a page in this virtual city for other renegade souls to ponder:

Punk ass brat boy seeks good-humoured Daddy figure for NSA *fun times.*

It was a crappy day. Outside where I was working, in the tangle of the downtown core, the streets were a toxic grey, as in foreboding, as in inhospitable and possibly even judgmental. Who is to say, then, whether the weather played a factor in my death? If it was a sunny day, a sunny August day, might I not have simply gone down to English Bay and tried to hook up at the beach?

Within the hour I had seven responses. Seven pics. Seven unique threads, with varying shades of excitement, and more typos than any grade school. Guy's was the most promising. Guy the guy. He wore a tight baby blue T-shirt that said *Father Knows Best.*

You sound sweet, he wrote.

We made arrangements. He lived on the West Side, said I could stop by after nine. This is the twenty-first century, where desire and technology dance to the same backbeat tango. It's sex as a PayPal transaction. It doesn't have to mean much. All you need is a reliable Internet connection, a strong desire to travel and vaguely the right sort of lines.

I think I'm your man, he wrote.

I was excited, the way it's easy to get excited before the first soft yawn of the unknown, the dark cool music in your head, the Death Cab for Cutie soundtrack, the Hare Krishna electronica.

I won't be able to stay late.

No worries, he wrote. *Whatever you want bud.*

One little e-mail is where it all began.

Thank you, from my deepest heart of hearts, to our early pioneers, to Jesus and His friends, to all our corporate talent scouts, and to Bill and Melinda Gates, who made this evening possible.

No One Else Really Wants to Listen
by Heather Birrell

HI ALL YOU MOMS-IN-WAITING,

I felt the baby move a little, I think, but I'm sort of worried because I'm having some spotting. Not a lot, and it's not bright red, alarm, alarm! But I feel a bit concerned. I'm wondering if anyone has any advice, or suggestions. I have an appointment with my OB-GYN on Wednesday, but I can't sleep right now. It's just on my mind, y'know?

—*New Country Girl*

WRT the bleeding – it could come from sex. I don't know about you chickadees, but since I crossed over into the second trimester I've been crazy-horny. It's like everything is super-ripe, y'know? No offence or anything inquiring about your love life – it's just normal to have a bit of blood from the friction. Sorry again if this is TMI.

—*Craving City*

No such thing as TMI in this forum, my friend. All info is good info. Yeah, ripe is one word for it. NC, the blood is likely coming from your cervix which is probably quite swollen and tender at this point. It might also be the result of straining on the toilet. Are you constipated at all?

—*Straight Shooter*

Nope, the elimination pipes are clear, and the bleeding continues – not heavy or anything, but it's there. I'm thinking I'll call
TeleHealth and see what they say.

—NC

Good idea, NC. IMHO it's totally better to be safe than sorry.

—*Craving*

New Country: I wouldn't worry too much – when I got pregnant not only my sense of smell but also my sense of tragedy
became more acute. By this I do not mean, as some women
exclaim, that I became more sensitive to the plight of others
or that I was compelled to turn headlines involving the maim-
ing of children face down on the kitchen table. Quite the opposite. During my first trimester, I devoured stories wherein
the unlucky fledgling protagonists were killed – instantly –
in a head-on collision; I spent afternoons imagining the last
moments of infants left to freeze in some alcoholic father's
backyard wasteland. You must understand, none of this was
malicious or gratuitous. Perhaps it was a test of my mettle –
I wanted to feel the worst, to encompass it. The pregnancy
made me feel expansive, as if I had grown new ribs, longer
ribs, that my chest cavity and not my uterus were expanding. I
felt sure that at my next visit, the doctor would ask to measure
my wingspan. Something moving inside me made it impera-
tive that I understand it all – not the week-by-week stirring of
the speck that had lodged itself like a grain of sand inside an
oyster but instead the bold cacophony of the outside world,
which, it appeared, was no longer outside, but instead a country of blood and tenderness and terror and chemicals and a
strange softness before dying within the scope of my very own
body. The country smelled of cardamom, shit, exhaust fumes

and a man's scalp, and if I spread my wings wide enough, I could embrace it all, all of it, my wingtips touching, feathers tickling the dust.

—*Wings*

Wings: Whoa! Pregnancy has made you all goth, eh? Which is funny because before I got knocked up I used to listen to a lot of punk and old-school angry hiphop. I loved that shit. Especially NWA. Then, it was so weird, as soon as those hormones got pumping, I was flicking the dial to easy listening. You know who I can't get enough of now? Faith Hill! She's this really nice white Barbie who sings about stuff like heartbreak and tractors and Jesus. WTF! I guess it's true what they say about pregnancy being "miraculous." Anyway, the nurse at TeleHealth asked me too many questions, then told me, in a super-solemn voice, that I should go to the hospital. But they always say that, right? I'll check in with you guys when I get back. The bleeding seems to have let up a little, so I'm not too worried...

—*New Country Girl*

Hey NC – let us know what the docs say, eh? We're rooting for you.

—*Straight Shooter*

Thanks, SS. Can I ask you guys – what does it feel like for you when the baby moves?

—*New Country*

When I was a child, my father packed us all into a van and we headed down to Florida, through Ontario, Ohio, then all those friendly-waitress states with the fat people and big brass belt buckles. We stayed in a pink hotel near the beach and I remember my parents as distant figures prone on beach towels. One evening my father showed me a photograph of a diamond-shaped sea creature in a glossy pamphlet. He told me the creature was a stingray and I should beware of stingrays. I had never been told to beware of anything before and I liked the sound of it – I felt I had entered a dark and brambly thicket, a new and exciting chapter of the quest that was my life. The stingray was silver and translucent, a dangerous sea treasure. It could lie quietly, stealthily on the ocean floor. A person could step on a stingray and be in mortal danger. How do they move? I asked my father. They flap, he said, and performed the most amazing and strange movement I have ever seen, his arms fluid from his shoulders, pulsing slowly up and down as if the air were water. It was beautiful and dangerous, and so unlike my father, and I understood immediately why I must beware. When I first felt my baby move I was reminded of that stingray, and of my father. It was the most astounding thing, those dangerous wings undulating in my belly. I will never forget it.

—*Wings*

Wings: GOYHH! Women have been giving birth to babies for millennia. What's with all the figurative language and self-importance? What makes you so special? I, for one, could do without it.

—*Straight Shooter*

Dear Wings: You might want to consult your midwife about these mood swings you are experiencing. It's possible there are deep-breathing techniques or yoga postures that may help you feel more grounded and calm. Maybe even talk to your partner about the feelings you are having – and there are some great resources on the Internet, agencies you could talk to. You have a new life growing inside you – how *blessed* is that? Congratulations!

—*Spiral Woman*

Spiral: I will not tell my husband about the wings, extra ribs or morbidity of my thoughts – although he, like me, delights in theory and fancy that bucks convention, and it is likely his scalp scent that perfumes my world. As for the Internet – we have both been busy with it. The "facts," panic mongering and treacly reassurances I could do without, but I have some interest in the lists of baby names from the 1920s. There is a sense of both giddy optimism and hard-won stoicism following the great war that is reflected in the era's monikers. Who could help but admire an Albert? And could a Ruth be anything but trustworthy? I have told very few people about the pregnancy, which is why I am using this anonymous forum to get some "feelings" off my fierce and cavernous chest. You sound like a moron.

—*Wings*

PS Grounded? Isn't that what happens when airplanes get stuck on the tarmac? PPS I don't have a midwife.

I know maybe this is off topic or in the wrong thread or whatever, but I wanted to tell everybody that I finally felt it – the baby – sorry, Country Girl, not to make you feel bad or anything – and it didn't feel at all like they said, like ripples or waves. It felt like something with lots of right angles and willpower. It felt like maybe it was angry. Do you think a baby can be angry in uteri?

—*Spiral*

Hello, my sisters! I am a member of another forum for new Christian mothers, but I LOVE the openness of these posts. So welcome and *refreshing.* Don't get me wrong; I still love Jesus, but I love the way all you ladies can *connect*, even when it's through a keyboard. NC – I'm praying for you!

—*Christian Mom!*

PS I have all of Faith Hill's albums!

Wings: Also – I think you are reading too many serious books. They say when you are pregnant you should skip the evening news and just try to watch fun TV shows and read light magazines (like maybe *Cosmo* or that other one that's about shopping). Otherwise it can be overwhelming. Maybe get your husband to run you a bath. But not too hot – you don't want to raise your body temperature. And light some candles – but not too smelly, I know the nose is sensitive! That way you can float away your troubles for a while. (Oh, and I kinda think Buddhism might be more your thing. Christianity is just so *fraught*, y'know?) *Love Your Bump!*

—*spiral*

Spiral: What can be overwhelming? You sound like you've been watching too many "fun" shows. I think I hate you.

—*Wings*

Does anybody else think Wings is just a *teensy* bit abusive?

—*Spiral Woman*

Hey gals! Just waiting to be seen by the OB-GYN – they have these nifty heavy-duty laptops attached to the waiting room chairs

– très Japanese. Spiral: Wings is just telling it like how she sees it. That's okay. We need to have someplace we can do that. And dissent is healthy, even among pregnant chicks. I mean, there is a level of niceness, generosity and solidarity I can appreciate... But we need to be honest with each other, because no one else really wants to listen, do they?

—*New Country*

NC: You are so right! We can exclaim all we like about equity and gender equality, but when it comes to it, when it comes to this – being a vessel – we've got a lock on the correct (or unlucky) XY that allows us to ferry another human around while they form bones, bloom lungs and grow soft, downy hair like strange and darling amphibian monkeys, their tiny eyes squeezed shut, their hiccupping bodies gulping down what they know and stuttering it up again. So it seems strange to me that we would not find a bond, but stranger still that what bonds us is the outer trappings – the teensy bonnets and plastic gadgets, the miniature bits and bobs that clutter up aisles in jumbo stores and infringe on dreams by amplifying them. Isn't it enough that we are colonized by our own bodies?

—*Wings*

Wings: *You* are so right! All those products demand sameness instead of discussion, they make us want and want and talk about the same things. It's better, no, that we disagree and tussle with each other once in a while? OTOH, I have them at home: onesies with yellow daisies embroidered on the bum, one of those newfangled carrier wraps it would take an origami expert to master. I am far from immune.

—*New Country*

Oh, NC, I have one of those wraps! I can totally show you how it works! It took me nine hours over three days, but I finally got it! It broke me, though; I cried. I wouldn't want anyone to go through what I went through. I'll email you detailed instructions, some pics and good vibes.

—Sheila K.

Hi everybody. NC here. So, the bleeding has let up a bit, but I've been ordered on bed rest. I'm to stay off my feet, lie on my left side and "do nothing." I've been doing nothing except thinking for the last six hours, lying here while Devoted Husband is at work keeping himself busy. And I'm pretty sure doing nothing is no good for the soul, even if it helps with the leaky womb. Maybe it's not the time or the place for this, but I can't sleep and I can't help wondering if my troubles today are somehow related to some work I did once… if a job, duties of the past, can somehow – like asbestos or mould – seep into a person's blood-stream. I keep thinking of that line Hamlet's mother said when she was feeling all guilty – for some reason it sticks in my head, always has. Spots on her heart that will not leave their *tinct*. I feel like maybe I'm tincted – or tainted. Whatever.

Here's why: I spent some time – seven or eight months I guess – as an escort. Not the kind you might be thinking, although that sort would probably be less offensive to some of you… Oh, gotta go, more later! dh home, phone ringing. Must get vertical, but slowly.

—*NC*

Girl! I did the escort thing for four months in university. It's the reason I was able to take Anthropology of Sex, Gender and Power and Feminist Perspectives on Pedagogy and Academe.

I'll leave you to parse the irony in that. Hey – don't feel tincted! We're humans here; we're allowed to follow our noses,
our hearts, our cunts, our convictions. We're even allowed to
fuck up. I mean, as long as you're no serial killer, right? Karma
doesn't work that way, friend. Actually, I'm not really sure karma works at all.

—*Craving City*

Oh, thanks, Craving, for your response! But I was actually a
different kind of escort – sometimes I think it would have been
better if I was some kind of high-class ho. But I was no fancy
hooker, nope.

I worked at a downtown abortion clinic escorting the "clients" to their appointments. My woman and I would march
from the foot of the path on the sidewalk, through the picketers,
up the steps to the clinic's doors. It was a pretty physical job – I
kept my elbows cocked like guns at my sides, my strides short
and powerful. I had to keep us both steady. Sometimes the path
seemed endless, the march forward so relentless. At these times,
I looked down at my army boots, with their steel toes and round
clown tops, and really felt myself a soldier, disconnected and
pure. The enemy was everywhere, lurking in a booby-trapped
underbrush. I didn't understand exactly what it was they said
as they waved their picket signs. (cc: Funny, but not ha-ha, what
you said about serial killers, because a couple of protestors had
signs like this: ABORTIONISTS = SERIAL KILLERS.) I could
read the signs, but for some reason I could never make out the
words they spoke; their shouts came at me in angry staccatos,
the machine-gun fire of the righteous. So there was only the
march forward, my prisoner and charge at my side. You know,
I'm not exactly a physically strong person, but my thighs are
big in relation to the rest of my body. I've clipped hundreds of

articles from magazines, tips on the camouflage and slimming illusions that should be applied to these things. But in this job my thighs were my secret weapons; my pretty haunches gave me a heft I didn't think was possible. They helped me to push through. I thrust them forward, and they carried me.

Okay, getting sleepy. More later. Why does lying in bed make me so tired?

—*New Country*

New Country: They have done studies that show that unwanted children grow up to be criminals, miscreants, molesters and general fuck-ups. They clog our prison systems; they come into this world unloved, wreak havoc and go out the same way they came in, in a cloud of ambivalence and shame. Do not feel bad about the work you did. Even on a purely practical level, you did the world a favour, saved us all some tax dollars and prevented a small societal seam from bursting.

—*Straight Shooter*

Straight Shooter: I feel sorry for you. Your soul has fled your body, left you all scooped out and sad. What brash arrogance you show, what blatant disregard for human family. It has been proven in numerous studies that in fact the enormous guilt women feel after aborting a precious baby later leads to child neglect and abuse. If you would like more information, you are welcome to join me at a meeting with my brothers and sisters in Love.

—*A Concerned Citizen*

Um, WADR, since when do we care about the opinions of one 'Concerned Citizen' (ahem, and WTF Christian Mom?) with a whole pile of Bibles to thump? When I was fifteen I had an abortion. BFD. Some shithead took advantage when I'd had one too many swigs of peach schnapps. My mom came with me to the clinic, and afterward we went for Swiss Chalet. I remember how I cried a little into the special sauce and my mom pretended not to see except she passed me an extra serviette. We never told my dad though. New Country, you're a hero in my books.

—*Craving City*

Ladies, I swear on my pile of Bibles (I really do have a pile, different editions and such...) that Concerned Citizen is not me. Really, truly. I mean, I don't approve exactly of, you know, the A-word, but I would never be so mean. That is totally not God's way.

Please believe me.

—*Christian Mom!*

Hi y'all! Thank you for your responses, but I feel like I ran out of steam before I reached the end of my story, and being bedridden makes me obsessed with finishing things... And because I am here, in this unofficial waiting room, on the brink of something, and I consider y'all my family of sorts – my sweet bodiless friends, with nothing to talk about but your bodies – I feel the need to confess. Once we reached the clinic, I would lead my charge up the stairs and help to check her in. She never looked at me and I never thought this rude. I did get the occasional clinger, whose grip on my arm became claw-like during our approach and whose weepiness I could feel without having to look at her. I allowed this like a man, giving several brisk, open-palmed pats to the back. I was stoic and strong until later I found myself trembling in the parking lot lighting up a cigarette – at least a pack a day during those months. After the procedure was complete, sometimes I was asked to escort the woman from the clinic to her car. The women, as they left, shook off my gallant overtures. They were spent and miserable, or relieved and giddy, but felt they should walk alone with the weight of their decision. I was paid very well for the job and there was only one time when I felt I could be in real danger. I remember the day so well, more vividly even than my wedding day. Is that strange? I think it is strange.

The particulars are all shiny in my mind's eye. It's bizarre I know, but I hold on to those details so tightly. I turn them around to look at them so much that sometimes I think I must change them just by holding them. But here it is, as I remember it: it was an overcast day, and it had rained earlier, a sudden downpour that sent the protestors scurrying to find shelter under a few earnestly planted municipal trees and shop awnings. I was glad to feel the rain; it cleared the way and gave me the opportunity to create an oasis under my big green umbrella. I had perfected the angle that kept us both dry, tilted slightly forward, positioned a foot or so above my companion's head. We were moving forward up the path, keeping a steady pace. She was tall, this client, and it was a challenge keeping the umbrella steady and in place. There were signs the sun might break through the clouds, and I knew this type of light was not a good sign for us. If the protestors were not too soggy they would be more riled up than ever – the sight of light struggling through dark clouds made them bold. I was just about to take the umbrella down so that we could move more quickly when I noticed a young woman break from the crowd and stand underneath a nearby tree. The woman was petite and brunette with corkscrew ringlets that brushed her shoulders – she was like a cherub carved into the top of a church pew. Her eyes were blue and blank. Her certainty made her so beautiful, which is why, I guess, I didn't think of her as a threat.

It wasn't until she was right next to us that I realized her intent. She had a switchblade clutched in one hand, flipped open and at the ready. It glinted like something from a 1950s musical – the moment felt all macho and melodious. I nearly laughed, but then I felt my woman tense and heard her sharp intake of breath. The world slowed down. The sun was still struggling in the sky. I wondered then if I was prepared to die for her, for this, for an idea of freedom and future that gives humans so much agency. I decided I was not, but neither could I allow the cherub to run and slash unchecked. It was too ridiculous. I shoved my woman behind me and squared my shoulders directly in front of my attacker. Then I punched the cherub, quickly and efficiently, in the nose. Odd, but I was thinking of sharks – how best to disorient one if it ever becomes overly aggressive while you are snorkeling in the tropics.

I broke her nose. The tears and the blood mingled on her lovely cheeks and she staggered away. My charge dusted herself off, took my arm again and pulled me toward the clinic. Thanks, she muttered, once I had seated her. No prob, I said. I never saw either of those women again.

And now here I am, leaking blood, confessing to strangers, already tallying all the moments in my life that might have been.

—*NC*

NC: Wings here. Thank you for choosing us to hold your story. To allow these shadowy corners access to the light is perhaps the most meaningful gift we can give each other. I say this with true feeling and conviction and – I hope – courage. You have inspired me to share my own story, you see. The fact is, I could have been one of your companions on your walks from sidewalk to doorstep, from relative innocence to murky knowingness. When I was twenty-three years old, I opted to end a pregnancy. I will not say it was a difficult decision at the time – you could say I saw no other option.

I had been travelling for eight months, backpacking for a few weeks with a childhood friend and then for various segments of time with other friends, who came to seem to me – in clouds of hash smoke, on train station platforms, in the lounges of youth hostels, on stone benches in public squares, sprawled on the grass that surrounded famous monuments – as friends I had known forever, as my soul's true companions.

When, back home in Toronto, I first began to feel queasy, I assumed I had brought back a souvenir, an opportunistic worm or virus simply playing its own role in my body's ecosystem. But then I was Late and Later, and I began to think about all the times in the last six weeks I had allowed myself to be seduced by the wave of sensation that meant I could gather another human into me. When I peed on that wand and saw that crucifix, it did seem to me just another short-term burden to bear. I had to get rid of it. And if I had not? I don't know. I think I might have married my cousin's ex. He had a wrinkle on his forehead that made him seem kind, and he listened to me when I drank too much Gato Negro. But he was not what I needed. I knew that then, and I know it now. I wish I could say I mourned the loss of life but I could not, not when all I knew of my own past, present and future was the result of my own arrogant spirit tentacling out to touch as much of the world as I could… Sometimes I think I should be asking someone or something forgiveness, but instead I am overcome by a gut-wrenching gratitude. Who is it I'm thanking? I'm not sure. I'm still not sure.

—*Wings*

Holy crap, Wings! Why don't you give it up and write a novel already?

—*Straight Shooter*

Oh Wings! Thank you so much for sharing. I knew that bristly exterior was hiding something mushy and vulnerable. You don't have to respond to this note – I just wanted you to know I understand and I forgive you for your earlier cranky posts.

—*Spiral*

Spiral: I definitely was not asking *your* forgiveness. And I still think you've been sniffing too much incense.

—*Wings*

Hi Everybody! Sheila K. here. I've been reading your entries like crazy – when I get home from work or running errands I sometimes have to stop myself from running first to the computer before stopping to pee – and believe me, I really have to pee! I guess I just felt like I had to put my two cents in as far as this whole debate or discussion is concerned. I know there are as many opinions out there as there are birds in the sky, but I feel like maybe I'm different. You see, I don't have a Bible to my name, never mind one I'd like to thump, but I also don't believe abortion is right. I'm not sure I've always felt this way; in fact I don't think I had an opinion, or at least not a fully formed one until very recently. I wonder sometimes if it was the birth of my first child that changed my outlook, but somehow I don't think so. I think instead it is a brand of certainty that comes with maturation, a commitment to a set of views that, when I was younger, I might have attributed to the stubborn rigidity of middle age, but that I now see as a kind of bravery. It's just that I believe that something, once started, should be carried through to the end. Maybe it's because everything in our lives has become so easily disposable. And I think – no, not *this*, you should not be allowed to do *this*. And I understand, I do, that there are issues of freedom, of gender, of a person's parameters being curtailed by others, of desperation and back alleys. But are we not an innovative, creative species that adapts, that finds ways to manage the unexpected? Should we not persist in filling gaps where gaps exist, evolve to take care of what we have created? What I'm trying to say is there must be more than one way to tidy our own chaos, no?

—Sheila K

Sheila: I hear you! I try to respect a person's choice, I really do, but I don't think any woman who's ever endured IVF – all that poking and prodding and waiting and wondering – would ever choose to end a pregnancy. It just seems like squandered opportunity, something wanton and wasteful.

—Spiral

POST REDACTED BY FORUM MASTER

What does "redacted" mean? It sounds kind of French.

—Straight Shooter

Who is the Forum Master? I didn't know we had a Forum Master.

—Spiral

I think it might be God.

—Craving City

It's so weird to think of God using a computer!

—Christian Mom!

Why would God bother censoring us, anyway? When has he ever cared about women's whinging?

—*Straight Shooter*

Ah, the ghost in the machine. It's actually the perfect place for god to hang out, isn't it?

—*Wings*

I lost the baby.

—NC

Oh, New Country, what happened? What happened?

—*Spiral*

Apparently my cervix is incompetent – along with my tear ducts. I know I should cry. I should be crying, right? Instead I just feel like someone has stuffed dry straw into the hole where my heart is and I wish like crazy for a word that might burn it up, make me feel something, anything. That so much liquid could gush from me, that my little one could escape me on a tidal wave of blood, and I could be left feeling so arid and artificial... This can't be what it means to be human.

—NC

My heart goes out to you, New Country. And Jesus SEES you, He really does. He understands your anguish and loves you and feels your repentance even if you've not yet recognized it. My God is not a punishing God, but there are reasons, there is sense and order in this world, a plan, a structure of sorts that emerges if we take a moment to understand the scaffolding of our lives. It was SINFUL work that you did, helping abortionists to commit abominations. But you are beginning to understand now and that is what is IMPORTANT. You know all too well, I'm sure, considering your CONDITION, that what we carry in our wombs as women is NOT GARBAGE. You know, I am certain, that what stirs within you is LIFE. By eleven weeks a fetus is waking, sleeping, eating, DREAMING. Dreaming of a life outside his mother, but bathed in the light of mother's love, of God's love. Please be strong and understand that although you have made terrible mistakes, there is room for you here in the fold, that we will enfold you and keep you and your baby from harm.

—*On the Side of the Innocents*

Holy mackerel! Who is this nutjob? "On the Side of the Innocents"? A bit unwieldy as a handle, no? I know we try to respect diversity of opinion here, but I have one word for you, New Country: ignore.

—*Spiral*

To ignore the word of God is to court disaster. *But when Jesus saw it, he was much displeased, and said unto them, Suffer the little children to come unto me, and forbid them not: for of such is the kingdom of God.* The souls you helped banish are with Jesus now. You will not be so lucky. There is a table reserved in a restaurant called Hades for you and your devil spawn. A special place reserved.

—*Concerned Christian*

New Country: Don't listen to these assholes with all their flaming fire and brimming brimstone. I also dreamed about your baby. He was small and dead. I held him in my palm then laid him on the ground. With my wings, I formed a kind of canopy over top of him. I wove my feathers together to give him shelter. I protected him.

—*Wings*

New Country: Are you still there? Please don't go away because of a couple of kooks with some Internet savoir faire and too many holy axes to grind. We're still here. And we love you.

—*Spiral*

Oh NC! I had to have a smoke when I read your news. About six "ladies with handbags" (you know the type) gave me the dirtiest fucking looks as they passed me on my stoop, knocked up and sucking on a cig like my life depended on it. I'm so sorry, NC. Is someone with you? Where can you go? I hope you have pals there besides us, all stuck in our virtualness.

—*Craving City*

NC: This is probably not the right time to tell you this, but just the fact that you could conceive in the first place, well, that's a good thing. You'll have more chances, you will. Take good care.

—*Straight Shooter*

New Country: You should crank your old music – as loud as possible – until the neighbours make 911 calls. Then you should beat on things – your own breast, tabletops, the fridge door. Do not stop until you are entirely spent. Once you've had a rest, turn up the volume again.

—*Wings*

It is not fair that your baby died. It happens more than people like to admit or talk about, but it is in no way fair. DO NOT let anybody tell you any differently. Stay away from parks and avoid schoolyards. Maybe take a vacation.

—*Straight Shooter*

PS Table Reserved?!?

Thanks, everybody, for all your props and kind words. I know that you are all speaking from your own truth, and that's what's important, even if it is difficult for me to absorb. I am writing to say goodbye as I don't quite fit in around these parts anymore. I wish you all the very best with your challenges, your joys, your wonderful tumult, the times when your faces are not lit by these crass, compelling, miraculous screens. Remember to talk to and touch each other whenever you can. As Faith would sing: "The secret of life is there ain't no secret / And you don't get your money back." Peace and Punk Rock,

—*NC*

New Country – I'm guessing you are in Toronto... If you are, would you like to meet me for tea (or something stronger) one of these days? That is, if you're still listening...

—*Wings*

Wings: I'm still here. I tried but I can't turn off my laptop. I don't want to believe... I just don't want to. So Wings, I want you to keep doing your crazy-assed, lyrical, love-me-or-leave-me thing, I really do, but I don't want to meet you. I don't want to know you. It's just that – even though we're networked, connected, I guess – you're really NOT my family, are you? I don't even know what you look like, or what your voice sounds like or what hair products you use… And, to be honest, I'm just not sure I could deal with it – with you and your, well, your CONDITION, I guess, and by that I mean no offence I really don't.

—*New Country*

New Country: I know I am probably the last person you want to hear from – but I don't judge you, I don't! Gosh, just saying that makes me sound so sanctimonious, doesn't it? I am so sorry for your loss. I've been praying for you. I didn't want to jump into the fray before, with all those loony-tunes giving us God-fearers a bad name. I don't know what God wants us to do, or why He might have chosen your baby, or why He'd want to "redact" anyone's post. I just believe in Him, and His Great Good Grace is all. I just have to believe in Him. Anyway, I just wanted to tell you, before you left, in case you didn't know, that I am also a Faith Hill fan!!! Especially the songs "A Baby Changes Everything" which is totally not about what you might think – it's Jesus who is the baby! – and also "You Bring Out the Elvis in Me" (not sure if you're really into Elvis…). Take care of yourself, and God Bless.

—*Christian Mom!*

Taking Flight
by Ben Tanzer

It starts on Facebook, and why does everything start there now? You suppose you're too old to understand it, just as you have no idea why you signed up in the first place. You're not actually interested in what anyone from high school is doing, how many kids they have or how much they love Jesus. You don't want their gifts or care about the farm they're building. There is a reason why you live nowhere near home and haven't, there was a bigger world out there, a world where new memories could be made and the old ones could be left behind and packed away.

And yet, here you are and you act like you don't know why, even though it's not so hard to figure out when you look across the dinner table at your husband, the husband you love, but are not sure you still want, the husband who sometimes feels like a sibling or friend, which is fine in some ways, there's no animosity or sadness, it isn't even stale exactly, it's just good, comfortable, the date nights, the movies, the trips to his family's cabin and the brunches at The 3rd Coast, every Sunday, copies of the *Tribune* and *New York Times* strewn across the table.

Still, you won't be your mom, putting on your happy smile, waiting, dealing, only to be left like your father left her, with nothing and nowhere to go. So, yes, there are moments when you get a glimpse of something more, or different, the way another couple looks at each other, or the random drunken moment at work parties when a younger male co-worker looks at you across the bar and pauses, holding his stare for that extra breath, taking you in, and wondering what you, an older, married woman, might be willing to do under the right circumstances, and not just what, but how much, and how often, and you have to wonder whether it would all be worth it, because that co-worker doesn't usually gravitate toward women older than him, but for that moment you're different, you're an object of desire, and it's exciting, and fresh, because being wanted is wonderful, especially when the person doing the wanting is exciting and fresh themselves.

And yet, as much as you wonder whether you would truly do something, even losing afternoons at work, running through all the possible permutations, you know you wouldn't, it will never feel safe to do so, never foolproof, things will go wrong, feelings will be hurt and at a minimum you will have to confront someone, maybe the co-worker, but maybe your husband as well, something that seems impossible to imagine, the pain and confusion on his face and his efforts to hide it, because that's what men do, they hide things, run from them and how could you ever do that to him, you couldn't, you won't allow yourself to, right, no, never, not.

Facebook though is safe, a look into other people's lives, new connections with friends from the past who don't care about who you were then and don't think about the insecurities that wracked your every moment when they first thought they knew you, because they didn't know about them anyway. And who knows who's out there and what they might be up to or into, and who knows what they might be into with you, something sketchy, but not exactly, these are just messages, though, ephemera, things that might cross a line, but for just a moment, because once you're done reading you hit delete and the feelings pass, nothing, like magic, or a bird taking a flight.

That's your thought anyway, because you of course would never initiate such an exchange, that's not your thing, never was, if there was an opportunity back then, usually drunken, you would grab it with a ferocity that was rarely matched in your regular life, the life that involved school, parents and work, the one that never seemed to have anything to do with getting high and drunk and hooking up regardless of the situation, the circumstances or the feelings involved. Having sex was fine, but not something you pushed, not really, not always, you were more of an air-traffic controller, or curator, you made things happen, it was organic, without being organic, random, but not exactly, and here you are again, making friend requests, sending messages and pretending you care about the trips they take and their dumbass jobs, all the while waiting, waiting for an opening, a weakness, something you can grab hold of, and then twist, pull, prod and arrange into something different and useful, because the fact is you may not want to end up like your dad any more than you want you want to end up like your mom, but if you have to choose, and you do, you won't wait like she did to see what happens.

There's nothing though, and no one takes the bait. You wonder how much the stories of Facebook flings and the rekindling of old romances are just folklore or urban myth, everyone seems so fucking happy, married to this person or that one, little hearts and hyperlinks everywhere. It's infuriating. And just like high school, everyone has something you don't, and yes they are happy to connect, but after that first exchange, nothing, it all fades, and though they update their status and leave wall messages for other mutual friends, they're gone, moving on to new relationships, and new sets of photos, the promise of excitement and release, just one more click away.

And so it goes until he comes along. Scott from senior year, Scott who liked to break into people's houses and have sex on their kitchen tables and in their bathtubs. Scott who said he wanted to do everything, do it everywhere and do it with you as often as you'd let him. He friends you and he is full of exuberance and energy, his messages at first the same dopey ones everyone sends, but as he doesn't go away, they change, he is not happy with his wife, he loves their kids but their relationship is staid and boring, old, it's so much work, work he can barely stand to do, but might if she showed more interest in him, and not in his inner life necessarily, because he's fine, and he's there for her in so many ways, and the kids, and there's no anger, no sadness, but she doesn't touch him like she used to, or even look at him like she used to, and they haven't had sex for a year, and she's fine with that, but would you be fine with that he says, setting the trap for you, no, of course not you say, right he says, and you know what I'm like, or was anyway, insatiable, crazy for it, yes, you know you say, you remember, I bet you do he says, you do, and that's game, set and match.

What about us he says later on, what about us, what, you say, you think things could have been different he says, I don't know you say, we were young, drunk, high, and obsessed with sex, things change, sure he says, but it's a start, right, right, and maybe some people have to take a break from one another he says, find themselves, learn from their time apart, and then come back together. Sure you say, seems possible, why not, exactly he says, why not, so that could be us, you guess you say, holding out on him, stretching it out, being subtle, not too aggressive, not too crazy, or pushy, organic, always organic.

This is good. It's going well, until you slip. So, why did we break up you say, not remembering, not really, not thinking it even matters, it was so long ago, and you were so young, and it was so nothing to either of you. You don't remember he says, really, the whole thing with Dan? Dan, your hot friend, yeah, you say, starting to remember. You suggested we have a threesome with him, he says, but I couldn't share you, I wouldn't, it couldn't be like that. Right, you say, because you had tried to initiate that and it hadn't gone well. It was a long time ago, you say, it was, he replies, and maybe it wouldn't have been that big a deal if you hadn't fucked him anyway, but you did fuck him, like I wasn't enough for you, how couldn't I have been enough? And this is a question you can't answer, because it was never about that, he said he wanted to do everything, but he didn't, he pussied out and let you down, and you acted out.

That destroyed me he says, and you say you're sorry, it really was a long time ago. You know my dad was a raging alcoholic he says, did you know that, no, not really you say. I would do anything to get out of the house, I just wanted to be someone else, and live their life, even if it meant breaking into their home, and you, for a moment, you got that, and you wanted to be with me, and then you ruined it, killed it, killed me in some ways. I'm fine now he says, it took a long time, and a lot of healing, but I'm fine, and I'm whole, and at peace. Good, you say, but you're scared, this isn't light or sketchy or organic or anything, it's crazy and wrong and nothing you want anything to do with.

Should we get together he says, pretend it's a business trip or something? That could be cool, you say, but now isn't so good. Why not now, what, what was this then, he says, and you say you don't know, it was fun, but it can't be more. Bullshit, he says, this means something, no it doesn't you say, you misunderstood. The hell I did, he says, when can we get together, and where, I will leave my family for you, he says, I'll show you what kind of man I am now, I'm not scared any more he continues, not scared, just let me prove it to you.

You ask yourself how this got so far, but you know how it did, desperation and fear and not wanting to repeat your mother's mistakes. The thing is though, we don't learn from our parents' mistakes, we say we will, and we try to be different, but we don't and we can't, and sure, you're not like your dad either, but that doesn't matter, because this is about your mother, it's always the mother, and you are her, and now you just want to run away and hide, which you can do because this is Facebook and all it takes is one click of the mouse to unfriend someone and act like you never reconnected with them at all.

SO MUCH FUN
by Megan Stielstra

Taken with an iPhone 5, posted to Instagram @shelbyliveshere:
Shelby, Becky and Bree have their arms around each other, smiling for the camera. They're in their late twenties, old college friends who don't see each other as much as they'd like because of demanding jobs (high-school teacher, PR exec, and arts administrator, respectively). But earlier this week, Bree had called, saying, "It's been too long," and now it's Girls Night Out. There are empty martini glasses on the bar. There are low-cut shirts, shiny lip glosses and dangerous shoes. Becky has a hard time walking in hers, but they're hot so who cares? Shelby's pants are so tight she leaves the top button unbuttoned. The hemline on Bree's silk dress hits mid-thigh; if she leans over, you can see garters holding up netted stockings and a teasing line of smooth white skin.

This photo of the three of them is totally perfect. They all look beautiful and you know how hard that is to pull off. Somebody's always blinking or their mouth is open in a weird way, but this? – this is how they'd like to be seen. It's how they see themselves: independent and sexy and powerful and free, reconnecting with old friends, burning off steam, maybe on the prowl – not Bree, of course, Bree's got a boyfriend – but the other two? Why the hell not! Becky doesn't want a relationship but she's always down for some fun (wink wink) and Shelby – well,

Shelby hasn't been on a date in forever.

"It's time," Becky tells her. "Tonight's the motherfucking night!"

After the photo is posted to Instagram, it's liked thirty-seven times by various friends and followers. There are comments, too: *RAWR* and *HAWT* and OMG *I wish I was there!* and *Get my girl back to me in one piece!* and *You guys are going to have SO MUCH FUN.*

Taken, not posted:
The twenty+ photos it took to get that perfect photo.

Taken, posted:
A close-up of three full martini glasses.

Taken, posted:
A close-up of three empty martini glasses.

Taken, posted:
A close-up of two full martini glasses and a whiskey, rocks.

The comments say *Awww shit* and *#round3.*

Taken, posted:
The moon, full and bright above Chicago's famous skyline, a thousand lights in a thousand buildings. It's mid-May; newly spring. The streets are full of people, of music from cars and bars and clubs with thrown-open windows, of relief at being outside. The girls are outside now, on the move from the bar to a nearby dance club. Becky's feet hurt like hell so she goes slow, one foot hobbling after the other, and Shelby and Bree walk ahead. They talk about their jobs. Their families. The things you talk about so you don't really have to talk.

Taken, posted:
Here is the obligatory wide shot of the crowd inside the club: a hundred-plus people sardine-packed under the strobe lights, their arms in the air as though they could climb the sound. There are men and women and both and neither, bare skin and thrift store and no-credit-limit Neiman Marcus, middle-aged 80s rave-scene throwbacks and eighteen-year-old kids who snuck in on stolen fake IDs. For a second, Shelby's sure she sees one of her high-school students from the year before, some baseball player who kept failing math. What was his name? It was a J-name – Josh, John, James?
    Fuck it. Who cares.
    Have fun, JoshJohnJames. Have so much fucking fun.

Taken, posted:
Several arty shots of Bree and Becky on the dance floor, each one a different colour 'cause of the fast-flash lights: red-blue-pink-gold-white. Becky's got her shoes off, holding them high above her head by the straps. She loves dancing. Lives for it. Shut your eyes, arms in the air, and everything else disappears. Bree moves slower, feeling the music match her heartbeat, feeling people's eyes slide over her body. There are always eyes on Bree. Always have been, ever since college. She used to think it was because men wanted to fuck her and women wanted to know where she got her clothes, but now she knows better.

Not taken:
Shelby's at the bar by herself. She needs a moment, away from the beat and the lights and her own stupid heart, her own stupid hope. A few hours earlier, getting ready to go out, she'd had a conversation with herself about the things she would and would not do tonight. She'd been so strong then, so resolved, but now there is whiskey. There's the moon. There's music and bodies and darkness to hide behind.

Shelby orders another whiskey, downs it fast, and turns back to the dance floor. Tonight's her motherfucking night.

Taken, posted:
A close-up of Bree dancing.

Taken, not posted:
Many close-ups of Bree dancing: garters and fishnets and smooth white skin; sweat plastering long hair to her neck; sweat gluing that silk dress to her ribcage, her abs, her ass.

Taken, not posted:
A close-up of Bree staring into the camera.

Taken, not posted:
Bree walking away from the dance floor, looking back over her shoulder to make sure the camera is following her.

Not taken:
Now they're locked into the club's single-occupancy bathroom. Bree's backed against the wall. Shelby's on her knees, her hands sliding the sweaty silk high over those perfect thighs, up around that perfect waist, a thin layer of lace panty is all that's between her tongue and its target. She breathes in and in and in; the thick, wet, stinking beautiful fog of this woman who makes her crazy in every possible way, the joy and the fury and the mess, and she tears at the lace with her teeth. Bree's moaning now, hiking one perfect leg up onto the sink to open herself as wide as possible, and she digs her fingernails deep into Shelby's shoulders. She likes leaving marks. She likes doing damage. She likes watching her half-naked body in the mirror on the opposite wall, the back of Shelby's head buried between her legs, hands gripping her ass and pulling deeper, hands in her hair and pulling down,

whose hands are whose and why does it matter in all this sweat and sliding and hunger and climbing and closer, Shelby's knees aching as they grind into the concrete floor, and in the mirror Bree smiles as she screams.

Not taken:
Both girls wrapped together in a ball, an indistinguishable blend of arms and legs and hair. The crowd outside the bathroom feels a thousand miles away. Slowly, their heartbeats sync. They breathe into each other. They hold each other. There is nothing else but this.

It's a really lovely moment.

Too bad no one was there to take a picture.

Not taken:
Life's not a still shot. It always, always, *always* moves.

Shelby says, "I wish—" and Bree says, "Don't."

"Don't what?"

"Don't ruin it. You always ruin it."

Shelby, hurt: "I don't—"

Bree, annoyed: "You *do*," and then gets out her mental list, the one she's carried since college of all the times Shelby tries to corner her, to make her talk through it, to say something aloud that she was still too terrified to admit to herself. "Why can't we just have *fun?*" she asks for the gazillionth time, struggling to separate herself, to pull away. Shelby holds tighter, hoping for the warmth of Bree's body for just another minute. Thirty seconds, even. She could stretch thirty seconds into a month's worth of memory. "Let me go!" Bree is yelling now, pulling backward too hard and banging her head on the underside of the sink. There's a crack of bone on porcelain. There are tears. Hard, awful words. Another entry on Bree's mental list. And Shelby, for the gazillionth time, loosens her grip and lets her go.

Taken, posted, and immediately deleted:
A selfie of Shelby, holding up her iPhone to the bathroom mirror. She looks like a demilitarized zone. Her shirt is bunched around her waist, her shoulders scratched raw, her pants shredded at the knees. Her hair is matted with sweat and cum; mascara and eyeliner and shadow streak purple and black; and the bottom half of her face is swollen from sucking and smeared lipstick and the stupid, angry sobbing that started after Bree slammed the bathroom door behind her, nearly a decade of Bree slamming doors behind her, Bree walking away, Bree going back to whatever man she was with at the time and still Shelby waited, crying her eyes out in public bathrooms, or pantries at dinner parties, or the backseats of the taxi cabs that take her back to her apartment, alone.

Taken, posted:
A selfie of Shelby, holding up her iPhone to the bathroom mirror. She's cleaned up now: clothes back on, face washed, make-up re-applied, hair wet in the bathroom sink and slicked back. What you see is a girl sweaty from dancing all night. What you can't see doesn't matter.

Not taken:
Crowd, lights, music, beat. Over the noise of it, Becky yells, "I've been trying to find you!" and "Where's Bree?" and, once she's close enough to see Shelby's face, "Are you okay?" Becky's not stupid; not blind, either. Feels like a thousand times she's cornered Bree in a bathroom at the bar or the bedroom at a party, saying, "What's going on with you two?" and every time, Bree cracks. It's awful seeing a friend like that: curled on the floor, sobbing uncontrollably, trying to find the words. She doesn't know what to *do*. She's so *confused*. She needs more *time*. She loves Shelby, *but*.

Feels like a thousand times Becky's stood there, waiting for the end of that sentence.

Such a fucking mess. So many fucking lies. Even now with her clothes torn, her face swollen, her balance zigzagging, Shelby yells, "I'm totally fine!" and "Bree had an early meeting!" and "She said to tell you goodbye!" Becky's tired of it. Exhausted by it. How much longer can this go on?

"Listen," she yells. She grabs Shelby's shoulders to steady her and looks into her eyes very intently. What she's about to say is important. It will, like, *mean* something. "It's time, you know?"

Shelby tries to focus on the bridge of Becky's nose. "I know," she yells.

"Do you?" Becky yells. "Do you, like, *know* know?"

"I do," Shelby yells. She wants to nod but her head is too heavy.

Becky lets her go. She's not stupid; not blind, either; but the music is so *loud*, the conversation so *big*, and there've been so *many* drinks. Easier to just shut your eyes and put your arms in the air.

At the end of the song, they hug, promise to call, and then Becky's gone. She has a busy day tomorrow. She has what you call a *life*.

Taken, posted:
A close-up of a plastic cup of whiskey.

Not taken:
It's the part of the night when the beat hurts your chest. Decision time: Home to sleep it off, or drink more to push it all away? Shelby's got her elbows on the bar and her head in her hands, working up the energy to go outside and hail a cab when it happens: "Ms Elliot?"

Shelby looks up. She laughs, because of course! Why not! The way this night is going, why the hell not! "JoshJohnJames!" she says, loud over the music, and laughs again.

He looks confused. "Jim, actually," he says.

Shelby laughs again. "Jim Actually," she says. "That's perfect."

Still confused, but he presses on. "I wanted to ask you not to tell anyone." He leans into her. His mouth finds her ear. He says something about being underage, about his brother's ID, about sneaking out in his dad's car. His breath is hot. He's wearing a sweaty tank top and his biceps are perfect.

"Remind me, Jim Actually," Shelby says. "You play baseball?"

"Ms Elliot—"

"It's Saturday-fucking-night, Jim Actually. Ms Elliot is off duty." Shelby is proud of herself for coming up with this line. It's a very good line. Were she grading herself on this line, she would give herself an A. She laughs at the thought and touches his bicep. "Call me Shelby."

"Shelby." He's a little uncomfortable with her first name but you can tell he likes it, too. He likes the power. He likes her thighs. He likes the liquor, and the danger, and the darkness to hide behind. "Do you want to dance, Shelby?"

Shelby's still laughing. "Actually, Jim Actually," she says. "I have a better idea." She slides her fingers from his arm to his chest; then down. "What were you saying about a car?"

Taken, not posted:
Lots of blurry, tilty photos of moving cars, taken from the passenger seat of Jim's dad's VW Passat: in the center of the city, surrounded by buildings; then on Lakeshore Drive, open and fast with red brake lights streaming; then parked near the Montrose Beach at Lake Michigan.

Taken, posted:
A close-up of Shelby's feet in the sand, faintly illuminated by the combination of street light, flash and moon.

Taken, not posted:
The moon over the lake, high and full in the sky. Below it, its mirror image reflects across the water, casting a long gold path from the edge of the sand into the dark horizon. Shelby stares at this path while Jim fucks her from behind. They were on a ledge of jagged rock, and she'd found one that had a smooth-enough surface to bend over without digging in to her stomach. She'd pulled her pants down herself, had reached around to help him inside her and is now pressing the meat of her palms into the rocks, bracing herself so his thrusting won't push her over the edge. Shelby's been with enough men to know to keep her mind busy, and imagines running down that golden path and climbing up into the moon. She wonders if she'd get her feet wet. She wonders if the reason we can't walk on water is because we were told as children that it's impossible, and the doubt causes us to sink. She wonders if JimJohnJosh is finished yet. She wonders if she's his first and how sad that would be – your first time without love – but then: *Fuck it. He's fucking his teacher. That's a great fucking story to tell.*

Taken, not posted:
A full-body shot of Jim pulling up his underpants. Shelby doesn't know why she took it. One second she's shaking sand out of her shoes; the next second she's reaching for her iPhone. Both of them are shocked when the flash goes off, his teenage body pale and awkward in the glare.

"Why'd you take my picture?" he says, pissed.

He says, "Give me that."

Taken, not posted:
Jim is closer now, hand outstretched and reaching. "You can't take a picture of me like this," he says.

He says, *"Give it to me."*

Taken, not posted:
A close-up shot of his palm. "I'm fucking serious. Do you know how much trouble I can get into?"

He says, "I'm not going to ask again."

Taken, not posted:
Several blurry, messy shots. Upside down and sideways. Too dark to really see anything. Later, Shelby would look through them, trying to work out what happened, to match the photos against her black-out, drunk-soaked memory: He came at me. That's his hand. I held it away from him. We were yelling. He was grabbing at me and I dropped my phone. That's the ground, right? And that's the moon. I must have had both hands free 'cause I remember reaching out and pushing him – right? Maybe?

There's one image she couldn't find in the Camera Roll. It lives in her mind. To this day, it's there; in her dreams at night or, when awake, burned on the backs of her eyelids: a pale, awkward teenage body, sprawled face down across the jagged rocks.

Or maybe she just imagined that part.

Not taken:
This is the backseat of the taxi cab, taking Shelby back to her apartment alone. She's barefoot, her feet raw and bloody. Her clothes hang off her. She's covered in sand and dirt and smeared make-up. No purse – when she gets home, she'll let herself in with the hidden key and grab a twenty to pay the cabbie – but for now, she slouches down to hide her headache from the rising,

unforgiving sun and pulls her iPhone from her back pocket, opening Instagram. There is the first photo of the night: her and Becky and Bree, arms around each other, smiling into the camera. It's a perfect shot. They all look beautiful and you *know* how hard that is to pull off. Somebody's always blinking, or their mouth is open in a weird way, but this? – this is how they'd like to be seen. It's how they see themselves. Shelby starts to cry then, fast and easy as an auto update or copy/paste.

The cab driver has seen many things in his day. A girl crying in the backseat isn't anything new.

It's not new for Shelby, either. She's been in this moment before.

It always, always, *always* moves.

The Wedding
by Sonal Champsee

My fight with David had gone late into the night, and I was tired. I'd skipped breakfast in favour of sleep, counting on getting to Deepa's wedding early enough to grab some hot coffee and sweet jalabi, but when I arrived the groom was already off the white horse and the jaan had started. Hungry, I stood at the fringes of a group of women in red and gold bandani saris – all the women in my family, each wearing the sari given to her on her wedding day. Family members smiled hello, and I nodded back, fiddling with the palu of my green net sari. My cellphone was in my purse, but I couldn't step away to discreetly call and fix things. The scene was strangely quiet. Some of the women were singing nasal-sounding wedding songs, but there were no musicians or drummers. Had I missed them? Or did they skip that part so the Bowman family wouldn't embarrass themselves trying to dance along in the groom's procession? Or maybe Madhu, my cousinsister and the bride's mother, cheaped out.

Ryan the groom looked strangely comfortable for a white guy in an embroidered sherwani and a manly pink turban. They were at the part where he had to step on a brittle clay pot to break it. If David were here, I'd explain that breaking the pot proved that Ryan was strong enough to withstand marriage. If David were here, I'd have spent last night assuring him that he wouldn't need to wear Indian clothes and in fact most men wore suits to these things anyway. But if David were here, we'd at least be engaged, since Indian people do not bring dates to Indian weddings.

Pot broken, the procession started so we all followed Ryan into the banquet hall where he slipped his jutis off his feet and ascended the two steps onto the mandip to sit alone. His side filed into orderly rows, while our side mingled and chatted as they jockeyed for seats near the front. My mother attempted to sit quietly at the back, but my cousins noticed and insisted she take a better seat. She told them not to bother, but with the whole family fussing over her she eventually gave up and – pulling me with her – took a seat in the second row, behind my father who turned and waved happily at us. "So wonderful, Deepa getting married," he said. "She's grown up so much."

My mother shrugged. "She's twenty-eight. This is the time when most girls get married."

I reached into my purse and gripped my phone. Soon, I could call him, smooth everything over.

The pandit stood on stage in a grey-blue jhubo and dopey white tube socks. In lightly accented English he announced that once the doors closed, the ceremony would begin and no one would be allowed to leave. What the hell? Normally at Indian weddings, the guests got to leave and have tea and snacks while the bride and groom suffered through hours of ceremony. There was no way to call him. I'd have to text him, and I hated talking about important things over text.

The pandit managed to hush the excited crowd and we chanted the Namokar Mantra five times as a group before he chanted other mantras solo. I flipped through the wedding program. We were on item four out of fourteen, and the pandit seemed to be sticking closely to the actual program; most pandits changed things around on their own whims. Still, it was impossible to predict how long the ceremony would last. My mother pulled out her iPhone and checked her email.

Even if I hadn't stayed up to argue with David last night, I'd still be tired. I had to get up at 6 AM to go to my cousinbrother's to get my hair and makeup done and my sari draped properly, and then I had drive all the way to Brampton to the wedding hall. And for what? Just so I could sit through the wedding of the girl I used to babysit.

On the mandip, the pandit directed the bride's parents to wash the groom's feet in a brass bowl. The groom's side watched Ryan's fish-white feet while the bride's side, knowing that this wasn't a critical moment in the ceremony, gossiped quietly amongst themselves. I glanced at my mother, who was now playing Bookworm on her iPhone.

I pulled my phone out of my purse and wrote David a text:

Are you okay?

I clicked Send, and then waited for confirmation that the message had been sent. I stared at the phone, willing a response to come, but nothing came. I texted again:

I'm at the wedding, but can you text me? Please?

There was still no instant response. Don't send a third, I told myself. Three messages goes into crazy territory. I folded the phone in the pleats of my sari to stop looking at it, but kept my hand wrapped around it.

On the mandip, the pandit instructed Madhu to feed Ryan a mixture from a plain white kitchen bowl, which he ate with good grace. She was using a toonie as a spoon; evidently, a five-rupee coin was too devalued to bother. Once they were done, the pandit spoke. "By feeding the groom a mixture of yogurt and honey, the parents are telling the groom that they are giving him their most precious possession, their daughter. By eating the yogurt and honey, the groom has committed to accepting her and caring for her in the same way her parents have cherished her."

I leaned over to my mother and mumbled: "It's nice that they told him what he was agreeing to after he's already committed to it."

She didn't take her eyes off Bookworm. "That's how they do things in India. Agree first, tell you later." I glanced at my dad, who was entranced by the ceremony, and then looked at her iPhone. After a minute, I pointed out the word "THREADS" to her.

Music began playing – a whiny version of the wedding march. Uncertainly and unevenly, the crowd rose. I couldn't remember if it was normal at an Indian wedding for people to rise for the bride, but I rolled my eyes when the small blonde flower girl walked down the aisle. Really? A flower girl? As if an Indian wedding wasn't enough pointless fuss without adding in some kid to throw white rose petals over the red rose petal-festooned aisle. And of course she had three bridesmaids (one Indian, two non-Indian) in identical purple saris – like those non-Indian girls would ever find a reason to wear a sari again.

My cellphone buzzed in my hand. All eyes were on the bride, my cousinsister's daughter Deepa, who was walking in wearing a heavy white sari and a very non-traditional smile. I checked my messages.

im ok

I exhaled. He was talking to me. I considered my next text as Deepa slipped off her high-heeled sandals to walk up the steps to the mandip. The pandit's assistants held a white cloth in front of Ryan's face so he couldn't see her. In an arranged marriage, like my parents, that might have been a sensible precaution but this bride and groom had dated through high school and college.

I texted back:

I was so worried when I couldn't reach you.

Deepa was arranged on stage so that she and Ryan were facing each other, but separated by the white cloth. Both were given garlands of red flowers, like heavy Hawaiian leis. The audience sat down again.

My cellphone buzzed:

sry

Why didn't you answer the phone?

i was asleep

The soft hum of whispered conversations on the Indian side stilled; this was an important moment. My father was so caught up that he'd forgotten about the camera around his neck, and even my mother was watching. The pandit's assistants removed the cloth, and with the pandit giving directions, the groom solemnly put his flower garland around the bride's neck, taking care to keep it from getting caught on her hair jewelry. She, in turn, placed her flower garland over his turban and around his neck. The Indian side applauded, joined soon after by the other side of the room. Ryan and Deepa relaxed and grinned. "By putting the garland around each other's neck," said the pandit. "They have accepted each other and agreed to be husband and wife. But the wedding is not over yet, we have more to go." The crowd tittered, and resumed conversation.

I didn't know what to say to David next. The only words in my head were "Do you still love me?" but that was such a pathetic question to ask. So I wrote:

It's just natural to worry about people you love.

The pandit spoke: "A single pure cotton thread by itself breaks very easily. But a thread woven twenty-four times is strong; it is unbreakable. So we place this thread around Deepa and Ryan to symbolize the unbreakable nature of their union to each other." Unbreakable. Ha. That string wouldn't withstand a pair of scissors.

There was no reply, so I explained further:

Like last night, I was only trying to help you. You would do so well if you joined in business with me.

It would be so amazing for you.

On the mandip, there was a thin white cord around the bride and groom, who were now seated side-by-side in large Queen Anne chairs. The pandit was busy setting up the next step, and the bride and groom were joking together to pass the time. They must be bored up there. They should have thought of that before putting us all through a long wedding.

David?

The pandit invited the groom's family to give Deepa the red-and-gold bandani wedding sari to show that they had accepted her into the family. The groom's mother, a tall woman, stumbled on the hem of her burgundy sari going up the steps to the mandip, messing up the carefully folded pleats. "Didn't anyone teach her to walk in a sari?" I said to my mother.

"She doesn't look graceful at all," agreed my mother.

I wondered how David's mother would look in a sari. I'd imagined her as a short, warm woman who teetered in six-inch heels, someone who'd reach up a little to hug me, and who'd have to hold on tight to keep her balance. David hadn't picked up on my hints to introduce me to her. Meeting her was overdue; we'd been seeing each other for eight months.

I saw the next message before the phone had a chance to vibrate:

we went thru this last nite

89

I know we talked about it, but you just got up and left so suddenly. Why did you just walk out like that?

idk

The groom's mother held a loudly crinkling plastic package containing the bride's sari. Another one of my cousins hopped up on stage to help her open the package and drape the sari properly over Deepa while the pandit continued to supervise and chant.

It's really important that we have good communication. All relationships need really good communication.

we communicate alot

But not good communication! I never know how you feel. You just shut down all the time.

"In an Indian wedding," said the pandit. "We literally tie the knot. Once we do that, then they literally become one, and they are married, and can go forward in life together as one."

u always say that

Can you please tell me how you really feel about us working together? Start with "I feel"

On the mandip, the knot was tied and the pandit announced: "And now, they are married. But we are only halfway done." The crowd chuckled. On stage, the pandit began setting up the sacred fire in a small metal pot. For a second, I hoped the smoke alarms would go off; I'd be able to call David.

i feel u don't listen

That's not how "I feel" is supposed to work.

thats how i feel

That's not how you feel.

yes it is

David just never understood the plans I had for us. He was a terrific graphic designer, but stuck in an office with people who didn't appreciate him the way I did was so wrong for him. Once we got through the initial hiccups it would be so great for our relationship. I could set him up with all my clients, he could build up a freelance network from there, and we could spend all of our time together. It was so perfect for him. He'd make more money, he'd have more interesting projects, and he'd see what a great team we'd make together.

Please take this seriously.

i feel u r nagging me

I'm not nagging!

yes u r

I heard a loud "Woo-hoo!" and looked up to see Deepa's younger sister holding Ryan's jutis in the air. The Indian side chuckled, and Deepa's sister began demanding a ransom from Ryan to get his shoes back. I couldn't believe Deepa condoned this juvenile tradition, but she was laughing. Was she really mature enough to get married? Even the pandit, who still hadn't got the fire lit, was smiling and encouraging this. They were turning this wedding into a circus.

I only want what's best for you.

u dont know whats best 4me

Yes I do.

no u dont

Yes I do! You have to trust me. I love you.

Friend. Follow. Text.

On stage, Deepa and Ryan had cupped their hands together and some of the male members of our family were pouring coriander seeds into their open palms. The pandit was chanting and on a signal from him, they poured the seeds into the fire. The flames flickered but didn't go out.

David?

David, please reply. Just say something.

I hate it when you do this!

Somewhere, a tabla and harmoniums started playing and Deepa and Ryan began to circle the sacred fire, with Ryan leading. Once they completed their round, the music stopped. The pandit began chanting again, and more seeds went into their hands.

u need 2 calm down

Then you need to talk to me. What's wrong with us working together?

this isnt about working tog

Then what is it about?

every month its something new with u.

What do you mean?

Music started again, signaling Deepa and Ryan were starting their second round.

*we should work tog go on vaca tog move closer
2 each other u r never happy*

I started writing, I am happy when I'm with you, but it sounded lame. I changed it to:

I just want us to be close.

we r close enuf

I don't feel like we are close. I feel distant from you.

thats not my prob

Of course it's your problem!

u don't understand this is 2hard

Because you keep shutting me out!

There was no response by the time Deepa and Ryan began their third round. I sent another text:

Why do you keep doing this to me?

For the fourth round, Deepa was leading Ryan. Everyone else was craning their necks to see who would sit down first, since on the last round, the person to sit first rules the marriage. My mother complained about the videographer stepping into her view, and my father gently asked the videographer to move, but I didn't look up. It didn't matter who sat down first. The person who ruled the relationship was always the person who cared the least, and that was never me.

this is 2hard.

maybe we need a break

There was a metallic clatter, and I started. The pandit had put out the sacred fire and was packing it away. He took out a mason jar of betel nuts, and laid out seven along the cloth-covered mandip floor. "Marriage, in the Hindu tradition, is about friendship. If you cannot be friends, you cannot be husband and wife. By taking seven sacred steps together, Deepa and Ryan will assure their lifelong friendship together and vow their eternal friendship to each other." He turned to them and asked them to place their right toes together on each betel nut, and repeat after him. They both extended a foot and lost their balance a little. They grinned stupidly at each other, and then leaned on each other and tried again, taking one hop between each incomprehensible Sanskrit phrase. They looked like idiots, hopping from betel nut to betel nut.

The pandit announced: "And now, they are married. But we still have just a little bit more to go." Jeez, couldn't they have just eloped and saved the rest of us time?

The phone buzzed in my hand. There was a new message from David.

> *r u ok?*
>
> No.
>
> *sry*
>
> What did you mean by a break?
>
> *we fite 2much*
>
> We can work this out.

The pandit was chanting again. I checked over the program. We were on the last page, and he was asking for blessings from the North Star, so that the couple would remain steadfast and constant. Like anyone can find the North Star anymore.

I texted again:

> Don't you want to work this out?

Madhu was on the mandip. She fed her new son-in-law some laddu, and then he fed laddu to his new wife, so that their first taste of marriage would be sweet. My stomach growled.

> *do u rly think thats a good idea*
>
> What do you mean?

Around me, married women were getting up to whisper marital advice in Deepa's ear. My mother stayed seated. My father turned to look at her, but she waved it off. "They have enough people to give her advice." He shrugged and turned back around.

"Are you sure?" I asked her.

"You don't even listen to my advice," said my mother. "Why would she?"

"I listen."

My mother tapped a word into Bookworm. "At least you saved us from going through all this fuss."

i think we need a break

Are you breaking up with me?

The pandit called for the rings, and began to read off a set of Western vows.

Don't shut me out now. Please.

"By the power vested with me by the Ontario Marriage Act, I am proud to introduce for the first time, Mr. and Mrs. Ryan and Deepa Bowman!" Everyone applauded and bustled around the mandip to congratulate the bride and groom and their parents. I was enveloped in a sea of smiling relatives, clinging to my phone as people jostled me out into the aisle. My mother hugged Madhu, who had a huge smile on her face and shiny eyes. I nodded my congratulations at her, pushing the corners of my lips outward, before shoving my way out of the crowd.

I checked my phone and there was another message from David:

im turning off my fone enjoy the wedding

A steel coffee urn sat in the lobby, probably left out from before the ceremony. I could pour myself a cup. I hoped it wasn't cold. The phone was quiet, a dead block in my hand.

People began to trickle out to the buffet in the adjoining hall. There was still lunch, tea, another clothing change, the reception dinner and dancing to get through. At least there would be food. I was so hungry.

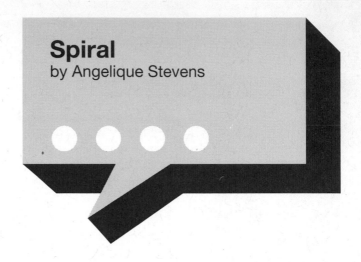

Spiral
by Angelique Stevens

Tuesday, March 22nd

Voicemail: From Regina Stevens Received at 5:15 PM

"Hi Angieee. It's your sister, GinaRegina. Ummm I just want to let you know that me and Bill, we're getting married. You're welcome to come to the wedding. We're gonna do it umm Christian style at a church and stuff. NO I'm not on the cocaine, I haven't done that in 17 days. I won' lie, I did a little of the marijuana tonight, but that's it. I've been on the tobaccy and the caffeine now and that's it. NOO I didn't take your money and use it for drugs. I did mah laundry like I said I would. I wouldn't ever do that to you Angee, I love ya you know. You're the best sister in the world... Nooo I'm not prostitutin'. I gotta give it to Judge Cuban, he um he he he has my vote, he said if he ev'ah catch me again on the street, he gonna put me away so quick. But I signed mah papers and did mah time, so I'm clean. You ain' gotta worry about me bein' in no jail ok? So I'm just lettin' you know. Bill maybe wants to meet you and have you an Ika, mah best gurl, for brunch someday. We're thinkin' about a cruise, I hope you can come. Wal gimmie a call and maybe you can take me to Walmart this weekend. I love ya. Peace out."

Tuesday, April 5th

Voicemail: From Brad Erden Received at 7:45 PM

"Gimmie that thing. Angiee Jesus Christ. It's Brad. It's Brad. Whaddya doin? Whaddya doin? This is my new number. 585.555.3252. For hells bells call me when you don't have any clothes on for hells... for crying out loud wouldya? I'm out here havin' a beer with Billie Sennet and we couldn't stop thinkin' about ya and touchin' ourselves in a public place. Allright, gimmie a call. Talk to ya later. Hope all is good baby, seeya be cool."

Text: From Angelique Stevens Sent at 8:58 PM

"What the hell brother? Where is your drunk ass calling me from?"

Text: From Brad Erden Received at 9:00 PM

"Brewskis spencerport... girl... houw u livin... Trippin the LIVE FANTASTIC WITH BILLIE AND NEIL... They r callin u out..."

Text: From Angelique Stevens Sent at 9:32 PM

"Hey! I'm ready right now for some hangin' and some chillin' with the old crew! I need some serious fun these days! And I think the next time you three drunkards go out for drinks you need to call me before you get drunk!"

Text: From Brad Erden Received at 9:35 PM

"Allright then. It's a bet. We'll see you soon!"

Text: From Diamond Boy Received at 10:51 PM

"Hey Bella"

Text: From Angelique Stevens Sent at 10:52 PM

"Hi sexy. How's things? Still sellin diamonds?"

Text: From Diamond Boy Received at 11:07 PM

"Yeah. When r we gonna stop messin around and start hangin a little more serious?"

Text: From Angelique Stevens Sent at 11:10 PM

"Haha you're cute. I'm always here. You just have to text me."

Text: From Diamond Boy Received at 11:11 PM

"Well I know but I need to stop texting at 11 and a more reasonable hour. I haven't seen u in so long and I love being with you!"

Text: From Angelique Stevens Sent at 11:15 PM

"Yeah that's true. I don't mind you texting late, tho it seems hard for us to get it together like that... I would like to see you again. I like the way you feel."

Text: From Diamond Boy Received at 11:20 PM

"I actually like sleeping next to u... and I have been thinkin' maybe I want to do it more often not just the sex but the companionship... you're a sweetheart and I just do like you... thoughts?"

Text: From Angelique Stevens Sent at 11:22 PM

"That's sweet. I'd like to see you more too. Why me though? You're young and sexy and accomplished. There's got to be some young and sexy girls all around you."

Text: From Diamond Boy Received at 11:32 PM

"You because I don't think about the age or anything like that I think about the way u make me feel and I love that. I know you work early but will you come sleep here nothing more than cuddle together. We can go right to sleep. I have to be up by 6. Just wear pj's... I really just want to spoon."

Text: From Diamond Boy Received at 11:42 PM

"don't ignore bella..."

Text: From Angelique Stevens Sent at 11:42 PM

"ok, give me 15 mins... Can't stay all night though..."

Text: From Diamond Boy Received at 11:43 PM

"can you just sleep with me.... And leave in the morn?"

Text: From Angelique Stevens Sent at 11:52 PM

"I just feel bad for my dog... I left him alone 12 hours today. I'm leavin' in a few. Still awake?"

Text: From Diamond Boy Received at 11:53 PM

"yes I am... if you don't want to you don't have to, but I would love it if you stayed... I'm excited to see you! My house number is 148 in case you forgot"

Wednesday, April 6th

Text: From Angelique Stevens Sent at 8:27 AM

"g'morning. I'm sorry I left last night… I'll stay next time, and I hope there is one soon cuz you were so freakin sexy! Have a safe trip today. Ok?"

Text: From Diamond Boy Received at 8:27 AM

"Thanks girl"

Fwd. Text: From Angelique Stevens Sent at 8:35 AM

"the next buncha msgs are from Diamond Boy last night. We hooked up, isn't he funny?"

Text: From Jacki Scroger Received at 8:40 AM

"OMG!!!! He totally wants you!! OMG How cute, I'm sooo excited for you to be dating again. I mean it's been like what two years since your divorce? It'll be sooo nice for you to have someone to have dinners with and spend time with and talk and chat…"

Text: From Angelique Stevens Sent at 8:46 AM

"Umm ahem… aacckck (sticks finger down throat) stoppit! You're making me sick. He's like 12 years younger than me. He wants sex and comfort when he's drunk. The next time I talk to him the trees'll already be bloomed!… still he's cute

"I really did try to stay the whole night, but afterwards, he fell asleep and the TV was on and I couldn't stop laughing at Conan and then it was 3 AM and I was like, I could go home now and get an uninterrupted 5 hours of sleep so I snuck out."

Sunday, April 10th

Voicemail: From Gina Stevens Received at 7:39 PM

"Yeah um Angie. I hope I'm not pushin' my luck. Um I'm getting married I got the ring on they said I have to pry the shit off me till I'm dead. Anyways, you invited to the wedding I was wondering pretty please if you don't mind um just tell me now, but I was wondering if you could ask Chris if he could come to the wedding. He's more than welcome annn um don' worry about it you're invited to the… I want you there, at least. um Soooo yeah. I love you very much, um, this is your sister. Gina Stevens. Livin' it up on South Avenue. Imaabout to call 103.9 and see if I can get a shout out. I hope you lisssnin to this as soon as you can. Peace out babeeeeee."

Monday, April 11th

Voicemail: From Nora Received at 5:04 PM

"Hi Ms. Stevens my name is Nora. I'm a social worker calling from the Psych E.D. over at Strong Hospital. And calling regarding Regina who was just admitted today. Um was hoping you could give me a call at 585.555.4800 to hear how she's been doing lately. Thanks a lot bye bye."

Voicemail: From Gina Stevens Received at 9:13 PM

"Yeah hi Angie, this is your sisterrrrHahahahahahahhahaha. I'm home now purrin like a pussycat up in heaven. Littlelolorlo Reginaaaaaa got proposed to. She getttttin marriiiii… soooo. Please don't make me, don' make me wait and beg an, I love you honey. I'm home. I just signed the um the terminations, thu the the agreement. Annnd I took my insulin… I got me a AIDS test. They dun sent shots and satellites, and and and *Enemy of the State*. I want it for Christmas baby gurl. Girl puh lease. You gotta get me that movie. That is the funniest fucking movie I have ever seen in my life. So lisssen umm I love you so much. I hope you have a wonderful life wherever you are. Give me a call right back and an let me know, you you you and and big brother Christopher, Christ to fur, if if you won't you you you're all invited to the wedding. I got plenty of money. And and I need a new couch, an an and an an, soo, I wanna mothafucking waterbed. I want a fuckin house. I want a condominium. And I I really really do hope that um that that you can find me a nice ring an engagement ring honey. I would love it if you do that pleeeease… uhh I know you ain't no millionaire but but I'm disabled and and and I'd love to have a ring. So anyways, um I love you very very much. I'm waiting for your phone call. Give me a call as soon as you get this message. Toodalooboopdeboo. I love ya Finnaknockyaforaeverlovingloop. Signin off. Peace out. Breakoutttt Call me love you."

Text: From Angelique Stevens Sent at 10:18 PM

"Gina is realllly fucked up… I don't think she's gonna last long… I really don't"

Text: From Sean Stevens Received at 10:59 PM

"Y wut hppnd?

Text: From Angelique Stevens Sent at 11:04 PM

"IDK I think her mind is gone. She's been drinking a lot and doing some drugs, not a lot… But even when she's sober she sounds gone… Very manic and….

"Whatever… Apparently she was evicted from her place and mental health arrested today.

"She says she's getting married

"She's gonna drink/or drug herself into oblivion or end up at Rochester Psychiatric Center or Jail… or whatever"

Text: From Sean Stevens Received at 11:06 PM

"Getting married huh? She smile at some bum on the corner somewhere?"

Text: From Angelique Stevens Sent at 11:08 PM

"Don't be such an ass. She's just delusional I'm sure. She invited Chris to the 'wedding' too"

Text: From Sean Stevens Received at 11:09 PM

"Chris? Ur ex?"

Text: From Angelique Stevens Sent at 11:09 PM

"yuh"

Wednesday, April 13th

Text: From Jazz Concert Guy Received at 8:15 AM

"Good morning. I'm going to the jazz concert tomorrow night. Any interest and desire for dance and music midweek? We could ride together"

Text: From Angelique Stevens Sent at 12:19 PM

"I'm not sure yet, I'm supposed to go out later with my friend, but I could cancel that. What time is the concert?"

Text: From Jazz Concert Guy Received at 1:18 PM

"starts at 7:30 PM"

Voicemail: From Kim Horth Received at 3:18 PM

"Hello Angelique umm my name is Kim Horth I'm Gina Stevens' um new neighbor in 17H and um I fed her breakfast this morning. Made sure she ate. She got all dressed up she was gonna go to church um, but we went to an AA meeting on Monroe Avenue annnnnd I didn't know she was an insulin diabetic annnd her sugar crashed. I guess she didn't do her insulin right and if I had known that she had problems doing that I would have helped her 'cuz I was a mental-hygiene therapy aid for over ten years. Long story short, she is at RGH Emergency ummm diarrhea throwing up um her umm mental health her her mood swings are out of, total out of order. And I have to leave because I have got things I have got to get done. Umm we've been here for several hours, umm could you please call me back. My number is 585.555.7777. The number again is, 585... thank you very much I need you here ASAP cuz I have things to do. I have five children and I have things I cannot cancel so please call me back immediately."

Email: From Angelique Stevens Sent at 3:20 PM

"Hey sister! I have an extra ticket to the play at Geva tonight. I'm going with my intro to lit students and one of them cancelled. You have any desire to go? Email or text soon if you can."

Voicemail: From Kim Horth Received at 3:34 PM

"Angelique hi um this is Gina Stevens' new neighbor yes in 17H. I don't know her that well yes I did work mental health for the state of NY. But she would feel much more comfortable if you were here. They're gonna put a IV in her due to dehydration, she's had diarrhea probably ten times, I was here, the whole nine yards. I don't mind doing it, but I, you know she... She really needs you here 'cuz she's sick ok? Could you try to get here please? Thank you. We're at RGH. Yeah, Rochester General Hospital. Thank you very much. Have a wonderful day. Hope to hear from you by 4:00."

Email: From Nydia Perez Received at 3:50 PM

"Hey, thanks for asking, but I can't go to the play tonight. Jordy has violin and Ryan has dance and James is working late tonight, so I have to drive both the girls. Let's try to get together over spring break though for dinner and wine, ok? We get back from New York next Wednesday. Let's do massages and then dinner and drinks. Have fun tonight."

Voicemail: From Kim Horth Received at 3:57 PM

"Hello Angelique this is Kim Horth, um Gina Stevens' new neighbor in 17H... I had to leave because my daughter was in a car accident in few days ago and she needs me, soo umm Regina is alone there with the nurses, they are watching her. They are taking good care of her, they know her. They know her mental health, physical health, etc. her diabetes, you name it. OhhhhhKay. Umm it would be really great if you could get there. They'll call me back in three or four hours if you don't get there ummm. You know. She's your family and family's really important... please... please try and get there. Thank you. Or at least please call me back and let me know what's going on. Thanks. Cuz I need some more background information if I'm gonna do my best job doing what I can do, ok? Thank you."

Email: From Angelique Stevens Sent at 4:15 PM

"Ok Sister, sounds good. I'm home during all of Spring Break. I may spend a couple days dog-sitting on Jacki's farm, but I'll be around if you want to get together for drinks."

Text: From Jacki Scroger Received at 4:54 PM

"Did you know Gina is back home? She was evicted because she is continually breaking the rules by smoking in the hallways and elevators, mutherfucking everyone loudly

"and prostituting out of her apartment. Her unit doesn't have bed bugs but I'm told it smells so bad in there that maintenance refuses to go

"in ☹ we're gonna need to work on this. Also she's very politely spouting her craziness to staff. If they had a heart, they'd be worried about her... this is the only thing I miss about working there at Southtown.

"They said she's wayyyy off the deep end and they are done with her ☹"

Text: From Angelique Stevens Sent at 4:59 PM

"yeah I know all that... she's in the hospital right now... her caseworker will have to find a place for her."

Text: From Jacki Scroger Received at 4:59 PM

"I just heard today that she is back at Southtown apts. today. Are you sure she's still in there??"

Text: From Angelique Stevens Sent at 4:59 PM

"No. She's back in the hospital again. She's at RGH now. Diabetic shock or something today. Yesterday it was the psych E.D. at Strong..."

Voicemail: From Kim Horth Received at 5:33 PM

"Helllo um Angelique this is Kim Horth um I had to leave due to my own daughter's emergency. Your sister is at uhh Rochester General Hospital E.D. Ummm You can call them or call me, but um she could probably really use you right now. She really needs a friend. And I have to take care of my own daughter 'cuz she got into a car accident today so um I pray that you got there and everything's ok and she's with you and she's feeling, you know, safe and not scared. So um… Cuz Regina's a good kid. Um I know she's 41. I'm 52. But uhh she could really use you right now, umm give me a call. Um and let me know that you got there so I know what's going on. Ok take care buh bye."

Text: From Jacki Scroger Received at 6:45 PM

"Oye… I hope they help her. I hear Andrews Place is moving people in with subsidy. That's the shittiest part is that she loses her discounted rent. I hope they keep her for a while. I hate Natasha, the manager at Southtown who took my position

"and Patricia too. Somebody could have gotten her some kind of help before it got this far. Jim said Gina would get dirty and you ride her to clean and check up on her and she would do what you asked her to do.

"she's not a mean person nor is she defiant when you treat her with kindness."

Text: From Angelique Stevens Sent at 6:47 PM

"Yeah… that's all true, but I think she's just declining… and there's probly a lot more everyone could be doing, especially me… But whose got the energy? It's easier to just let her slip through the cracks"

Text: From Jacki Scroger Received at 6:52 PM

"I hate it more because the site has a service coordinator paid for by HUD for exactly this purpose. They suck over there since I left. Tell me about this diabetic

"thing. is all the drinking causing the craziness because her sugar is dangerously affecting all her organs?"

Text: From Angelique Stevens Sent at 6:53 PM

"Maybe the sugar is affecting her craziness too. Some of it could JUST be her sugar, who the fuck knows."

Text: From Jacki Scroger Received at 6:56 PM

"Yeah bummer. Natasha says Gina's been non-stop drinking which I know is terribly dangerous to a diabetic. Anyway, did you hook up with anyone lately? U probly

"have your period now huh?"

Text: From Angelique Stevens Sent at 7:36 PM

"There's only two choices for her now... die or go to RPC

"no haven't hooked up with anyone, but the guy from drinks last week wants me to go to the jazz concert tomorrow..."

Text: From Jacki Scroger Received at 9:12 PM

"Cool. Are you gonna go?"

Text: From Angelique Stevens Sent at 9:15 PM

"IDK. I'm at a play right now with my intro to lit class and then I have to go see it again with my honors class on Friday. Tomorrow's my only day to chill. I haven't decided yet. But break is coming.

"maybe I'll just say yes... but then again it feels weird, like a date... and he wants to pick me up, which is code for 'I want to get you drunk and fuck you after the concert'"

Thursday, April 14th

Text: From Jacki Scroger Received at 7:27 AM

"you should go, drive yourself. And then if you decide he's worthy, bring him back to your place afterward"

Phone Call: From Gina Stevens Received at 8:28 AM

"Angieeeeeee *(crying)* I'm hooome. I don' know what I'm gonna dooo."

"What do you mean honey?"

"I mean, I don' know where I'm gonna live *(sobbing)* aan aaand I think I got AIDS"

"Gina, what did you say?"

"I think I got AIDS." *(sobbing)*

"What?"

"I think I got AIDDSSS." *(sobbing)*

"What do you mean, Gina, 'You Think? How can you think you have AIDS?"

"The doctor said I had a virus."

"What kind of virus?"

"They don't know."

"Gina, the doctor did not just come into your room and say 'you have a virus, we don't know nothing'? What is it connected to? What made them look for it? What does it affect? How does it make you feel? There's got to be something?" *(gets louder)*

"They said it might be pneumonia." *(sobbing uncontrollably)*

"What's wrong honey? Pneumonia is not AIDS. How do you get AIDS out of pneumonia, did the doctor say AIDS?"

"No. I'm jusssssssoooo scared Angeeeeee. I'm gonna die. I don' wanna die. I mean I'm not homicidal or suicidal, I'm just scared I'm gonna die. I just feel it." *(sobs)*

"Oh honey, you're not gonna die. Now have you talked to your caseworker?"

"Yeah I gotta limo pickin me up at 11:00. They gonna take me outta here."

"Gina, who's coming to pick you up?"

"The Medicab is gonna pick me up and take me there so I can meet my caseworker, I don' know what they gonna do with me, maybe I'll go to RPC. *(sobbing again)* I just feel like I'm gonna die and I don' wanna die Angeeee." *(phone clicks off)*

Text: From Angelique Stevens Sent at 8:45 AM

"I haven't decided yet if I'm gonna go with him or not. Gina just called. She's home this morning. She's going to see her case worker today. Hopefully they'll put her in RPC."

Text: From Jacki Scroger Received at 11:35 AM

"They'd be ridiculous not to. They should also get someone to store her stuff and move her out."

Text: From Angelique Stevens Sent at 11:37 AM

"Ah yep. That's what they do"

Text: From Jacki Scroger Received at 11:41 AM

"They suck at it. Just so you know. She will probably end up losing all her stuff because they're lazy. If you talk to them tell them that she has no bed bugs. They'll be more apt to do something. Poor Gina."

Text: From Angelique Stevens Sent at 11:42 AM

"Won't be the first time. What's she have now anyway? Nothing worth keeping. Some stinky clothes maybe… pictures… nasty ass hand-me-down filthy shit?

"She was crying this morning…

"Scared she's gonna die soon"

Text: From Jacki Scroger Received at 11:43 AM

"God I hope not"

Text: From Angelique Stevens Sent at 11:44 AM

"You hope not what??"

Text: From Jacki Scroger Received at 11:46 AM

"I hope she doesn't die!! I always hope they can make her feel better even if it doesn't last forever. She's so great when she's clean and sober.

"I know those times are few and far between lately, but I want happiness for her"

Text: From Angelique Stevens Sent at 11:47 AM

"She will… that's what I've been saying. She doesn't have long.

"she knows it too."

Text: From Jacki Scroger Received at 11:49 AM

"I don't understand though. Why would you think that? What is different about this time than the others? I mean if they let her out of the hospital she

"has got to be doing better physically. Can't she pull out of this again if she gets herself some help to get clean for another stretch?"

Text: From Angelique Stevens Sent at 11:52 AM

"It's just a feeling. And it's all very different. It's never the same… each time it gets worse and harder. How is it that after watching this and me

"and my family fuck up and die again and again all these years that you still have some fucked up Pollyanna sense of hope?"

Text: From Angelique Stevens Sent at 11:55 AM

"sorry"

Text: From Jacki Scroger Received at 11:56 AM

"it's ok. I just do."

Text: From Angelique Stevens Sent at 11:56 AM

"Well at this point there's not much helping her I don't think."

Text: From Jacki Scroger Received at 11:57 AM

"I haven't seen her since we brought her that mattress last year. My mom and dad saw her on South Ave a month ago but couldn't get her attention to say hi."

Text: From Angelique Stevens Sent at 11:58 AM

"She was probably laughing and talking to herself... 25 years of hard drugs and psychosis takes a toll on a mind and a body. Some things just don't heal."

Text: From Jacki Scroger Received at 12:01 PM

"Yeah. How are you dealing with it all? Are you ok or are you starting to spiral?"

Text: From Angelique Stevens Sent at 12:04 PM

"Ha ha. Clearly I'm fine... I'm just gonna be angry at you for being so fucking sunshiney and deluded though"

Text: From Jacki Scroger Received at 12:04 PM

"I prefer optimistic."

Saturday, April 23rd

Voicemail: From Joann Received at 11:41 AM

"Hey Angelique this is Joann from Brooklyn Teen Challenge, your sister is here with us in Brooklyn and we'd like a little bit more information about her and how she got to Brooklyn and what she is like, how she has been lately. Any information you can offer will help. She's very hard to understand right now and we would like to help her. Please give us a call back at 718.555.2222."

Text: From The Bartender Received at 9:46 PM

"Hey girl what you doing? You want me to come over and do dirty things to you?"

Text: From Angelique Stevens Sent at 9:52 PM

"Hey there sexy. I haven't heard from you in a while. Sure, come on over. I love it when you do dirty things to me. I just opened a bottle of Jack."

Text: From The Bartender Received at 9:52 PM

"great. I can't wait to see you girl. Your house is the big yellow one with brown shutters right? I'm gonna take a shower and be over about 10:30. That ok?"

Text: From Angelique Stevens Sent at 9:58 PM

"Yep. Yellow house. Text when you're leaving. I'm gonna take a shower too. See you soon."

Monday, April 25th

Text: From Angelique Stevens Sent at 10:30 AM

"So Gina's in Brooklyn. Apparently she called a pastor from Free Village, some Christian place for runaways she stayed in like 25 years ago and the fucking pastor gave her 65

"fucking dollars, drove her to the bus station and told her to find her way to this Brooklyn Teen Challenge Place. Told her they'd help her!"

Text: From Angelique Stevens Sent at 10:31 AM

"What the fuck is wrong with people?! I mean really?! Put a motherfucking psychotic crack addict on a bus to fucking Brooklyn with $65?

"Yeah I'm sure it's a much smarter idea to send someone 500 miles away where there's only strangers than it is to call her motherfucking caseworker or her sister!"

Text: From Jacki Scroger Received at 10:40 AM

"What the hell? Really? I don't even know what to say to that. Did you talk to her? Did she say why she went to Brooklyn?

Text: From Angelique Stevens Sent at 10:43 AM

"She said she's never coming back to Rochester, hates it here. I think she's a bit freaked about her last prostitution charge. It's not finalized yet. Has one more court date.

"So much for that. And now she can't stay at that teen place because she's umm not a teen, fucking idiots! She's a 41 fucking year-old woman!

"So apparently they're looking for a place to put her. who knows."

Text: From Jacki Scroger Received at 10:45 AM

"People are assholes. That doesn't make any sense. So what are you gonna do honey?"

Text: From Angelique Stevens Sent at 10:44 AM

"What is there to do? Nothing. Just sit back and wait I guess. Maybe I can find a way to get down there and bring her some things. Who knows."

Text: From Jacki Scroger Received at 10:46 AM

"I'm sorry honey. Let me know if there's anything I can do."

Friend. Follow. Text.

Text: From Angelique Stevens Sent at 10:48 AM

"no worries sister. It is what it is. I saw the Bartender."

Text: From Jacki Scroger Received at 10:48 AM

"OMG you did?! How long has it been since you have seen him? How was he? Are you going to see him again? Hows it goin with Jazz Concert guy too? You guys still hanging?"

Text: From Angelique Stevens Sent at 10:50 AM

"Ha, you're funny. I'm sure I'll 'see' him again. Who knows when though? It's not like we're going out for dinner and long walks on the beach any time soon. It was good.

"That guy is sexy as hell. His body is nearly perfect. I mean there's not one ounce of fat anywhere. I saw jazz concert guy a few nights ago.

"We met for drinks in the afternoon and stayed at the bar like all day drinking margaritas. We went back to my place after and got crazy

"...and somehow I cried during sex... So weird."

Text: From Jacki Scroger Received at 11:00 AM

"Really??? He made you cry? That's so unlike you? What is it do you think? You like this guy? What did you guys talk about?

"The last time you two went out, you said he was really smart. I mean maybe this guy has all the stuff you need honey. Some great conversation, good sex.

"Does he like Jack Daniels too? Haha just joking. I'm so glad I can live my life vicariously through you. My god. My life is so boring compared to yours."

Text: From Angelique Stevens Sent at 11:10 AM

"yeah he's very smart and I loved talking to him. The sex was good, but honestly he's gonna be a clinger.

"He clearly wants more. I'm not even sure I'm going to see him again. I think the crying was because I'm getting my period."

Text: From Jacki Scroger Received at 11:11 AM

"yeah, I'm sure that's what it's from"

Wednesday, June 22nd

Voicemail: From Peeta Raji Received at 11:14 AM

"Helloo my name is Peeta Raji at the Bronx St. Barnabas Hospital. I'm calling about your sister? Regina Stevens. I need to get some information about her health care in regards to the accident she was in. I would appreciate a call back this afternoon. I will be available before 2:00 PM at 718.555.3265. Thank you very much."

Text: From Angelique Stevens Sent at 2:20 PM

"WTF Gina was hit by a fucking Hummer in the Bronx! She's in the goddam hospital.

"She's ok I guess, well her leg is fucked up pretty bad, they had to do some skin grafts on it and now she has a MRSA infection.

"She was just walking her cracked up ass across the street not paying attention and some dumb ass in a hummer hit her."

Text: From Sean Stevens Received at 2:30 PM

"Great Gina. A Hummer? Hey maybe she'll get some money out of it. Are you going to go see her?"

Text: From Angelique Stevens Sent at 2:35 PM

"Well I can't I'm leaving for my trip to Cambodia in a week. I've got too much to do. I'm not even going to be back until August.

"I'm going to spend the first week volunteering in an elephant sanctuary, then I'd like to try to spend my 41st birthday on the beach somewhere in Thailand...

"and maybe the rest of the month visiting ancient ruins in Cambodia."

Text: From Sean Stevens Received at 2:36 PM

"Your sister's in the hospital and ur leaving to go galavanting around the world and ur not even going to go see her? Nice."

Text: From Angelique Stevens Sent at 2:40 PM

"Shut the fuck up. She's your sister too. half-sister is still a sister. I don't see you getting on a plane to fly your poker playing ass to go see her either."

Text: From Sean Stevens Received at 2:42 PM

"Whatevs dude. How's Tim been doing?"

Text: From Angelique Stevens Sent at 2:44 PM

"I'm pretty sure he's been drinking again. I got one of those 'I love you sis' texts the other day. He only gets emotional like that when he's drinking."

Text: From Sean Stevens Received at 2:45 PM

"Yeah I got one too. He'll probably be in jail soon. Or maybe he can share a hospital room with Gina."

Text: From Angelique Stevens Sent at 2:46 PM

"or a cell"

Thursday, August 18th

Text: From Tim Stevens Received at 2:00 AM

"you there?"

Text: From Tim Stevens Received at 2:12 AM

"hey. You around?"

Voicemail: From Tim Stevens Received at 2:30 AM

"Hey it's me. Call me back as soon as possible."

Text: From Angelique Stevens Sent at 3:30 AM

"What happened??"

Text: From Tim Stevens Received at 3:31 AM

"DWI. Arrested. Again."

Text: From Angelique Stevens Sent at 3:31 AM

"Jesus Tim! You're going to jail. Are you ok? What happened besides you were trashed?"

Text: From Tim Stevens Received at 3:33 AM

"Ran a stop sign at 60 miles an hour and umm almost hit the sheriffs waiting at the corner. They let me go home. I think that was just a courtesy because of Jess's dad.

"Even though he's retired, they all still kno him. I think they wanted to help his son-in-law out a lil. I get arraigned tomorrow. They'll probly put me in jail

"I've become my father and I hate myself. I said I would never be like him"

Text: From Angelique Stevens Received at 3:33 AM

"oh Tim. Dad was not so bad you know. He did some really good things before he died.

"You could be like him, the good parts you know? You're only 30. You have your whole life. Be happy you're not dead and take this as a sign that you need to change your life. I love u."

Text: From Sean Stevens Received at 3:33 AM

"Hey u hear from Tim?"

Text: From Angelique Stevens Sent at 3:34 AM

"Yep. I'm up. I just found out. Jesus Christ. That fucking brother. He's going to jail this time for sure."

Text: From Sean Stevens Received at 3:34 AM

"I told him that. I hate to say it but maybe he needed this. He's been too lucky for so long. Now Jess is gonna lose a husband and his daughter is going to lose her dad.

"I told him he should b happy he's still alive.

"I want to see if we can get him bail. I remember being in jail for six months. It was the worst fucking feeling in the world.

"U feel like no one gives a shit about u rotting in jail on a cold hard cot. I don't want that for him. He's not like me. I don't know if he can handle it"

Text: From Angelique Stevens Sent at 3:40 AM

"I know. I know. I told him the same thing. He gets arraigned tomorrow. I don't have any money left, Sean. I just got back from Cambodia for Christ sake

"Is this ever gonna end??"

Text: From Sean Stevens Received at 3:45 AM

"IDK Ang, I really don't.

"I have some money from the last poker tournament I played in. Let me know what happens when he gets arraigned. I can send some western union if need be."

Text: From Angelique Stevens Sent at 3:46 AM

"ok"

Text: From Diamond Boy Received at 8:00 PM

"Hey Bella! Long time no see. Are u back in town?"

Text: From Angelique Stevens Sent at 8:15 PM

"Hi there sexy. How's it goin?"

Text: From Diamond Boy Received at 8:15 PM

"It's going good. How was your trip?"

Text: From Angelique Stevens Sent at 8:16 PM

"It was fantastic. I had an amazing time. What are you up to these days? Got a girlfriend yet?"

Text: From Diamond Boy Received at 8:17 PM

"no one serious. I miss you and the way you feel and the things you do to me. You are so good at it. We had a good thing for a little while didn't we?

"Maybe we can get 2gether soon?"

Text: From Angelique Stevens Sent at 8:20 PM

"Ha! Well of course. Yeah it's been fun. It'd be great to see you too."

Text: From Diamond Boy Received at 8:20 PM

"Tonight? Can I text u later??"

Text: From Angelique Stevens Sent at 8:21 PM

"Sure. I'm going out with the girls. I should be home around midnightish."

Text: From Diamond Boy Received at 8:22 PM

"Great! I can't wait to feel your body next to mine."

Text: From Angelique Stevens Sent at 8:22 PM

" ☺ "

Grindr
by Clayton Littlewood

Soho Athletic gym.

7:15 PM. There's hardly anyone around. The café bar is empty. The only sound, the receptionist washing glasses, the manager ringing up till receipts and the distant sound of club music floating through the gym.

I try to catch the receptionist's eye. He's slim, toned, hair perfectly parted, the obligatory beard. In his late twenties. Probably from Shoreditch. He looks over. "Can I help you?"

"Can I have a towel please?"

"Sure," he smiles. "That'll be a pound."

I hand over a coin, sign in and then head toward the changing room, passing a tall, well-defined woman pounding away on the Stairmaster, the Brazilian trainer "spotting" for a client and a face I know from some club or other. I'm feeling strangely nervous, as if something weird is about to happen.

It's busier in the changing room, some guys are dressing, some undressing, a smattering of bears and suited businessmen. A surreptitious glance here, a lingering look there. The usual casual cruising that you find in a gay gym. I find a locker. At the back. Near the showers (my usual spot). Then I unzip my gym bag. Inside is an empty bottle of medication, a black Moleskine notebook, a pair of Adidas tracksuit bottoms and a grey T-shirt with "Muscle" written across the chest, both items of clothing in complete contrast to the designer gym gear that most guys here wear (my gym etiquette is to always be unobtrusive as possible).

I'm about to close my locker when I remember my iPhone. I fish it out of my bag and as I do it vibrates. It's a push notification. From Grindr. I enter my passcode, tap the application and the sender's profile. The pic is slightly grainy, although it looks familiar. Like a gym. I tap Chat. The message reads, *Howdy! How's ur night going?*

I tap the Back button. There's no name on the profile, just a quote, "Life is short, so enjoy."

I contemplate what to do. Then a third message. *Don't block me!*

Actually, I wasn't going to. Blocking always seems such a passive-aggressive act. I have an aversion to it. But equally, if I don't block him, he sounds like the type that will plague me with messages. Fuck. Why did I even download this app? It's not as if I intend to meet anyone on here. What was it my friend Paul said, "Why don't you just put 'Timewaster' as your profile name?"

Then another message pops up, *Enjoy ur workout!*

I swivel round. Startled. Is he in here?

To my left is a Latino guy, blow-drying his armpit hair. Sitting on the bench nearby, an older guy, bearded again, in fatigues and a tight white vest, unties his bootlaces. Neither of them is using a phone.

I tap Back again. The profile reads:

Online

10 meters away

Ten meters!

I type, *Where r u?* Press Send.

He responds immediately, *Closer than u think*

I glance across at the toilets. There's no one there. He must be in the gym doing a workout. He must've spotted me coming in. I head back outside, intrigued.

I position a gym bench under the Nautilus equipment. Sit down. Wipe my hands on my t-shirt. Then stare straight ahead into the mirror, taking in my surroundings. There are five guys in here. Three working out and two chatting by the far window. None of them are looking in my direction. This makes me feel both safe and uneasy. Safe, because as I've said, I like to blend in. And uneasy because I remember a time when I'd walk into the gym and everyone would check me out. Now, no one does.

I stare at my scuffed trainers, thinking about my fading looks. I quickly shake the thought away. Clasp the barbell with both hands. Take a deep breath and push it upward in one dynamic thrust. I work out briskly, concentrating, not wanting to get wrapped up in negative feelings. After three sets I'm about to take the weights off the bar when I feel my phone vibrating again.

Not doing a 4th set then?

I scan the room. Everyone is either lifting weights or on a machine. I check the profile. It's still says he's 10 meters away! Where the hell is this guy? I type, Come on! Where r you?

U'll find out soon

I grin. But at the same time I'm getting mildly irritated. Now I can't block him. Wherever he is, he can see me and blocking him will just make me come across as uptight. I type, Give me a clue? Then I survey the oblong room again: a tattooed guy doing press-ups on a yoga mat and a stocky bear training his biceps. The bear's face is familiar. But then so many guys on the scene are these days, having seen them out and about for thirty-odd years, or having viewed them online. And now with this bear look, everyone has become one.

There's another vibration. *I'm not that bear if that's what u think!*

I press the Power Off button. Okay, I've had enough of this. I've got to finish this work out and get out of here. I've got work to do at home. Chores to be done. Plus I'm knackered. I really need an early night. What was it my boss said to me today? "Clay, you've been looking really tired and haggard lately. Are you okay?" I felt like saying, "Look, I'm just a bit run down, all right! Give me a break!" But of course, you can't say that. Not to your boss. You just have to smile sweetly and say, "No everything's fine. But thank you for asking."

Twenty minutes later, I'm dressed again, standing in front of the mirror, applying Dax Wax to my salt and pepper hair (more salt now I admit). My skin, although unlined, is starting to sag. I open my mouth, wide. Then close it, watching the flesh fall back into place. The phase I went through a few years ago of having Botox every six months, well, I thought it'd passed and that I was finally accepting the aging process. Now I'm not so sure.

There's a vibration in my pocket. I take it out. *U're getting older. Soon no one's going to want u*

Who the fuck does he think he is? I clench my teeth and press Block. Then I then shove my phone back in my pocket and march out of the changing room, the gym, down the stairway, onto Macklin Street, a self-satisfied smirk on my face. Vile queen. Well that put a stop to his stupid little game. And I make my way through the evening crowds to Soho.

+

Old Compton Street is a cosmopolitan melting pot. A Hogarth painting come to life. I pass a posse of G.A.Y. twinks, East End lads in Hackett tops, a group of bleached-blonde girls with pink rabbit ears, rickshaws parked outside the Prince Edward Theatre. Then I arrive at my favourite coffee shop, number 34B, on the corner of Frith Street. I take a seat inside, tucked up by the window and order a small black coffee. It's from this vantage point that I do all my thinking. My window to the world. The place I come to when I want to ponder life, my career, mortality. There're a stack of magazines in the corner. I pick one up. It's *The Clarion*. The local mag. It always has an interesting historical section and I'm engrossed in an article about Soho Square when I feel a movement in my pocket.

I reach for my coffee. Take another sip. Not in any particular hurry to answer it. I give it a minute. Then reach into my jeans pocket. It's another Grindr message.

In ur favourite spot I see...34B

I thought I'd blocked him! I press Block. Again. Turn off my phone. Then I scour the crossroads. But it's so busy, there are so many people laughing, or singing or arguing, it's like Gay Pride night. I exchange glances with a few guys. It could be any one of them. And they all seem to be looking at me, knowingly, as if they're somehow all in on it.

Normally I'd be here for at least an hour, writing in my notebook, trying to make the night last longer before it's time to face the drudgery of home and preparing for work the next day. But tonight my spell has been broken. My little oasis has been defiled. So I take a last mouthful of the now lukewarm coffee, thank the Hungarian assistant and leave.

I weave in and out of the crowds, down Brewer Street, past the neon-lit bookshop, the peep shows, the NCP car park, the health food shop, turning right at the end of the street, past Third Space and the Piccadilly Theatre, heading underground, down the stairs, the escalator, past the busker murdering *The Final Countdown*, until I'm on the Piccadilly Line platform (at the back and out of sight).

The train ride is uneventful. It's 9:15 PM. Fortunately I'm an hour ahead of the drunken passengers, with their out-of-tune singing and excessively loud voices, all breaking that Golden Tube Rule: Thou Must Not Speak. I get off at Earls Court and take the rear exit, away from the throng.

Now I'm above ground. The garish display of the Ideal Home Exhibition looms before me. It's all fake topiary, with a stately home backdrop. Tacky beyond belief. Although I've only been on the tube for 15 minutes, darkness has already descended. I walk down Warwick Road toward Holland Road, thinking about what I have to do when I get in. I'm just passing Tesco when my phone vibrates. It's a Grindr notification. The profile pic is of a building. I tap it. Then tap Chat. The message reads, *Thought u'd lost me did ya?*

Online

10 meters away

I spin round. Panicking. There's no one there. And no one in front either. He must be in Tesco!

I tap on the profile pic, enlarging it with my thumb and forefinger. It's a pic of… Homebase. The building ahead! Oh God. He's somewhere ahead of me. Probably hiding behind that wall! Now what? I could press the Report button, but what am I going to say? That I'm being stalked on an app? That's what Grindr's for, isn't it? So guys can stalk each other? My mind's racing now. What should I do? Double back? Take another route home? The questions hit me like a stream of arrows. I'm aware too that I'm breathing much faster now and that my right eyelid is twitching. Wait a minute. This is ridiculous. Just jump in a cab. What's he going to do? Run after it?

I wait until the traffic has subsided, then run across the road, doubling back on myself, turning left onto Cromwell Road, checking behind intermittently that I'm not being followed. A few seconds later I spot a black cab with a yellow vacant sign. I stick my hand out. Please stop! It hurtles toward me and pulls over.

"Holland Road please!" I say, diving into the back. "The High Street Ken end."

The driver indicates. I quickly turn in my seat, looking out the back window, still breathing heavily. The street's deserted. I sigh and sink back in my seat.

"Just past the pub please. Wherever you can find a space. Yes. Just here's fine, thanks."

I hand the driver a tenner. "Keep the change." He looks at me in disbelief, as the tip is more than the fare. But I'm not really thinking straight at the moment. I just want to get inside my flat. I slam the cab door. Run the few yards up the street, down the checkered tiled steps, into the basement. It takes me a few seconds to find my keys. I can hear them jangling in my bag somewhere... Here they are! I'm about to put the key in the lock when I feel my phone vibrating. I hesitate. Then take it out. It's another message. I tap on the profile. The pic is of a bedroom. Hold on, that's my bedroom! That's my Jean Cocteau lithograph above my bed. He's inside my flat!

I back away from the front door. Rush back up the stairway.

A short, red-headed woman is about to enter the main building with a young man.

"Please! Can you help me!"

She stops, key in the door and turns her head. The young man whispers to the woman. Then he walks toward me. "What's the matter?" he says politely.

"Listen, I know this sounds weird. But there's someone in my flat. He just sent me a photo on my phone. Of my bedroom! He's in there!" I point down to the basement.

"Do you know this person?"

"No! No, I haven't a clue who it is."

Now the woman walks toward me. "You've got to calm down a bit Clay," she says, as she strokes my arm. "Ian'll go down and check."

I hand him the key. Once he's in the basement I turn to the woman. "Thank you. You're very kind. And I'm sorry for being such an idiot. It's just that—"

"Don't worry Clay," consoles the woman. "Everything's going to be alright." She looks down into the basement area. "Maybe we should go down too."

"No, I err, don't want to."

"Perhaps you should've called the police."

At that moment Ian walks back up the basement steps. He frowns and scratches the back of his head. "There's no one in there." He looks embarrassed. "Whoever it was must've left."

"Ian, don't be silly. We've been standing here the whole time and we would've seen…" she stops abruptly, for Ian's glance is sharp. He nods at her when he thinks I'm not looking.

"I searched everywhere," he says. "In every room. And there's no one there. *Nobody.*" He says it with finality.

And then the woman, as if delivering her verdict, says. "Oh well, that'll be that then…"

+

The key goes in the lock in one swift movement. I push the door open. Step inside. Shut it. Locking it again behind me at the top and bottom. I throw my gym bag on the sofa. Walk into the bedroom, shut the door and collapse on the bed. Within seconds, I'm in that world which is half dream, half sleep. NREM sleep I think my doctor calls it. I'm vaguely aware of a sensation in my pocket. But now I'm drifting, drifting. There it goes again. I think it's a vibration. It is a vibration! I jump up. Switch on my phone.

Took ur time getting here didn't ya?

Online

1 meter away

Sixteen-hundred Closest Friends
by Steve Karas

I friended Billy Dallas on Facebook. He accepted. To think it'd taken me this long to join the social-media revolution.

"I can't believe you're not on Facebook?" my younger brother had said. Had taunted me. "Everybody's on Facebook."

I got harassed about it by the one of the girls who worked for me at the diner, too. Then the dental assistant when I went in for a routine cleaning, before finally giving in. My first friend request was less than twenty-four hours after launching my account – Raj, an Indian dude from my tenth grade physics class I hadn't seen since '92. I found Billy, my old childhood pal, a few days later.

My profile picture, carefully narrowed down from several possible choices, was of me and my wife, Irene. A self-take on our honeymoon, faces pressed against one another, the Mediterranean Sea behind us. "Who's the chick, bro?" Billy commented on my wall. Apparently he hadn't bothered to look at my relationship status.

I spent an hour sitting in front of the desktop in our basement, navigating through Billy's page. It had been about four years since I'd last spied on him via MySpace. I wondered periodically if his vast social network had come crumbling down with the demise of the site. Maybe I secretly hoped it had. But, he'd clearly come back bigger than before – 1,617 Facebook friends. From a dozen Angies to a handful of Zoes. I'd never even come across one Zoe in my entire life. The guy had always been popular, but goddamn.

"Sam, what are you doing?" Irene called from the living room. She was watching *Dancing with the Stars*. It wasn't like me to miss it.

"Paying bills online, baby."

Billy's profile pic was the expected: linen shirt unbuttoned past his chest, skin Miami-tanned, teeth white as a wedding dress. He looked like he was still twenty-five. His interests: traveling the globe to listen to the best live DJ sets, beach volleyball, reading a good book. The Billy I knew couldn't even get through an audiobook.

A post from a girl who went by the name Karolina Poland popped up on his Wall: "Hey cutie. Sound-Bar tonight?"

It was a Tuesday.

+

Unlike some people, I was up at four AM the next day. Shit, I was up at four every day. I'd hit the snooze button twice, be at the diner by five. Never liked getting up that early, but it hadn't ever bugged me as much as it did that morning. I wondered if Billy and Karolina Poland had even gotten home yet from the night before. Or maybe they were naked, rolling around under his silk sheets while I was opening shop and getting the coffee pots brewing. I really needed to get the Internet hooked up there.

Dan, a retired electrician, came in at 5:45 with the *Sun Times* tucked under his arm, just like every day. Diner Dan. He sat at the counter, his back hunched, sipping on his usual cup of black coffee.

"What's on tap this week?" he said. "Any big plans?"

"Just hanging out with the wife. Same thing I always do."

"You're still young. You should be living it up, married or not. When I was your age, I was out every night. Everyone in this city knew me – every bar owner, cocktail waitress, bookie."

Dan used to meet up at the diner with his buddies. They'd guzzle down pots of coffee, devour skirt steaks (all the way down to the fat), and go through packs of Marlboro Reds. But one by one, his friends started dropping off. Paul the Painter was serving three years for tax evasion; Gus, the long-time maître d' at a swanky downtown restaurant, stopped coming around after his wife caught him with an Asian masseuse; Vegas, who made his living at the track, had disappeared two years earlier between March Madness and the Kentucky Derby.

I slid Dan a piece of pumpkin pie. It matched his dyed hair. "I'm here twelve hours a day," I said. "Been working since I was thirteen, you know that. Never had the time to chase around cocktail waitresses like you."

"Wait 'til you have kids. Then you can really forget about it."

For the last month, Irene and I had been in talks about when we'd start "trying." By trying, she meant visiting the doc for pre-conception planning, keeping track of her menstrual cycle on the kitchen calendar, graphing her basal body temperature, and stuffing a pillow under her ass while we made love so my boys could make it to their destination. She wasn't messing around.

"Kids," Diner Dan said. "Now that's a game-changer."

For most of the day, I sat in the booth closest to the register, getting up to ring out customers or shoot the shit with my cop and firefighter regulars. I downed five cups of java by day's end. Talked to Irene about ten times, figured out what we were going to have for dinner, what we'd watch on the tube. By late afternoon, I wondered if Billy and Karolina Poland had even started the day yet. Maybe they were in the shower now, Karolina's hands leaving prints on the steamy glass, Billy behind her giving neck kisses, while I was at the bank on the way home, making the day's deposit.

+

Every night that week I ended up in the basement spying on Billy. I couldn't help myself. On top of that, I was amassing new friends every day. People I barely even knew – dudes I met at the gym, customers from the diner, my dry cleaner. I was already almost at twenty.

"What are you doing down there?" Irene would say.

"Checking e-mail, sweetie."

I swear, within the week, Billy's relationship status had changed from "single" to "in a relationship" back to "single" again. It took me days to get through his photos – all 968 of them. *The guy's a loser*, I said to myself. *He doesn't want to ever grow up.* I kept clicking through his pics. *These girls he's with look like teenagers, the predator!* I kept clicking. I scanned through his friends again. My nineteen-year-old busboy, José, was even on his list. José, for Chrissake! Was there anyone in this city Billy didn't know?

One night Irene snuck up on me before I could click back to the ESPN homepage. On the screen was a picture of Billy, sun-kissed, waist-deep in the Atlantic Ocean, palm trees behind him, an open coconut in his hands. Pretty sure he was flexing his abs. I muttered the caption to myself: "Fresh coconut anyone?"

"Who the hell is that?" Irene said, like she'd busted me looking at gay porn.

"Just some guy I used to know, honey."

She sat down next to me in her pajama pants and baggy T-shirt, glasses on. She browsed his latest postings: Billy Dallas "just ate twelve hard-boiled egg whites and is about to hit the gym, baby!" at 7:05 PM; Billy Dallas "has sore fucking abs" at 8:15.

"Our dads were from the same village in Greece," I explained. "We lived right down the street from each other so, you know, the old men would get together to play backgammon and shoot the breeze. Billy and I would play videogames and street football, breakdance. We were practically best friends until junior high."

"Wait, you used to breakdance?"

"Yeah, I was a b-boy for about a year in '84." She laughed.

I didn't have the balls to tell my own wife that by the time Billy and I were in high school, he wanted to have no part anymore in videogames or street football or breakdancing. Or me. He was going to parties experimenting with booze and sex while I was having sleepovers on weekends with the only two close buddies I had.

Before long, Irene and I were clicking through Billy's pictures together, following him on his adventures from Mykonos to Ibiza to Bangkok. Two voyeurs. We read the comments below each pic from his circle of female admirers: "Amazing," "Holy abs. Yummy!", "Oooh don't you look gq?", "Nerd. Jk. (kinda)."

"Did you used to be like this?" Irene said.

"No, of course not, baby." I wished. "We grew apart in high school. I've barely seen him since. I started working with my dad at the diner, I was busy all the time. You know how it goes."

"I can't believe you were *ever* friends with this guy."

"Well, he kinda changed after puberty. He was actually a pretty nice kid."

In the time it took us to go through Billy's pics, he'd added four new friends. Irene eventually got bored and went upstairs to do the dishes. I told her I'd be right there. I stared at a photo of Billy in some random packed club, God knows where on the map. His arms were wrapped around two bleach blondes half our age, all three with shots in hand. His face looked swollen from the sun. The girls' eyes were practically shut, hair wild, tits spilling out of their tops. He'd probably ended up working his way through an assortment of Kama Sutra positions with both of them that night, I imagined. I was disgusted and envious at the same time. Irene's tits were the only two I'd ever see again in my life and they'd be shrivelled to nothing after six months of breast feeding, from what I'd heard.

"*American Idol*'s starting, Sam!" Irene called. "Hurry up!"

+

Irene left a few days later to visit her sister in Philly who'd just popped out her second kid. Field training in swaddling, burping and diaper changing. I had to stay back and keep an eye on the diner.

"You probably won't even miss me," she said. "You've been so glued to that Facebook lately."

It took me a second (I was updating my list of favourite movies), but I shut off the monitor and stood up. "Of course I'm gonna miss you." I leaned in to kiss Irene's forehead and smudged her glasses as I often did.

"When I get back, I guess we'll start trying ourselves, huh?" she said.

I nodded. "Will do, honey."

I drove Irene to O'Hare. She wheeled the suitcase behind her. I waved as she passed the security checkpoint. When I got home, the house was dark and quiet. We hadn't spent a night apart since the day before our wedding. I turned on the TV, but it wasn't the same watching *The Kardashians* without her. I shut it off, walked down the creaky steps to the basement, and sat down at the computer.

+

Irene made it into Philly. I stayed up past my usual bedtime, spying. Voyeurism wasn't quite as much fun alone, though, either. I scrolled down Billy's wall: "Crobar tomorrow night with DJ Inphinity! Email me if you wanna be on the guest list."

I found some old pictures on my computer from a bachelor party in Vegas Billy and I had both ended up at six years earlier. Some guy who'd grown up with us down the block. It was the last time I'd actually seen Billy. I decided to post one of them. Called it "Back in the Day." It was a shot of me, Billy, the groom (since divorced), and a few other guys. We were standing in front of a line of showgirls, our arms across each other's shoulders. I had a cigarette tucked behind my ear even though I didn't smoke. By the end of the night, four people had liked the pic, flashing the "thumbs up" symbol.

On a whim, I decided to IM Billy. I wrote: What's up? The wife's out of town. Why don't you swing by the old neighbourhood for a BBQ before you go out tomorrow night?

He responded, to my surprise.

Billy Dallas: Cool. You can roll out with me to the club afterward.

Sam Nikas: Wish I could, but gotta be up at four.

Billy Dallas: Come on, your woman's out of town. She'll probably be out dancing at the club herself.

Sam Nikas: Her sister just had a –

Billy Dallas: When was the last time you partied, dog? You should take advantage of the freedom. Return of the Mack.

I loved that song.

+

The next morning, I woke up before the alarm even sounded and got into the diner early. The coffee was brewing, machines running, before the employees got in. I watered all the plants. I even started shredding the hash-brown potatoes myself. Diner Dan came in at 5:45.

How ya' doing, Dan-o?" I said. I poured him a cup of coffee. Decided to let him have it on the house.

"What's on tap this weekend?" he asked.

"I'm heading downtown with a friend tonight. One of my boys. Should be fun."

"Good for you. About time. You should stop by the Como Inn. That was one of my old stomping grounds. Tell 'em Dan sent you." I didn't have the heart to tell him the place had been torn down about a decade ago to put up townhouses.

When I was done working, I ran to get a haircut, then stopped by the mall to find something cool to wear. I'd dug through my closet the night before and came up with nothing. I popped my head into stores I'd never even heard of – H&M, Urban Outfitters, Forever 21 (which apparently was for girls only) – before finally finding a shirt with images of skulls and wings and lightning that looked like something out of Billy's photos. I swung by the grocery store and picked up a case of Bud Light and a pack of stogies.

By the time Billy made it over, forty-five minutes late, I had brats sizzling on the grill and Armin van Buuren playing in the background (the 2003 album – most recent one I could dig up).

From the backyard, I heard his Harley roaring down our quiet suburban street. I happened to glance over at our garden tucked away in the corner of the yard. I remembered when Irene and I went to Home Depot to pick out our plants. There were so many choices: San Marzano tomatoes, beefsteak tomatoes, cherry tomatoes. "Isn't this so much fun?" she'd said. It was, but now I couldn't help but envision myself earlier in the summer, on hands and knees, planting lettuce while Billy was probably just leaving some club after last call.

I cut through the house, tongs in hand, and eyed Billy through the screen door. He was in a tank top, sleeve tattoos covering both arms, empty-handed with the exception of an open can of Red Bull.

"Yo, yo, where've you been, dog?" Billy said. He clasped my hand and gave me a back-slap. His hair, brushed up and molded into place with firm-hold gel, scratched my cheek as he reached in.

"I've been around," I said. I literally lived three-quarters of a mile from my childhood home. I gave Billy a good once-over from close range. He looked different than I'd expected from his Facebook pics. His face was leaner; wrinkles radiated from the corners of his eyes down to the corners of his mouth. I was relieved not to be the only one with a receding hairline. "You don't age," I lied. "When I saw your pictures on Facebook, I thought you'd discovered the Fountain of Youth."

"Aw, I Photoshop all those pics. That's just my brand."

I grabbed a couple beers from the fridge and we moved to the backyard. Billy sat at the patio table, while I stood at the grill dodging smoke.

"I forgot how quiet it was out here in the country," he said.

"We're only like twenty minutes from downtown..."

"Maybe it's just 'cause the city's always poppin'," Billy said. "I have an apartment in the Gold Coast. It feels like we're in the middle of Wisconsin right now." He took a swig of beer. I noticed him take a long look at the garden from behind his Versace shades.

"So, what's been going on with you?" I said. I turned the brats. The juices dripped onto the coals, aggravating the flames. "I haven't seen you in years. Since Vegas, I think."

It took him a second. "Oh yeah, Vegas. The bachelor party. I forgot you went with us. That was off the chain. I slept with that Cirque du Soleil dancer." He looked off into the distance like he was trying to evoke images of the encounter. "Anyway, I was bouncing at a club for a while, now I'm kinda managing it. I'm still out every night, travelling like crazy. My friends just keep getting younger, that's all that changes."

I took a couple brats off the grill and dropped them into buns.

"So your dad's produce store – you guys got rid of it, right?" I said. My dad had already told me the land had been sold to Costco when Billy refused to take the business over.

"Couldn't do it, my man," Billy said. "I might as well have been in the clink. Waking up at the ass crack of dawn,

139

surrounded by the same four walls, smelling fruit all day, every day. I'd be bored as hell. I'd go crazy."

There was silence. Crickets chirping.

"You? What do you do?" he asked.

"Me?" I could feel my face turning red, like the big boy tomatoes hanging in the garden. "Just at the diner still. Yeah, I run it now, so…"

"No shit?" Billy said. "Good for you, buddy. Good for you. Took the plunge. Own the diner. Nice and settled. Good for you."

After dinner, we walked around the yard, examining the garden, smoking stogies. Billy pulled his iPhone from his pocket and looked at it. "We should probably head out," he said. "You ready?"

I was on my third beer. "Most definitely," I said.

+

Billy insisted on driving. "You ain't gonna find a spot to park your mini-van downtown, dog," he said.

Irene would kill me if she found out I'd been on the back of a motorcycle going ninety on the Kennedy. We stopped by Billy's place, a seven-hundred square-foot junior one-bedroom on the twentieth floor, with floor-to-ceiling windows and a sprawling view of Lake Michigan. He had a monster canister of whey protein on the granite counter and some furniture arranged around a 52-inch flat screen TV. Above his black leather sofa was a life-sized portrait of himself smoking a cigarette on a beach.

"Cool painting," I said.

"This Spanish chick that I hooked up with in Majorca gave it to me." It was based on a picture she'd taken of him just after they'd had sex in the sand, he said.

I peeked into Billy's closet while he showered. He had two dozen belts with various buckles hanging from the back of the door. There was a Native American Indian buckle, a bald eagle, a Texas Longhorn. Crazy how different our lives had become. His biggest concern was probably which one he was going to wear to the club that night; mine was when exactly my wife would be ovulating. He chose the eagle.

We sped down the elevator packed in with five other people, no one saying a word. I was excited. A little nervous, too. I told Irene I was going to see a movie. I thought it'd be best.

When we got to the club, there was a line out the door. Billy knew the doorman, though, so we didn't even pay. He pushed his way through the crowd towards the VIP section. I tried not to lose him. Bodies pressed against one another; hands reached up to avoid spilling cocktails.

"It's my friend's birthday," Billy yelled over the blaring music. He gave the VIP attendant a kiss on the cheek and a little small talk, and the velvet rope was lifted.

A group of people stood up from a small table as we walked in. There was a bottle of vodka chilling in a bucket of ice and carafes of cranberry juice and OJ. I recognized faces from Billy's friends list. There was a lanky dude who went by the screen name Muscles. There was an emaciated blonde with 600 CCS in her chest and orange skin.

"Is that Karolina Poland?" I leaned in and asked him.

"Karolina who? Oh, no. I kicked that chick to the curb."

I stood behind Billy while he chatted. He tried to introduce me, but I could tell he didn't know all their names.

"This is one of my dogs," he told the birthday girl. I swear she must've been turning eighteen.

We sat down at the table. They talked about DJs, who was hooking up with who, which clubs were hot that night. We took shots together. Jägerbombs, Kamikazes, Red-headed Sluts. I got tipsy for the first time since a wedding Irene and I had been to the summer before. We fist-pumped, me and my new friends.

"Are you on Facebook?" someone asked me.

Of course I was. I was one of Billy's sixteen-hundred closest friends.

The girls all jumped up when a Lady Gaga remix started
pounding over the speakers. Billy and Muscles followed them
onto the dance floor.

"I'll meet you out there," I said.

It was already after midnight. I had a headache. Could barely
keep my eyes open. I stood at the bar sipping on a gin & ton-
ic. Billy posed for pictures with the birthday girl, lips pursed,
chest flexed. Those pics would make their way onto Facebook,
no doubt. I bummed a cigarette from some kid and almost lit
the wrong end. At about 12:30, Irene sent me a text. "Going to
bed," she said. "Love ya." I started to text her back when I felt
a hand on my shoulder.

"Mr. Nikas?"

I turned around. It was José, my busboy.

"Man, didn't expect to see you here, boss!" he said.

Billy approached and ordered another round of shots from
the bar. His face was sweaty, the bags under his eyes more pro-
nounced. He bobbed his head to the music and stared at the
bartender's cleavage.

I leaned in and yelled into José's ear. "Actually, I'm here with
an old friend. I think you guys know each other. I saw you're
one of his Facebook friends." I turned to Billy. "Hey, don't you
know my guy over here – José? He works for me."

Maybe I should I have been embarrassed to be seen there –
tied for oldest guy in the club and likely the only one referred
to as "Mr." that night. Or maybe I'd have a newfound respect
from José that would trickle down to the rest of the busboys,
the cooks, the waitresses. Maybe I wouldn't just be the boring married dude with the five o'clock shadow who sat around
drinking coffee and barking out orders all day.

Billy gave José the once-over. He shook his head. "No, I don't think we've ever met." He extended his hand. "Nice to meet you, dog."

"But I thought–" I began to say.

It didn't matter. José slid off into the crowd. Billy and his crew downed another round of Jägerbombs. I went to take a piss and bumped into some girl who spilled her green-apple martini all over my brand new designer T-shirt. As I swayed in front of the urinal, I stared at the picture on my cell phone of me and Irene at a corn maze, mid-October 2008. I texted her goodnight.

+

Billy stood looking at me, hands on his hips. "You really gotta go? DJ Inphinity, man! You can crash at my crib. I've got two Cubs tickets for tomorrow."

"Yeah," I said, "gotta open the diner at five and I'm picking up Irene in the afternoon."

He clasped my hand and wrapped his arm around my back. "That sucks, my man. Oh well, we'll do it again, right?" His eyes darted through the club; his hand stayed rested on my shoulder. "I still can't believe it – married, own the diner, pretty soon you'll probably have a house full of kids. Good for you, brother. Good for you." His breath smelled like Jäger. Before I left, he reminded me to check his Facebook page the next day for pictures from the night.

I hailed down a taxi and jumped in. When I told the cabbie I was headed to the burbs, he muttered something under his breath. Something about the "fuckin' country" and didn't speak for the rest of the ride. I called Irene's cell.

"Honey? What are you still doing up?" she said in a whisper.

"I'm actually just heading home."

"So late? How was the movie?"

"It was all right," I said. "Nothing like the previews."

Irene sent a picture of our new nephew to my phone. "I'm so excited to start a family with you, Sam. Our own little family."

I leaned my head back and kicked off my shoes. My feet were sore. My wet designer T-shirt clung to my chest. I secretly dreaded sleeping in our old two-storey colonial by myself, the floors creaking all night long, the king bed big and empty without Irene spread out across the other half.

A Collection of Ill-Advised Facebook Status Updates
by Kate Baggott

Dora Foster is no longer in a relationship.

Dora Foster figures if promises of more oral sex can't save a relationship, the break should be as swift as it is inevitable.

Annie Levinski hears Thailand is a great place to default on student loans. They never find anyone in Bangkok.

Dora Foster wishes you good luck on the pregnancy plans, but remembers when her ex-boyfriend used to sleep with your husband.

Thomas DunLeary won't be putting a ring on anyone's finger this Christmas.

Dora Foster is giving **Thomas DunLeary** the finger.

Moira Cohen-Emilion tries to fit in by shopping at Giant Tiger, but can't figure out the difference between "the good" jogging pants and the regular kind.

Annie Levinski dreams of defaulting in Thailand, has the budget to get to Niagara Falls. Is the casino a decent place to hide?

Jennifer Allen-Foster was up with the baby six times last night. Very tired.

Dora Foster is relieved to see everyone she went to high school with can obviously afford to Super Size it.

Annie Levinski likes the Group of Seven, Recovering Graduate Students Anonymous and Unconventional Sex in Classical Arts: the film.

Miranda DunLeary might have one cuckoo in the family tree, but that's below average in this town.

Steve Foster can't figure out why people think new parents are sleep-deprived. Our baby doesn't wake up at all.

Jennifer Allen-Foster posted on **Steve Foster**'s wall. "Have you been paying attention to anything? You better give your sister a call."

Annie Levinski earned her PhD in Art History and discovered she's really only interested in making money.

Herbert Emilion thinks **Annie Levinski** should call him.

Moira Cohen-Emilion wonders if anyone can recommend a good divorce lawyer.

Jennifer Allen-Foster posted on **Moira Cohen-Emilion**'s wall. "I emailed you a list of lawyers who specialize in family law and have good reputations. I spent nap time doing the research for myself."

Herbert Emilion was talking about business, like always.

Moira Cohen-Emilion wonders if the red plaid lumberjack pyjamas at Old Navy are authentic.

Moira Cohen-Emilion joined the group Unconventional Sex in Classical Arts: the film.

Herbert Emilion left the group Unconventional Sex in Classical Arts: the film.

Craig Foster warns **Dora Foster** and **Steve Foster** to block **Greg Foster** and Thea Santinakis-Foster before they figure out how to work the Facebook app on their new iPhones. They've given themselves early Christmas presents.

Thomas DunLeary is not taking over the family business. Organs just aren't that interesting.

Dora Foster knows exactly which organs **Thomas DunLeary** is interested in and thinks he should just come "out" with it.

Annie Levinski is pretty sure at least three of the AGO's most popular paintings are fakes.

Hugh DunLeary is taking over the family business and reminds his brother that there's no reason for him to live by the rule "life's a bitch and then you marry one."

Dora Foster would like to thank the boys from school for ignoring her when they were young and cute because living with you old and bald now would be awful.

Miranda DunLeary tagged **Thomas DunLeary** in a wall post: "Tom? Did something happen between you and Dora? Her status updates have been kind of hostile today."

Greg Foster is now on Facebook. Suggest friends for Greg.

Greg Foster and Thea Santinakis-Foster are now married.

Greg Foster just sent friend requests to three out of four children and is waiting to hear back from them. Can't wait to keep up with their daily lives.

Thomas DunLeary is now friends with Thea Santinakis-Foster and **Greg Foster.**

Kate Baggott cannot believe the nastiness on her newsfeed today.

The Life Span of the 21st Century Crush (A Cautionary Tale)
by Lisa Mrock

Month One: You see him at a reading. He's tall, reads well, speaks well and is kinda cute. You go home and google his name. You find his two Facebook accounts, two Tumblrs and his Twitter. You are proud of your investigational skills. You go to the info page on his Facebook and find out he likes the same TV shows you do. He also has good taste in movies and music, a lot like your own, and he goes to readings like you do. You look at his Tumblrs and find the usual hipster stuff, but you can overlook such a hindrance. You determine from his Tumblr and Facebook photos that he is photogenic. You read his Twitter and find him to be hilarious. Judging from the content of everything you've looked at, you decide he is entertaining. You bookmark his two Facebooks, two Tumblrs and his Twitter, and hope to run into him again.

Month Two: You've been reading his blogs religiously for the past month. You now know without ever having spoken to him that he is a nice guy who has had terrible luck in relationships, that whenever he puts effort into a girl, he loses her. You think, "I wouldn't slip through his fingers like that. I'd stick in him like stitches." You see him at few readings, but he doesn't read and neither do you. He stands around talking to people and he's never left alone. You hope he takes the same way home you do. He doesn't.

The Life Span of the 21ˢᵗ Century Crush (A Cautionary Tale)

Month Three: He posts a picture of himself with a new nose ring on his Tumblr. It's not so great, but you can overlook such a hindrance. You see him at another reading where he reads a story about failing to seduce a girl. You think it's funny and tell yourself you're going to talk to him. Instead, your heart feels like it's about to turn itself inside out, and all you can do is stand next to him because for some reason, you can't say anything. You go home and a few hours later go on his two Facebooks, two Tumblrs and his Twitter. He posts about not being able to find anybody and you think, "But I was standing right next to him." On his Tumblr, he posts that he's starting a video blog and will make an update every week. You subscribe to his YouTube channel and are going to watch every one of those videos five times.

Month Four: You're at a reading, and you read a story. He compliments you on it. You refuse to delude yourself into thinking his compliment was spoken in a secret code which translates to, "Wanna go out?" You think about an interview in *Rolling Stone* with porn star Sasha Grey, how she once had a relationship with a man almost ten years older, and how he was the one who helped her explore her sexual fantasies. You think, "I want to be Sasha Grey and I want to explore with him." You're also beginning to imagine what your relationship with him could be like. You imagine sitting with him in his apartment, no roommates, and watching your favourite TV shows like *Community* and *Mad Men*. And afterward, you imagine him fucking you mercilessly and breathing hard, like he's trying to inhale your blood through the pores of your skin. And after the simultaneous orgasm, you'd bore your eyes into his and say, "I'd bury myself in you if I could," and he'd say, "I buried myself in you a *long* time ago."

Month Five: While procrastinating on writing a story about a woman's surreal experience having sex with a man who looks like Jared Leto, you go on his personal Tumblr. He's made a post about how great John Steinbeck is. You don't agree with him, but you can overlook such a hindrance. He has also written a long post about his dating woes, how the ones which should've lasted didn't and the ones that *did* never deserved to. He's vulnerable, as are you, and you know if you could only be vulnerable *with* him, everything would work like you imagined, where he wraps his arms around you while lying down on the couch and fucks you like it's illegal. You imagine getting the balls to write to him over his Tumblr, saying you think he should go out with you because of various reasons you'd articulate over the course of an hour, and then you'd hit Send and hope he reads your anonymous crush letter, not an anonymous love letter, because being in love with someone you've barely talked to is creepy.

Month Six: You check his Facebook and your heart immediately wants to jump out of your chest and beat the shit out of you – he's changed his relationship status from "single" to "in a relationship." But it's impossible. Just a few weeks ago he talked about how futile his efforts were. How could he have found someone so quickly? Now, forty of his Facebook friends have liked his status and are congratulating him. You check his personal Tumblr and see a new post. It's a photo of him and his new girlfriend. He's also made it his new Facebook profile picture. Your heart feels like how your stomach feels – hungry because it's empty. Even the area around it aches, as if gravel is grinding through your arteries. You haven't felt this way since high school, when the lacrosse jock you liked got a girlfriend the day after you met him and stayed with her for the rest of the four years, no matter how many anonymous messages you sent to him over his blogs, saying how his girlfriend was cheating on him, amongst other lies. You vow to stay off all of his blogs for a few weeks in order to take in the information and deal with it, though you refuse to stay away from readings, because he's not going to have that much power over you. Besides, with his track record they could be broken up within the month.

Month Seven: You go on his blogs for the first time in a few weeks. You see he's still with his girlfriend. You see a few photos of them on his two Facebooks, two Tumblrs and his Twitter. They look happy. You'd be lying if you said you didn't long to be the girl in those photos, but that's not all of it. You know what you really long for is the overall concept of being with someone. You want to have the proverbial partner in crime. You want to kiss someone and tell them everyone else is ugly. You want to pull streets out from under cars, bomb buildings and tear the windows off of skyscrapers to make glass houses with someone. You unsubscribe to his YouTube channel. You take one last look, close the tabs to his two Facebooks, two Tumblrs and his Twitter, delete the bookmarks and close the laptop. You go to a reading later that night. He's there with his girlfriend. You ignore them. You see a guy. He's wearing a Nickelback T-shirt, but you can overlook such a hindrance. He goes up to read. The guy's a little short, reads well, speaks well and is kinda cute. You go home and google his name.

Do You Want to Burn to Death and Look Like Steak with Hair?
by Greg Kearney

About me: Welcome to my sobriety blog! My name is Helene Savant. I have lived in Winnipeg all my life. I am a recovering addict and breast cancer survivor. I have been sober since May 2009, and cancer-free since August 2008!

I love to write, so I started this blog in the hopes that my story – my – the ongoing, thrilling story – will be of inspiration to other people living (!) with illness and addiction issues. There IS life – thrilling, thrilling L-I-F-E! – after drugs and alcohol and, in my case, real breasts. Read on!

February 28, 2010

A bad day. Not the worst day I've ever had, but a bad, bleak one nonetheless. I considered all my little diversionary mental tricks, my little Helene bits of business – cardio, shopping, on-line chat, masturbation – and nothing appealed to me. I think I am simply going to sit in my plush, comfy pink chair in the living room, motionless. This goes against my basic nature, which is GO! GO! GO! 24/7, but I need to try a new tactic. My old tactics aren't working.

I think might call a friend. Ekaterina is really my only fleshly, real-life friend. I don't normally reach out to fleshly, real-life friends unless I'm about to mount them or kick their sorry ass in racquetball. Maybe I will call Ekaterina, just to talk About Jack. About what Ekaterina does to help herself during difficult times.

Do You Want to Burn to Death and Look Like Steak with Hair?

February 27, 2010

Tonight, at the tail end of a lovely meal at Red Lobster, Jack told me that he finds me "vexing and exhausting," and he doesn't want to see me anymore, in any capacity, ever! I was blindsided. I asked him why he hadn't, at the very least, delivered the news before we had dinner. He said he was hungry.

I am despondent. If I wasn't so strong in my sobriety, I would relapse right now. Since coming home, I have cleaned the bathroom and pleasured myself twice. One day, one moment at a time.

I just don't understand. Things were going so well.

February 26, 2010

Dawn. Jack just left, the end of perhaps the most perfect date in the history of romance. My life is wondrous! There are dark, glittering, lilied troves here and there, everywhere, in my wondrous life.

We met up at 3 PM, played racquetball for two hours (I kicked his sorry ass – yessssss!), then I sat with him while he lay down on a courtside bench (he felt faint). While he recovered, I talked about my journey over (OVER, not through!) cancer and opiate addiction. I talked and talked; remembering that we had first met on a smoking cessation message board (even though I don't smoke and never have), I made sure to make up details about my journey over tobacco, too.

After that, we showered (separately! Ha ha!) and went to dinner at this vibrant new Mexican restaurant Screamies. All the food was incredibly spicy; Jack and I stared at each other, panting and fanning ourselves like two Sahara vagabonds on their last legs. So yummy.

After that, we went to see that new action film (I'm terrible with movie names) starring that blonde actress (I'm worse with movie stars' names!), the movie in which the blonde actress has to dig her way out of the centre of the earth with a spoon (or something along those lines; I wasn't watching the film, I was watching Jack!).

I looked at his face in the darkened theatre and thought, I could abide with this man. I could rest with him. We could sleep so sweetly together. I would pare his toenails if he asked me, I thought to myself.

After that we went back to my place, Jack took a Viagra, I climbed aboard and rode him all night. I rode and rode and rode and rode. Once or twice he mentioned that he was tired and sore, but we all know what that means!!! I kept right on riding! I climaxed twice! I think he came, too. I couldn't really tell; he's such a suave, discreet lover.

And he was completely unfazed by my reconstructed breasts. He fondly fondled them. So unlike my ex-husband, as you will recall if you've been reading my blog from its inception.

My ex-husband was initially very supportive when I was diagnosed, constantly reassuring me that he would always find me beautiful and desirable. But my implants frightened him. He'd accidentally brush against them in and shudder, as if my new boobs were electrical or something. Fuck him. I delight in the knowledge that he is languishing at the very bottom of the food chain in prison.

Back to Jack. During afterglow, I nuzzled against him and asked him to sleep over; he said he was "too tired." Too tired to sleep over! I love dry wit. No "wet wit" for me!

Sobriety ROCKS.

February 25, 2010

My blog is being followed by three people now! After only nine months of blogging! I am going to put on my joggers and jog to Winners and buy whatever the hell I want! I've earned it!

February 24, 2010

I love my sister, but talk about a stick in the mud! As you know, she came down last week to support me during the trial. I wanted to do fun things, to celebrate my ex-husband's incarceration and inevitable, repeated ass rape. I wanted to play paintball, go to the casino, the racetrack. I did NOT want to go to Mass and wring my hands and talk about my feelings and wonder aloud how it is that a loving God can allow a middle-aged man to blow a thirteen-year-old boy.

This was the first time I'd seen Judy since getting sober and I have to say, she's not how I remember her. She used to be a real good-time girl, full of one-liners, given to giddy gossip. She has always been devoutly Catholic, but she never has rammed it down my throat the way she did this visit.

"Oh," she kept saying, "you must feel forsaken, because of all you've been through."

"No," I kept saying, "I don't feel forsaken. I feel formidable." She just refused to believe that I wasn't angry at God. O she of little faith, is what I say.

And she was horrified by my behaviour at the courthouse. Every day I wore my mean, ironic Macaulay Culkin T-shirt and sat as close to the front as I could get. I stood outside the courthouse, and I gave my two cents to the *Winnipeg Free Press*.

From today's paper!

PEDOPHILE CONVICTED

A local man was found guilty yesterday of sexually abusing a thirteen-year-old boy over the course of several months in 2008.

51-year-old Claude Savant was convicted of ten counts of forcible oral copulation, and three counts of lewd acts.

Savant did not show any reaction as the verdict was read.

Outside the courthouse, however, Savant's ex-wife was jubilant.

"I'm like a child at Christmas," a beaming Helene Savant declared. "This verdict is a victory for the ex-wives of pedophiles everywhere."

Thrilled as I was to have been quoted in the newspaper, I'm still miffed that the nitwit reporter left out the part where I said that the verdict was also a victory for the victims of pedophiles everywhere. The quote in the paper makes me sound so self absorbed.

As Judy and I drove home from the courthouse yesterday, she said I'd handled myself "deplorably!" What the hell does she know about handling oneself in a crisis? So her stupid Springer Spaniel broke a leg last month – ooh, time to call in the prayer circle! I said as much and it really set her off: God this, Mary that. I told her I didn't want to hear it, that the very reason I avoid AA is all the higher power bull dung. I couldn't wait to drop her at the airport.

When I got home from the airport later that night, I literally ran to the computer to check in with my various online support groups. I went into all the chat rooms, posted umpteen times, but nobody responded. Some people actually left the chat rooms as soon as I'd post. I wasn't offended or hurt. I get it: sometimes other people's chaos is simply too much to cope with for the recovering addict.

I finally ended up in a Nic Anon chat room, for ex-smokers. I've never smoked, but I was desperate for contact.

I started a private chat with this man, Jack, who quit smoking New Year's Day. We sort of hit it off: he gave me the link to his eHarmony profile. He's seventy, a full twenty years older than I, but the grin he offers on all his eHarmony pictures hints at a playful sexuality. We've made a date for the 26th. I'm trying to not get my hopes up. How can I not, though? I'm ready for love again. Crazy, crazy love.

February 17, 2010

I'm sorry I haven't updated my blog for so long. I am perfectly well and strong in my sobriety, if anyone was worried. I've been mired in my ex-husband's trial (yes! It's finally begun!), and the last few details of my divorce settlement needed hammering out.

On that note, there might be another wee gap in my updates, because my sister Judy is coming for a visit! She's worried about me; she thinks I need "support." Ha ha ha! Ha ha ha ha! Oh well. Bless her heart. We're going to have so much fun. Judy's a crazy lady; we used to backcomb our hair into Bride of Frankenstein dos and then go out on the town to see who'd still bite! I haven't seen her since Christmas '06.

And Ekaterina called me! What a dear woman she is. Wanted to see how I was holding up through the trial. I told her that I'm flourishing, absolutely flourishing. Adversity hones and primes me.

Did I tell my "bottom story" already? I must have.

Oh well, one can never revisit one's bottom story too frequently.

Summer 2008. I was finishing chemotherapy, finally. Home early from my next-to-last session, I walked in on my husband performing oral sex on a thirteen-year-old boy who was squatting on our ottoman. My mouth went into a perfect O. I slapped my palms to my face. I looked just like the boy in that movie... lemme google it... Macauley Culkin in *Home Alone*. My face stayed that way for days.

My doctor prescribed a nice sedative, Clonazepam, for my tattered nerves. At first I took it just before bed. But soon I was taking it more frequently. Several times the maximum dose. I popped those babies like Tic Tacs. My doctor is elderly and has asked me out several times while examining me; he had no compunction about renewing my prescription every week.

With Claude gone (I kicked his sorry ass out pronto!), the house felt somewhat empty. I got a cat from the Humane Society; I thought a nice, plump cat would infuse my lonely house with warmth. Ha! The fucking thing was more high-strung than I was! It used to balance itself atop my wrought iron headboard and then leap onto my face in the middle of the night, claws dug deep in my neck and forehead. So I brought it to Loblaws and set it loose when nobody was looking. I am an animal lover, and I am not proud of that move. Yeesh, addiction really warps you like a motherfucker, doesn't it?

I was still working at the library back then. Ekaterina is the head librarian and a long-time friend; as my addiction worsened, she kept reducing my workload.

By spring of last year I'd been demoted from the desk and stacks; now I was Storytime Lady, reading once a week for a group of preschoolers.

One day in early May, I downed a handful of Clonaz right before storytime. Swooshy and mindless, I began to read aloud from *Hollywood Wives* by Jackie Collins. I got to a sexy part and – my shame blazes over this still – started pleasuring myself through my slacks. A little girl asked me why I was so itchy. Then I fell off my stool.

Ekaterina pulled me into the staff room. She said that the only reason why she wasn't going to fire me was because her sister had been an alcoholic, and she was the sweetest person in the world before she passed out drunk with a lit cigarette and burned to death. So Ekaterina gave me a last chance.

"Do you want to fall asleep and burn to death and look like steak with hair?" she said.

"No, I sure don't," I said.

She drove me home. She wanted me to go to the hospital; I refused.

After all, I've been on my own, doing things my way, ever since I left my alcoholic parental home at the age of seventeen.

Even when I was married, I was alone. Claude was always so ethereal, forever fading out of one room and into another. For years, I just thought he was gratuitously gentlemanly, maybe, maybe gay, absolute tops. I never caught even the faintest whiff of pederasty.

And so I kept house, and tried for children for fifteen years, night after night of dutiful, grueling pound, pound, pound, to no avail. I conceived once; I lost the baby three weeks in, bending over to pick up Claude's vintage hardcover copy of *Ricky Schroder: In His Own Words*, which had fallen from the bookcase.

That was the end of that. Claude was slightly forlorn about my barrenness; mainly he was floaty and… not around.

Then, in 2007, breast cancer. Double mastectomy. A year of chemo. Sometimes Claude drove me, mostly I drove myself. When you're seriously ill, fending off fevers and frailty that could end your life at any time, and you sometimes lie in bed and listen to your own breathing, and your breathing sounds hard and exotic, a great, brass wing flapping, and you wonder: is this breathing new to me? Is this the prelude to a death rattle? When you lie with that fear and never once shake awake the man beside you for comfort.

Well, suffice it to say, I knew that I could and would quit stupid fucking Clonazepam by myself.

So, after Ekaterina drove me home that day, I sat myself down, and I said to myself, "You are a powerful, powerful woman. There is nothing that you cannot conquer. There is nothing that you are going to be enslaved to – or there is nothing to which you are going to be enslaved…" I can't remember the exact syntax. I was drugged at the time.

It was rough – my hair went white – but I got off the damn pills. And then… I can't remember! I'm going to go back and look at what I wrote when I started the blog…

Ha! Here is what I wrote. **May 30, 2009**: "This is my blog. I am twelve days off the pills. Never again will I be subjugated. Never again will I kowtow. Goodbye, addiction! Goodbye, perverted husbands! Goodbye, breast cancer! I will be a furious blur from here on in. Constant motion, racquetball, and lots of sex, and the Macarena, and the Achy Breaky Dance, and the Hustle!

My real life starts now! SOCKO! POW!"

Wow. I was not lying! Was I?

Older entries >>

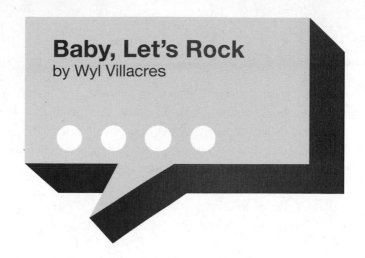

Baby, Let's Rock
by Wyl Villacres

The article would be my opus, my take down of the online-dating world. I'd set out to prove that women on the Internet were desperate and ignored flaws in potential mates lest they die alone, surrounded by cats. It never occurred to me to look at how men behaved. Men are pretty much always terrible, especially when it comes to dating, so it's a given, right? Women were still a mystery to me. I had dated my fair share, even been engaged once upon a time, but still had no idea what made them tick. And the Internet added a whole new level of deception and desperation, and hey, we can't all be the perfect feminists that we want to be. So there's that.

As part of my research, I set up two online profiles, one of what I imagined to be the perfect guy, and one who sounded like a serial killer. Where the perfect guy liked indie music and folk singer-songwriters, the serial killer preferred Marilyn Manson and speeches by Hitler. The perfect guy made between thirty and fifty thousand dollars a year, volunteered as a writing tutor for little kids and had a cat named Chairman Meow; the serial killer worked at a porn shop, enjoyed walks through alleys at night and practiced taxidermy in his spare time. I sat back, basking in the glow of my accomplishments. I used my own photos for the characters: the nice guy was me in a tie, the serial killer got a photo from a day I made rabbit stew – a glamour shot of me, tattoos and messy hair, holding a rabbit's ribcage. Soon the responses started rolling in. Within a week, the serial killer had received fifteen messages, most of them including "oh, you're so funny!"; the nice guy only one, a "you're too good to be real." with a sad smiley face. It was shaping up to be the perfect story, if anyone would buy it.

At the time, there were a few OK Cupid take-down articles out there, mostly dealing with people making fake profiles and saying "SEE! OK CUPID IS TERRIBLE! LOOK AT ALL THESE DESPERATE PEOPLE!" So, that could be why it wasn't selling. Something no one had done, however, was to embody their fake profiles, to become the monster they created and go out on a date with one of those desperate people. Sure, it doesn't sound like the greatest idea to try to attract crazy people and then meet those crazy people. But sometimes the story wants what the story wants. And sometimes, somewhere deep inside, the author of those stories is single, sad, lonely, and has heard stories of casual sexual hookups stemming from online dating. With all of this buzzing around, I decided to respond to one of the girls from the creepy dude's messages, and see what happened.

I picked "Kingsley." Her message had consisted of a link to a story of a woman in Texas investigated for taking pornographic photographs inside a dead horse (complete with pictures). The message was accompanied by: "Think you'd be into this?" *No!* I thought as I replied, "Sure. Anything with knives is pretty fun." After a few more messages and a couple texts, we decided to meet up.

I waited for "Kingsley," real name "Laura Goldstein," (not her actual real name), at the Belmont red line station. I sat in the December cold, hands in my pockets, pigeons pecking around my feet, feeling as dirty as the station around me. Grey slush splattered the concrete pillars and sidewalk. I wondered if it was a mistake to meet up with wannabe horse killer Laura.

But maybe she was just like me: faking her profile to cause a stir.

As I considered catching the next northbound train back to safety, a child sat next to me. Five feet tall, waifish, a mess of unbrushed curly hair, the closed-off posture of a fifth grader on detention. She looked over, smiled slightly and inched closer to me. "Hi, I'm Laura."

She looked nothing like her online photos, which were probably taken from strange angles and with some help from Photoshop. There was no bronzed, full lipped, smokey-eyed, "5'6", twenty-two-year old vegan." There was no turning back now, either.

During the walk to Argo Tea, the small talk was awkward.

"My parents are paying for me to study in China." She stared at the sidewalk in front of us.

"That's very nice of them."

"Yeah, they're, you know, Jewish. Goldstein: Jewish."

"Man, I wish I was Jewish. My parents are Latino, so, you know, we're poor. Obviously."

"Oh. So you're a spic eh? My parents won't like that."

Nice. But maybe not so strange from a girl who'd started our online conversation with a link to dead-horse porn. Shock value was probably her thing. And after all, I did have the nickname "Spicky" in middle school, in the almost all-white suburb where I grew up. (Given to me by my best friend. He eventually changed it to "Jose," which went down a lot better when we both moved to Chicago, home to many other Latinos.) And besides, I'd opened it up with the joke about poor Latinos. So I played along.

"I mean, we're also Catholic, so I can't bring home a Jewish Princess either. Not that this would even come to that..."

At the café we got our drinks and sat down to talk. Laura pulled out her invisible braces and set them on a napkin, long lines of spit extending from her teeth like telephone wires. She took off her jacket to expose a faded long sleeve T-shirt, "Las Vegas" printed across the front and down the sleeves.

I had elected to put on a nice sweater for this first date. Sure, I was playing the part of the creep, but that didn't mean I was going to look scuzzy. She leaned in while she told me about... China? DePaul? The weather? I don't really know. I spent more time tearing at my croissant, rolling my glass along its bottom edge, faking phone calls to step outside and escape her. Nothing she said resonated with me. Everything I said was met with a blank stare.

"Can we go back to your house? I think we should drink something." With that, Laura slipped the braces back into her mouth.

"You want to throw down on a jug of wine or something?" No matter what, no matter who asks, never, ever will I turn down an opportunity to drink. And I hadn't had anyone to drink with in a while. It might be nice to have some company, and she wasn't *that* bad...

"Oh, I thought you could just get it. Steal it like a good Latino." Wasn't there something about "negging" being a thing? Insulting someone which somehow became flirting? I think I remember hearing about this on the Internet.

"Ah. I see. So this is how the Jews keep all their gold. Stingy bastards."

At Jewel they were sampling wine with in-store coupons at an end-cap of the liquor aisle. We stopped, grabbed one-ounce cups, Laura again pulling the invisible braces from her mouth, the plastic popping as it came off her teeth. She liked the one called "Juliet" with roses all over the bottle, because of course she would. The employee handing out the samples, a fat, older man with a grey military haircut, said, "Well, you already have your Romeo!" in an impossibly high and nasal plea for this young couple to just fucking buy the wine already. I wanted to puke.

Back at my place, drinking from plastic tumblers, we sat in my living room in the only two pieces of furniture, a La-z-Boy recliner from the 1970s and an overstuffed green armchair, placed next to each other facing the TV. We talked about bullshit, my laptop on a milk crate plugged into the speakers, Black Flag playing fast and shrill. Not exactly mood music, as I drained glass after glass of Juliet. I might have also snuck off to my room to take a couple pulls of stale rum from my "emergency flask." We asked the requisite "so how did you get into online dating?" but didn't linger on the topic, neither of us wanting to confront those particular demons.

The overhead light had burned out a week before. The last few rays of daylight limped through the window. Laura extolled the many perks of being Jewish (did you know that Jewish women always have perfect hair?). I sat back in the armchair drunk, letting my cup fall against the empty bottle on the floor, wishing I had a coffee table. Laura turned to me. "Can I put on some porn?"

What?"

"There's this Czech guy and – oh my god, he's so smooth. He gives women money to show him their tits and then more to fuck them and sometimes he gets anal!" Her voice was smooth – no slurred speech, like she hadn't drunk any wine at all. Why was I feeling drunk, and she seemed stone sober? Had she even had a glass? Was this part of her plan?

"What?"

"Here." She jumped up, crossed over the cracked hardwood to the laptop and navigated to her preferred site. For a second, I was nervous she'd see my own in the browsing history, the first two drop-down results after "www." Then I figured it might have saved some time.

She was a slow typist. P. O. R. N. H. Y- backspace. U. B. Dot. C. O. N- backspace. M. Enter. Searching the "Czech" category, she gave quick critiques of each passing video. "This one is terrible" or "this one is okay but she giggles too much" or "this girl is hot" before finally settling on one.

She was not merely an ill-dressed Jewish girl. She was an ill-dressed Jewish girl who thought watching porn on a first date was an acceptable thing to do. I felt a stirring in my jeans. Maybe if I got her in bed I could close my eyes, pretend she was Sarah Silverman and enjoy breaking a dry spell. She sat down, riveted by the porn.

The porn was POV-style: a shitty, shaky hand camera showing the money, then focusing on the girl's breasts. The caption read "100 [koruna] for your breasts, yes? Beautiful." One-hundred koruna was worth about five dollars. I learned this from a friend who went to Prague that summer.

I felt awkward, as if the porn exposed my own intentions. Sure, I wasn't offering her money, but I only had one goal in mind at this point, drunk, horny and lonely. I started to feel sick. Researching an article was no longer my main objective. I'd fallen into the online-dating trap myself. Lured by easily made profiles, the flurry of messages, seemingly endless possibilities. Loneliness and desperation had taken over. I was ignoring glaring personality flaws in the hope to not end up alone and die surrounded by cats.

Laura moved behind me, straddling me in the chair, giving a sensual shoulder massage, moving her hands eventually to my chest. I started to wonder if maybe, just maybe, this whole online-dating thing might not be that bad. I mean, if it didn't work out with her, I could write about it – or not – and I could pick another girl – or not. There was nothing keeping me there, no monthly fees, no promises or obligations. There was always the possibility of getting laid. Laura breathed heavily onto the back of my neck.

The massage stopped as quickly as it had started. Laura spun in front of me, ordering me to lift my shirt. "I need to check your nipples."

"What?"

"I need to make sure you don't have weird nipples. Let me see them."

"What?"

"Here." She pulled up my shirt, examining my nipples like a jeweller inspecting a diamond, searching for the smallest flaw. Satisfied, she let my T-shirt fall back. She nodded approvingly. I felt my chances of sex growing.

"Well, since you saw mine, I feel like it's only fair that I see yours." I was a sly sonofabitch.

She paused. "All right."

Laura pulled her shirt up then off, taking the bra with it. She stood there, confident, straight, proud of her breasts. They weren't much, two halved peaches, somehow sagging despite their size and her age. More or less symmetrical nipples. Two short black hairs stuck out of the right one. It seemed like a good time to try and kiss her.

Put into that situation a thousand times, I'm fairly sure I would make the same decision every time. I went in slow, trying to be smooth. But I was drunk, so I'm sure I looked terrible. She stopped me, holding a hand between us, looking strangely satisfied.

"I think I've been giving you mixed signals." Laura replaced her bra and shirt and sat in the other chair again. I stayed half seated, puckered lips sliding back into place slowly, head still cocked to one side.

"Well, now what?" she asked. When I suggested that she leave, she agreed whole-heartedly.

I didn't kick her out because I was mad about not getting laid. I kicked her out because there was nothing really left to do. We didn't like each other and we weren't going to have sex; it was like sitting in a dentist's waiting room. With the addition of the exposed nipples.

She texted me the next day saying that our date was weird, and that we should go out again on a better date. She wanted to meet at the Museum of Contemporary Art in two days. I agreed. Then I deleted her number and ignored her calls and texts when I didn't show up. Not something I'm proud of, but at the time it felt great. I was in charge of my love life again. Back in the saddle, no longer worried about being alone, confident in my ability to have a terrible first date and yet still get called for a second one. The sense of grandeur was unwarranted and silly, but it still felt good.

I waited a few months before returning to my fake profiles. I figured I might as well try a date from the nice-guy profile. As I talked to "Babyletsrock," the urge to come clean pulsated beneath every message I sent, as I told myself the "nice guy" I had created would never lie about who he was.

So I told her everything. I sent her the rough draft of the story I was writing, gave her a list of things that were false on my profile – I don't make that much money, I like punk rock and hip hop, my cat's named Zombie not Chairman Meow, I'm a paid tutor for college students – and asked if she'd still be interested in meeting up. Her real name is Emily, and we've been dating ever since.

Coffee Owl
by Judy Darley

I see something today on Pinterest, like an optical illusion. It looks like a portrait of an owl. I like owls. The picture makes me smile. It has been created, the caption says, by dropping two Hula Hoops into a cup of coffee.

I enjoy the idea of seeing the owl in my coffee cup, but the thought of two soggy Hula Hoops, the swirls of salt, displeases me in a distracting way. It nudges me as I try to work, dilutes my focus so that the right words skim out of reach, leaving in their wake slower lumpier words that will just have to do.

Davey, my brother, loved owls when he was little. I remember taking him to a farm park when he was three or so, with the first of my boyfriends to have a driver's licence. We sat in the cold, watching daffodils bob their jagged heads as we waited for the raptor display to begin. An owl was brought out first – a huge barn owl. Davey was entranced, ran forward before I could stop him, wanting to meet this strange feathered beast. I froze in panic, but all that happened was that he came to a halt a couple of curious feet away, and the trainer solemnly introduced the pair of them. I never forgot that moment of fear. Davey never seemed to remember it, although he loved owls all his life.

When he was older, teenage, and almost fully grown, Davey loved coffee just as much as me. It was a small similarity I clung to – proof we really were related. In every other way we seemed like opposites, his crackle and bite against my whispering calm. He used to avoid the stillness, the quiet I always sought. It was as though he was afraid that if all were silent, he might hear himself think – hear the truth of his thoughts.

I wonder now if he could already feel it – the gradual unraveling; small holes appearing and letting out the light.

We went to the lake sometimes, when he still wanted to know me, with sandwiches and Hula Hoops and Davey's Superman flask of tar-strong coffee. The shore was covered with the prints of wading birds and bits of driftwood that Davey would collect and carve into creatures I couldn't quite recognize. He would whistle all the while, sing or just mumble to himself. I suppose I should have known something wasn't quite right, but he was just Davey, as he always had been.

I would bring an old crocheted blanket sewn together from granny squares: blue, green, lilac, yellow. Mom had made it years before and it was soft with age. Davey loved it – would lie down on it, rub his cheek against the ancient fibres, eyes half-closed in bliss. I'd smile, watching him, seeing him so happy.

I must stop thinking about Davey and write something I can hand in before 5 PM. My deadlines are like dark bare billboards that block out the sky.

There's a message on my cellphone I don't want to listen to. I heard it vibrate an hour or so ago, connected to voicemail and began to listen to the anxious lilt of Mom's voice, but I hummed to myself, using Davey's trick to keep the truth at bay.

I have a recurring dream about Davey, prompted by that time he went missing for almost a week, then I got that message from him on my voicemail. Where he's telling me how glad he is, how sad he was until he was walking and it was dawn and his socks were wet with dew and then the light rose up and swallowed him whole and the owl that lived in it told him to be happy, so he was. He thought he was making sense. He thought

I'd be pleased to hear him sound so full of cheer. But I knew by then how brittle his joy was – how easily it could shatter and cut him till he bled.

In my dream they find him in the lake, floating on his back like he's still living – buoyed up cruelly by the reeds. But his wrists are open, have let out all that important stuff. His Superman flask is on the beach, lying on one side, spilling every drop into the sand.

If I hadn't driven straight over there, the moment I heard the message. If I hadn't found him crouching on the sand, tear-stained like a four-year-old. If I hadn't…

But I did, and "if" is so much better than "if only," isn't it? Yet it haunts me, perhaps because he hasn't spoken to me since. It's almost as though he blames me. As if he wanted to die and I prevented it and he resents that, so he's done the only thing he can and made himself dead to me.

Not only did I make him live, but I think he felt I had punished him for his sadness, by making him go to his doctor, receive treatment. I remember Mom coming to see me once after visiting him, a hopeful light in her smile. "He's carving again," she told me. "Look, he made this for you." And she handed it to me.

I held it with distaste. I guessed it was supposed to be an owl, but to me it was just a small misshapen lump with roughly scarred, scared eyes.

I understood the message well enough to know how betrayed he felt by my efforts to save him.

At first I'd continued to send him the occasional text or email, just saying hi, suggesting we meet for coffee, retweeting witty things he posted to Twitter. Then he unfollowed me, and he never replied to a single text or email. One morning I realized that when I thought of him it was with resentment rather than regret.

I left him alone after that, Mom our only link. It was through Mom I knew he'd gone to France to help rebuild some crumbling monastery, through Mom I know he went missing the week before last. The first time he's done that since I found him at the lake, five years ago.

I've stopped listening to her messages, telling myself it's because of these deadlines when the truth is that I can't bear to hear her escalating unease, her bursts of false cheer, whatever will follow.

Instead I endure the dreams, each night – several times a night, sometimes leaking through in daylight hours too, till all the words in my head turn to sodden crumbs. I'm supposed to be writing up a feature from an interview I carried out yesterday, a mother and daughter reunited after forty years, but my mind keeps floundering, words sinking down out of reach.

I'd asked the mother how she felt when she saw this grown woman her daughter had become, whether it had been difficult to believe the truth her eyes were telling her.

She smiled at me with something like relief, like a woman exhaling after holding her breath for far too long. I had the sense she'd been wearing that look for days – ever since they'd met again. "It was easy," she told me, "Because I never stopped imagining her. Never stopped seeing her in my mind."

There, I think, there, that's the quote I'll use for the headline: *I never stopped seeing her in my mind.* Not overly sentimental, just as emotive as that particular magazine's readership likes.

I sit back; think of putting the kettle on, rewarding myself for this one small triumph. My mind flicks back to the coffee owl, and I remember that I have a packet of Hula Hoops in the cupboard. The thought makes me smile.

I stand there listening to the boiling water's rumbling song – two cups waiting, one to drink from, the other to turn into a work of owlish art. I think to myself that I should photograph the result, email the image to Davey. If he sees it, if he's still out there, it might be enough to prevent an "if only" moment, mightn't it? Enough to bring him home to me.

Three Tuesdays from Now
by Shawn Syms

Will you accept $500 to penetrate me?

Ben's Craigslist ad hadn't said anything about payment. Still, he was intrigued by this response in his inbox.

With a well-paid day job as a fundraiser at a pediatric oncology charity, he didn't need the money. But $500 for ten minutes work! Ben was sure he could last twenty if someone was paying that kind of cash. He'd just think about his grandmother. Or his gerbil.

Was $500 really the going rate to bury the salami these days? Ben had had two experiences with sex for pay in his early twenties – with men, though he definitely wouldn't have said no to an attractive woman either. An older guy with a moustache and a wedding ring, who he met at the bus station on the way back from visiting his family in Guelph, had offered the young man a hundred bucks to blow him in the men's room. It was late at night, there were no kids in the mostly deserted station, and Ben appreciated fatherly men with facial hair. He tried to imagine himself with a wife and kids.

Ben had walked out of the can with a fistful of twenties. No real urge to repeat the experience though. It was happenstance. The other time a random homeless guy started chatting Ben up on the street. He was looking to sell a transistor radio for ten bucks. Ben offered fellatio instead. Handing him the ten-dollar bill after servicing him between two cars in a secluded parking lot, Ben said, "Keep the radio." That guy had a big one. And he didn't smell too bad either for a homeless person. Kind of like soil from a flower garden.

Ben guessed those extreme close-up penis shots he'd taken with his iPhone had paid off. No face pics though, just in case any of the office mates in his all-woman department at work were trolling the Craigslist casual encounters section just like him. Ben had little trouble imagining that scenario, in fact. His colleagues were a pack of horny cougars and he'd even gone with them to the male peeler joint Remington's a few times. Working the cancer field all day meant you really needed to blow off some steam every once in a while. Ben popped a Wellbutrin every day to help him cope, but that didn't always cut it.

Though he was no John Holmes, Ben supposed he was worth paying for. To this one guy at least – who hadn't sent any pics in return.

I'll have to tell Charla, he thought. Best friends, they were training for a marathon, and would sprint up steep hills the next day after work. It would give them something to talk about instead of her tedious workplace drama. Charla was employed at an agency that gave money and subway tokens to former prisoners. How do-gooder is that? Ben loved having a friend he could tell *everything*. Well, maybe almost everything.

Fuck it. Why not? Ben clicked reply on his Gmail account and asked his suitor for more details. Said he only did "outcalls"; he'd seen that word in real escort ads before. The guy must live on the Internet because the response came back almost right away, including a low-res selfie this time. Handsome, with a shaggy goatee, blue-green eyes.

"I use a wheelchair. Got a problem with that?" the man wrote. "I'm on Skype. Ravercub77. Message me."

+

Three Tuesdays from Now

Got your email. Looking good there.

                                         thx

              u been with a guy in a chair before

No.

        its the same. i can run you over if ur boring though

LOL

        i need to get fucked raw so bad, i have 400 bucks

I only play safe, cool?

        ok, if you don't do it bareback maybe 300 then

Sure.

             u sound like a goody two shoes

      youll fuck a guy in chair, u dont care about money

                  r u sure ur a real top

I know how to fuck.

I've got good references if you want. :0)

                u sure you dont want it raw

        i could use a good load up me its been 2 long

Yeah, I'm sure.

        you have to lift me from my chair to the bed, got it

      i don't weigh 2 much tho. my arms and legs are short

Okay. I'm pretty strong.

                      cool man

                    can i trust u

What do you mean? I'm a decent guy.

        last guy who came over took advantage of me

What?

                  he robbed me

I'm not like that. I'm decent.

      sucks because im saving up to move to edmonton

             sucks that he stole from me

I'm sorry.

        ok so maybe we make it 100 for u to fuck me

          u sure u dont want to fuck me raw

Friend. Follow. Text.

i like cum a lot

I would rather be safe but let's see what happens.
Can I ask something?

what

Why did you offer me $$$?

i like to get what i want. i can pay for it
im just negotiating. whats wrong with that
do you think i'm broke or poor

I don't need money to get together with you.

even better

You seem nice.

ffs, are you getting all wimpy on me
ur a real top right... i need it up the ass bad
i like rough sex

I can be very dominant.
I'm not just a "goody two shoes"..

but ya are blanche, ya are

What?

never mind

My name is Ben.

raimundo here

I could come over tomorrow on my lunch hour.

bring it on if youre tough enough
no rubbers is better

+

Dr Jong-Essex was the whitest Korean guy Charla had ever met. He dressed like a Bay Street lawyer and had perfect elocution to match. His parents are Canadian-born like mine, she assumed.

"Your numbers are great as usual, Ms Chua," said Jong-Essex. "Nothing to worry about. We can probably keep you on this same drug regimen for at least a decade." He paused and fingered a paperweight on his desk. It was a miniature of a famous Henry Moore sculpture, made of shiny reflective metal.

Her viral load had been undetectable for two years. T-cells, over a thousand. "That's healthier than most HIV-negative people," the doc reminded her. She saw him twice a year for blood tests. And an annual flu shot. Each visit, the shelving unit next to his desk featured a new photo from his most recent international cruise. This time, she could see the Sphinx behind him and a husky white guy with a trim beard. That must be his lover. The white dude, not the Sphinx, that is.

Charla went on meds as soon as she found out. She'd probably had the virus for a few years already, the doc said, so in terms of microscopic battles to be fought and won inside her bloodstream, she figured she'd come out swinging. But she generally kept her medical information to herself. She told Ben obviously. They talked about almost everything, and he knew a few poz guys. Her dad knew; he was surprisingly tranquil about it. Charla sensed that she and her father both had the same unspoken thought: it's good your mother is dead so we don't have to tell her this. She'd come unhinged. Needlessly.

She would have told Erich, the guy she got it from, if he were around. They dated for nine months, and shot up together a couple dozen times. Charla was never a junkie herself. She was... what did they call it in that Al Pacino movie? A chipper. A part-timer, weekend warrior.

And a Tuesday here and there. She only got high with Erich; he shot her up each time. It would have seemed irrational not to share the needle; she was already letting him cum inside her. If anything, fixing together felt like a form of bonding. Their last month together, he couldn't get it up anyway and the warm downer sensation from a nice hit replaced sex as their communion. She didn't blame Erich, and doubted he even knew he was infected. Did he give the virus to her – or did she take it from him? Does it matter?

One day he told her he was moving to Thailand. The next, his possessions were gone from her Little Italy apartment, and she never saw him again. Never got high again either. She took a few days off work and locked herself in her bedroom. Charla had never bought dope herself and saw no reason to start. She missed it for quite a while, though. Especially on Friday nights after a long week in a claustrophobic office with her bipolar boss Patti. But she missed Erich more. She still had his email address but had not used it since he left.

"Ms Chua... Charla?"

"Yes, doc." She'd tuned him out.

"Is there anything else you'd like to discuss today?" Cufflinks glinted with reflected light as Dr Jong-Essex put down the iPad he'd been reading her test results from.

"What if I want to get pregnant?" she blurted out. Whoa, where did that come from? Charla thought to herself, cracking one of her knuckles loudly as her left hand grabbed at her right one. The office had a vaguely minty smell and she noticed this for the first time as she waited for his response.

"Five of my patients have had healthy, HIV-negative babies so far this year. I'd be thrilled to make that six. Is there someone new in your life?"

Charla imagined flying to Bangkok in search of Erich. Bailing him out of some sweaty, crowded jail cell and cleaning him up. Starting over. "No," she said, more primly than she intended. "I just wanted to know. For future reference." Stuff that she would easily spill to Ben over beers Charla still felt weird bringing up with her doctor. She'd been referred to Jong-Essex after her initial diagnosis, after Erich disappeared, after the miscarriage.

The doctor looked up from notes he was typing into her file on his laptop. "You don't have a Hep c co-infection, and your viral replication is minuscule because of excellent adherence to your meds. Your chances for a successful pregnancy are as high as anyone else's." He seemed to get excited. "I want you to see Dr Loutfy upstairs," he chirped. "She's an expert on HIV and fertility."

Charla hadn't even had sex in a long time. Two years and three months, to be exact. She hadn't quite been sure how to approach the idea of sex since her diagnosis. She didn't feel dirty, just uncertain.

"I'm not sure I'm quite at that point yet." Her hand in the pocket of her black blazer, Charla picked up a quarter that lay there, and toggled it back and forth between her thumb and fingertips. The ridged metal disc felt cold in the air-conditioned room.

"How about this," the doc suggested, typing rapidly on his keyboard. "What if we set up the appointment as a general information session? Let's start to get you some useful tips now, even if you don't use them immediately. If you decide you really don't want to attend, you can cancel with forty-eight hours notice." He stared at the screen for a moment, then reached for a card and his pen. "She's free three Tuesdays from now at 7 AM."

Charla nodded, dropping the quarter in her pocket and warding off a slight, unexpected tremor.

"When you are ready to get pregnant," he added. "There are ways to do it safely for you, your partner and your baby. Maintaining your low viral load is the most important thing in terms of keeping your virus to yourself, so don't miss a pill. And until then, just continue to play safe." Then he actually reached into his desk and handed her three condoms along with the appointment reminder.

The doctor meant well, but sounded like a high-school guidance counsellor. Charla tried to imagine the good doctor porking his fat lover, efficiently deploying a prophylactic then drilling at his big white ass like an oilman looking for black gold.

She stood up to leave. Jong-Essex shook her hand, as he did at the end of every appointment. On her way out, Charla felt a low, dull ache in her side. In the elevator, she closed her eyes and tried not to think of anything. Heroin had been good for that at least.

+

"The white one with the v-neck, please." Raimundo gestured toward a thin cotton T with a plunging neckline.

"Showing off the chest hair today? I see." Dave plucked the top off the hanger with a muscled, green-inked forearm and plunked it onto the bed next to Raimundo. "Pants?"

"My black sweats. No undies."

"You must have a hot date if you're going commando." Dave lifted the shirt over Raimundo's head, over each of his short arms. Raimundo could smell the lingering scent of fresh soap on his attendant's face and neck; it smelled like Irish Spring.

"I'm just trying to keep things simple for later, buddy. The less clothes you put on, the faster they come off, you know what I'm saying?"

"Makes sense, Ray." Dave was one of the attendants at the co-op; he usually worked mornings. Raimundo liked the guy. He was professional, still fun. Not every attendant was the same – some were unfailingly polite, but stiff as a board. Raimundo appreciated people who, like himself, had a bit of spunk to them. Why make life boring?

Dave pulled the short cotton pants off a shelf and got down and helped put Raimundo's truncated sweats on one leg at a time. Raimundo had a bit of a chub already, which Dave appeared to pretend not to notice. Raimundo tried not to focus on the slow sensation of engorgement for the moment; he would let Dave get his work done and get out of there.

Apparently the gayest that Dave ever got was watching *Glee* with his wife once a week, but Raimundo would occasionally give him glimpses into queer culture. Only when it was practical for himself, not for any kind of shock value.

"Need some condoms by the bed?"

"Nope, I told him to bring some. One last thing, please." Raimundo gestured with one arm toward the small glass bottle of Rush on the desk by the computer, a red-inked lightning

bolt strewn across its yellow plastic label. Dave unscrewed the
bottle and held it under Raimundo's nostrils one at a time for a
sniff, before replacing the cap and putting the bottle back in its
place. The odour of the sex-enhancing inhalant wafted through
the room, its distinctive scent evoking a pile of unlaundered
gym socks.

"Thanks a lot, man. That's all I need for now. Maybe put
on the news on your way out." Raimundo's face turned flush
as he smiled, his breath slowing slightly, the throbbing between
his legs renewed.

"Have a good one, Ray. Call down later if you need anything." Raimundo heard Dave walk through the living room
and click on the TV, then heard the apartment door open and
close behind him. Raimundo leaned forward toward the joy-
stick and propelled his chair toward the computer. He turned
on the small round webcam sitting next to the keyboard, which
aimed at the empty bed. Then he backed up and went into the
living room, waiting for his guest to arrive.

+

Magenta, green, blue, an approximation of yellow: grainy pixels shimmer and flash, trading positions. Blurred, fuzzy, they jit-
ter, toggle off and on, resembling fireflies in motion. Amid the
shifting distortion sits a man in a chair, wheels in front and rear.
A pair of black gym shorts on. Short legs. Before him stands a
man whose head is out of view, cut off at the top of the frame.
Wears a business suit. One head lowers toward the other; lips
meet and meld. As they kiss, the suited man's fingers roam the
body of the other: stubbled chin, naked chest, small arms that
end in rounded tips, the back of the neck. This diffuse image
moves across a flat screen monitor, atop a brown desk next to
a near-empty coffee mug and a half-full ashtray of thin translucent glass. In an office chair, a lone, bearded man is clad in only
a grey T-shirt imprinted with the insignia of the Indianapolis

Colts. One of his hands rests on the mousepad. The other moves slowly between his thighs, like that of a potter kneading a fat lump of clay.

+

"Yeah, he came over yesterday on his lunch hour from work."

Raimundo watched as Joe used his laser pointer to spell out a question on his communication board. *Did you get what you wanted?* Joe was hilarious. So blunt.

"Hell yeah I did, brother — do you want to see a video of it?
Dude no

Joe smiled and Raimundo laughed. Out the window, it was pouring. Before he came over to Joe's apartment and after he got screwed by Ben, he went up the street to the Rabba to get some multigrain Tostitos. When it started to rain it messed with the mechanisms in his chair, which was always annoying. Good thing he liked his best friend a lot, because he wasn't sure if the chair would start up again right away.

Tell me what happened I know you want to

"You know me too well." Raimundo loved having a friend he could tell everything. "Then you can tell me about your date with Kelly."

Joe rolled his eyes from his own chair, and the laser pointer affixed to his glasses scribbled the upper wall of his apartment, incidentally next to a photo of his girlfriend that was hung on the living-room wall. *I don't kiss and tell like you*

"You know you love me and don't want me to change in any way." Raimundo was eager to get on with his story. "So this guy, he was all right, pretty good-looking. He took his shirt off right away like he wanted to show off his muscles. Conceited much, right? So we start making out and he starts playing with my nipples."

Joe interjected. *Kelly does that too*

"I thought you didn't kiss and tell. Right." Raimundo scratched an itch on his chest with his left arm. "Anyway, then he starts rubbing his fingertips on the ends of my arms which drives me crazy because they are sensitive. But he wasn't like an icky flipper queen who would just be fixated on them, do you know what I mean?"

Fetish person. Joe spelled out the letters one by one, since the word "fetish" did not appear on his board.

"Yeah, exactly. One of those guys would be staring and masturbating onto them and everything. This was just nice, his eyes were closed while he was kissing me and I think he just did it because he could tell I liked it. I'm a moaner. He pulled my shorts off but I didn't let him touch me because I was so close already! He stood on the front wheels of my chair to get some oral. Lots of guys have done that, but it does require some balance so I was impressed. Then we went in the bedroom and did it. *Au naturel* as they say!" Raimundo giggled and Joe shot him a quizzical look.

Don't you worry about catching something

"Do you and Kelly use rubbers?"

Different. She wants to have a baby

"I'm just trying to live a little bit. Dennis knows. He was watching the whole thing on my webcam. He likes to see me having a good time. I'm going to be with him for good in two weeks anyway."

I will miss you when you go, friend

"Dude, don't get all mopey on me. Put yourself in my shoes. What if Kelly lived in Alberta and you never saw her? You would want to be with her. It's called, come for a visit. I don't care if you have never been on a plane. I do it, and so can you. Are you afraid?"

With his pointer, Joe indicated his answer. *Yes*

Raimundo stared his best friend down, with an arched brow. "But are you going to?"

A near-imperceptible pause, then the answer came. *Yes*

Joe changed the subject. *Think you will see this guy again*

Raimundo laughed. "He asked me on a date. Maybe the fluid exchange made him all emotional and clingy. I said no and let him know I have a boyfriend. Then I booted him out."

Want to watch some TV

"Okay." Raimundo drove over to the TV set and stack of DVDs next to it, relieved to find that his chair's motor wasn't on the fritz anymore. "Whatever you do, just don't say *Glee*. I fucking hate that show."

+

Charla expertly separated the meat from the bone of her curried chicken wing. No better way to cap off an hour's worth of exercise than beer and wings. She spoke loudly to be heard above the ambient noise of the bar, not to mention "Smoke on the Water" from the nearby jukebox. "Why do you think the dude kept asking if you were cool with the wheelchair?"

"I guess he's dealt with some crap before. Gay guys can be real assholes."

Charla didn't really see gays or bisexuals as especially different from straight men. They all have the capacity to be goofs or decent. She wasn't sure where to put Ben on that scale at the moment. Her mouth burned from the spicy wing, and she reached for the pitcher for some more Stella. Finished chewing the carrot stick in her mouth. "If you are so sensitive to the plight of horny men in wheelchairs, why would you take cash from this guy?"

Ben was staring at the muscular, middle-aged coach of a girl's soccer team loudly taking up an enormous table nearby. Always horny, Charla thought, a bit distastefully.

"It was his idea!" Ben's face reddened. "I figured I should accept the offer at face value. I didn't want to seem like I was pitying him for being disabled. And I didn't end up taking the money anyway."

"How magnanimous of you." Charla threw another drumstick aside. "You're not a high-priced call boy. I'm glad you slept with this guy for free, like you'll do with almost anyone else."

"Jealous much? Anyone would look like a slut compared to you, Mother Teresa." Ben got the server's attention as she moved away from the soccer team's table balancing a trio of empty plastic pitchers on a large tray. He made the sign to get the bill. "Truth is, I'm proud I have pretty broad tastes."

"Well, maybe you should fuck me if you're so open-minded. I've been thinking of having a baby. I can pretend I'm in a wheelchair if it would get you off."

"Are you serious?"

"Maybe." Charla could see the waitress watching them from a distance. She was pretty, with faint blue eye shadow; flat-chested in a plain black T-shirt.

"I've gotta take a piss." Ben stood and left the table. He brushed past a couple of Japanese guys on their way to the dartboard, almost knocking a pitcher of lager from one guy's hand. Charla rolled her eyes. She got off on Ben's nervous energy, it charmed her a lot of the time, but some days she struggled with his easy life and sense of entitlement. Still, he was a good person, even if he wasn't always the most self-aware. Charla looked down and noticed the server had stopped by and discreetly placed the bill on the table.

When Ben got back, Charla picked up the conversation about this Raimundo guy. She had more to say about this. "Ben, you get lots of attention for your looks and this guy probably is ignored half the time just because of the wheelchair. If you know it's wrong that you aren't both treated the same, maybe you shouldn't come across like such a golden prince," she said. "I'm not trying to be an asshole, but maybe the reason he offered to pay isn't because you are so amazing-looking, it's just that most people won't even consider him otherwise. Do you want to perpetuate that cycle?"

Guitars duelled in an old Black Sabbath number as the dart players hooted at one another, slapping each other's backs. Ben finished his sudsy mug and plonked it on the tabletop loudly. "Charla. We have known each other a long time and I love you, but can I tell you something? I don't know if it's because of your stupid job or what, but you spout so much PC bullshit these days."

Charla sensed the waitress staring at them again. Embarrassing.

"This guy is not the stereotypical helpless wheelchair person who lives in your imagination. Dude is a total player. He knows what he wants... he even talked me into some stuff I don't normally do. Speaking of which, do you seriously want to go get knocked up now?"

Charla looked over at her purse, then back at Ben. "Well, I'm not sure I'm in the mood for angry sex right now. Plus you can't just snap your fingers and be fertile. There is timing and stuff to consider. I have to talk to a specialist about it. Anyway, do you really want to do this?"

"Charla, you're my best friend. I screw around with randoms on my lunch hour. Why wouldn't I have sex with someone I care about?"

"Well, we can't do this right now anyway. I quit my job and I'm going on a trip. I'll be back in two weeks and we can talk more then." She couldn't bring herself to say the word Thailand out loud. "Want to come over and help me pack?"

"Have you got beer in the fridge?" Ben stood up to leave. "I'm glad you quit, by the way. That job was killing you."

"So am I." Charla grabbed a twenty out her wallet and put it down. Ben did the same, and they headed for the exit as the blonde waitress made her way to the table. She reached for the money without looking at it, watching them walk out the door.

Deletion
by Robert J. Holt

Most nights, when I came home, Nikki was there. Usually sitting on the couch in her underwear, looking through photographs. It was summertime then, and the apartment would be roasting. But she never opened the windows. When I came through the door, I'd head straight for the windows and open them, then go and sit beside her.

"Do you like them?" she would ask.

"Yeah, they're great," I'd lie. Nikki considered herself a photographer. She took pictures of streets and train yards and people she liked. The pictures were not very good but she worked hard at them, and I think sometimes that should be enough.

"Really?"

"Yeah," I would say, pointing at a photo. "Especially this one. I mean, these came out great!"

Then she'd smile and put the photos away. After that, if we both felt lazy and the fridge was running low, we'd order a pizza and I would go across the street to pick it up. When I came back, the apartment would be a little cooler and Nikki would be dressed and we would eat in front of the television. A little while after dinner, Nikki would ask:

"Do you think we're stuck in a rut?"

I would think for a second. "No, I don't think so."

"I hope not. I don't want for us to get boring."

"Are you bored?"

"No... I worry about it though. I don't want us to be bored, because then we'll break up"

"Well," I'd say, "we're not stuck in a rut."

"I know." It would be quiet for a minute. Then, "Babe?"

"Hmmm?"

"You're not just saying that, right?"

"Of course not, no! Nooo, I love ya."

"Really?"

"Really really. Same as I always have, since the day that I met you."

Nikki would look down, wiggle her toes a little. "You always say that."

"And I always mean it!" And then I'd wrap an arm around her and say, "I love you, Nikki. Okay? I love you I love you I love you, a whole whole lot."

Nikki would smile. "Okay. I love you too. And you don't think we're stuck in a rut?"

"We're not stuck in a rut."

"I hope not," she'd say, "sometimes I just worry."

We had that conversation once, sometimes twice a week.

+

It hadn't always been like this. I first met her at a noisy little bar on the east side of town. A friend was celebrating their birthday – I can't remember who – but it was late November. She came in with another girl who looked familiar. The bar was dark and crowded, and I only caught glimpses of her at first. She was thin and lovely, with curly brown hair and a deep, natural-looking tan as though she had been away for a while. I saw her step outside, out onto the patio with a cigarette. I waited for a minute and a half – I wanted our meeting to look incidental – then joined her out there.

"Hey."

"Hi."

+

"You here for the party?" I asked, lighting up my cigarette.
"Which one?"

I looked through the patio's glass door and pointed to a
table. "Uhhhh... that one." She leaned in toward the window,
peering through. Her eyes were light brown, and shaped like
almonds.

"You mean Don's?"

"Yeah." Don, it was his party, I remember now. Anyway, she
nodded. "How do you know Don?"

"Oh, I don't, really. I came here with Laura, we work together at the Portsmouth."

"You're a barmaid?"

"We prefer 'bartender.'"

"Sorry."

She laughed and shrugged. "I don't mind. What about you?"

"Don and I took some classes together in university."

"Yeah? What'd you take?"

It was a banal conversation, but I didn't mind. It felt good
to be alone with her. Then I got nervous – not because I was
talking with a beautiful girl, but because I knew that soon she
would ask me The Question. The Question was simple enough,
but I always had a hard time answering, and I knew that when
I tried, the girl's eyes would glaze over and our conversation
would be over. A moment later, she asked me.

"So what do you do?"

"You mean for money?

She nodded. I took a long drag of my cigarette, now nearly
finished. "Nothing special."

"Oooh," she drew her lips together, smirking. "How mysterious of you."

I laughed. "No, it's not like that. It's just boring, is all."

She stood a moment, staring, waiting. "Well? Go ahead. Bore me."

I felt around my pockets for another cigarette, and pulled out a pack.

"Could I bum one of those?" she asked. I handed her one, then pulled out another for myself.

"I work for a company that does document storage."

"Like, a warehouse, or...?"

"Sort of." I hoped she would drop the subject. Instead she stood there, staring again. Well, I thought, here goes:

"According to the law," I started, "every business has to keep their personnel records for at least seven years after the date they were signed or last updated. Contracts, written complaints, performance reviews all that – anything you sign at work, anything with your name on it, they have to keep for seven years."

"Why?"

"In case you decide to sue them, or something like that."

"Does that happen often?"

I shook my head. "Not really, but that's the law. Anyway, over seven years those documents pile up, especially if you're a big company with a lot of employees. Since most of those documents are about people who don't even work there any more, most companies can't be bothered holding onto them. So they pay us to do it for them. We hold on to all these old papers, and once they turn seven years old, we destroy them."

"Destroy them?"

"Yup. Shred 'em."

It was quiet for a moment. Then, she looked up at me. "You practice that, don't you?"

"What?"

"That whole thing about your job. It sounds rehearsed."

"No. Not really."

"No?"

"Maybe a little."

She laughed. "I'm Nikki," she said.

"Hi, Nikki."

We talked a bit longer, and after that we went back inside. The band was bad and noisy that night, and I didn't see Nikki again. A few weeks later she was at another friend's party, and this time I managed to get her number. I got to know a lot about Nikki after that. How she loves summer but hates spring, how her middle name is Catherine and she wishes it wasn't, how she lost her virginity when she was fourteen and that she likes to smoke cigarettes from countries she's never visited. She had been new back then, thrilling, and we were happy together. Maybe she was still happy. I don't know.

+

My father got me the job when I finished university and nothing else was coming up. I figured it would be short-term; that was two years ago. Most days, I didn't mind it. Every morning, I came in to find a freshly printed list sitting on my desk, showing the files that were expiring that day, and where to find them. Most of my day was then spent walking through the storage complex, with its endless rows and columns of tall grey filing cabinets, looking for files, tossing them in carts and bringing them back to my desk. Then, I'd double check, make sure I had the right ones, and send them through the shredder. Mostly, I was paid for the things I *didn't* do – I was valuable because I didn't try to steal anything, or sell one company's information to their competitors. It was mind-numbing work, sure, but it paid very well. Over two years, I had come up with a few ways to kill the time, little games in my head. One was to read the names off my list, and try to imagine what kind of face that person had. I read them aloud as I walked.

"Terrence Updike, Borland Corp." Terrence, I decide, is a stocky, round-faced man in his late thirties. He has a hooked nose he had broken as a child, which is now flattened to his face.

Below this, the beginnings of a moustache sprout. God, but he's ugly though. I move to the next name.

"Erin Krishner, Sierratech Industries." Erin wears large, square-rimmed glasses to distract people from what is – in his opinion – a nose too large for his face. Other than that, he has no real distinguishing features, save for thin lips, and noticeable dandruff in the winter. Satisfied, I read the next name.

"Emily Vaughn, Digital Imagery." I think about this one. Emily Vaughn. That's perfect. She will have sandy blonde hair, very straight, and her eyes will be green. I figure that when she smiles (which is often) little creases form around her nose. Emily Vaughn. I like that name. It has some poetry to it. I spend a long time working on the details of her face. When I'm finished, she looked quite beautiful, and I wonder if I'm not just remembering someone I've already met before. The feeling soon passes.

"Sylvia Mynarski, Atlear Group." Now Sylvia, she'll have...

A few days later I was deciding whether Janet Vickar's chin should be pointed or squared when the name came back into my mind. Emily Vaughn. It happened all afternoon, and in the evening when I got home. Each time, I would see her face again, the face I'd made for her. Maybe I had seen her before – she was so familiar – but I couldn't remember where. It nagged at me; I wanted to know for sure.

That night, I opened up my laptop and logged onto Facebook. In the search bar, I typed "Emily Vaughn" and hit Enter. The search came back with dozens of Emilys. I clicked through the first few results – none looked like the girl I was thinking of. Where was it she worked? I mulled it over, trying to remember. Was it "image"? It had an "image" in it. Let's try that. I searched again, this time typing "Emily Vaughn image." And there she was, the very first hit.

This Emily looked much as I had imagined her, except her skin was fairer, her hair a lighter shade of blonde. She wore a black dress in her profile pic, posing with some other girls. Her profile said she'd worked for Digital Imagery for a few years now. It was definitely the girl whose name I had seen on the file. But had I met her before?

She had hundreds of photos. I went through them. She was always smiling, always happy. I saw her on vacations, and at parties and at home with the family for Christmas. I read her bio, and her favourite movies, and her hobbies and her interests and her favourite music and books. I couldn't possibly have known her – she lived in the States and we had zero mutual friends. Still, after going through her profile, I felt like I knew more about her than I knew about Nikki after three months of us seeing each other. She was much more open about her life.

I found my way back to Emily's timeline, and began reading the messages there. The most recent read:

> i went to see your parents today. i tried to cheer them up but they still miss you. we all do. you were a great friend and a truly amazing person and i hope i see you again someday. ily

I read another.

> Emily, when God took you away, I was angry for a long time. I didnt know why He could take someone like you away. Now that its been awhile Ive seen that He has a plan for us, and I know you looking down on us from up there. Rest in Peace.

Another simply read, "Emily Sara Vaughn March 25 1982–July 16 2006. RIP". I continued reading for a long time. Then I closed the laptop and tried to fall asleep. Nikki snored quietly beside me.

✛

A few days went by, and Nikki was there again. The sun was just setting, the apartment baking. I ordered Thai food for dinner and went to pick it up. Nikki was on the couch in a tank top, flipping through channels trying to find a movie we hadn't already seen. When I came back, she was lying down with her eyes closed.

"Something wrong?"

"No." She sat up when she said it. The TV had been switched off. We ate dinner, saying little. Sometimes an ambulance would blare past on the street, but the apartment was very quiet. I turned on the TV. Finally, Nikki spoke.

"Why do you lie to me about my pictures?"

"What do you mean?"

"You don't like them."

"Sure I do."

"Sarah texted me. She told me you said they're no good."

"When?"

"When you were getting the pizza."

"I didn't see Sarah."

"No! That's when she texted me. She heard you say it last weekend."

"Where?"

"Laura's party."

"I didn't talk to Laura there."

"You weren't talking to her, you were talking to Alex."

"Oh. Well, I didn't see her there." Nikki didn't respond, she just stared out the window with her jaw clenched. "Which one is Laura again?"

"My friend, Laura. You've met her before."

"...Is she blonde?"

"Fuck you."

"What?" I asked. Nikki got up. She was picking her clothes up off the floor.

"You heard what I said I said fuck you! I introduce you to my friends, you talk to them and then you don't even remember them, ever. It's like you're trying to... I mean, why don't you care?"

Deletion

She put on her socks, then her shirt, wiggled into a pair of jeans. I thought it was funny, how the socks went on first. She kept on talking, snatching things up off the floor.

"...and they're *important* to me. So, when you act like you don't care about *them*, it's like you're saying that you don't care about *me*. You know?"

I sat up on the couch. "How come you put your socks on before your pants?"

Nikki turned around, fully clothed now. "What?"

"Nothing, no. I just thought it was funny, how you put your socks on before anything else."

Nikki looked at me for what felt like a long time. Then she said "Go to hell!" and walked out of the room. I stood up and put the rest of the Thai food in the fridge. I sat down on the couch, checked my email, then logged onto Facebook and changed my relationship status to "Single." It was as simple as that.

+

A letter:

July 16, 2006

Attn: Emily Vaughn

You are receiving this letter as a reminder re: our Company's Time Off Policies. Employees are expected to notify their Supervisor(s) as soon as possible if, for any reason, they will be absent from work. In some cases, your Supervisor(s) may request a doctor's note or other documentation to verify the reasons for absence.

This office's records indicate that you have been absent from work, without properly notifying your Supervisor(s), on the following dates:

Friend. Follow. Text.

April 13, 2004
June 7, 2004
June 21, 2004
July 16, 2004

Unexplained absenteeism is detrimental to the Company and puts increased pressure on your co-workers to perform your duties while you are away. Please consider your co-workers in the future. Failure to do so will result in termination of your Employment Contract with the Company.

Sincerely,

Derrick Isley,
Human Resources, Digital Imagery

It was Friday afternoon. I looked at the stack of papers on my desk all turning seven years old that day. I read the letter again. Someone had struck the whole page through with a red marker, and at the bottom had written "N/A" and below that "DECEASED." I reread the letter. It all seemed cruel to me. I fed the letter into the shredder beside my desk.

I didn't want to go out that night. Don told me I should – said it would help me get over Nikki, that I had been weird lately, distant. I told him that I'd really rather stay in. I opened a bottle of wine with dinner, and left it out when I was done. Late in the evening, it started to rain. The water came in through the open window. I started to feel better. I got up to shut the window and opened another bottle.

It got late. I was lying in bed, tired but not sleepy. My laptop was on the nightstand. I sat up and laid it across my legs. I checked and re-checked my email. I visited Emily's profile. A button below her picture read "Send Emily a message." I clicked it, and began:

Deletion

Emily:

I just wanted to say that I wish I could've met you in person, even just once. I think we might have liked one another. I'm a lot like you. It feels weird saying that, but it's true. We like the same things. We like the same bands. Your friends still post on your wall, even though they know you won't answer. I think you get more posts than me. I guess that says something. Anyway, sometimes one of them will find an old picture of you and put it online. They tag you, and people comment on your pictures like nothing is different. I think that shows how much they care about you. Well, that's all I wanted to say. Take care.

My legs were warm from the laptop. I felt strange at first, but reading it back to myself I began to feel good about what I wrote. I pressed Send.

We're sorry, something went wrong. Please try again later. I clicked OK, then Send.

We're sorry, something went wrong. Please try again later.

I clicked Refresh. The browser took me back to my news feed, not Emily's profile. In the search bar, I typed "Emily Vaughn image."

Sorry, no matches were found.

I searched again.

Sorry, no matches were found.

I tried over and over, but she would not come back to me. I looked at my watch. It was nine minutes past midnight. Emily had been dead for seven years and one day. In all that time, no one had logged onto her account. Emily had expired. I shut the laptop and got under the blankets. For a long time, I listened to the sounds of the city and the rain.

Google World
by Sara Press

I thought travel would be a good excuse to get away. I asked Jeff to come because we'd been buddies since forever and he was taking a gap year too. He'd become a real pussy since his girlfriend dumped him though. Still listened to her radio podcasts on his iPod. We'd been gone three months, *get over it.*

"Let's trade iPods," I called over to him. He stayed looking out the window and playing with that damn hemp bracelet she gave him. Looked like it'd been ravaged by termites. I threw my shoe at him.

"What?" He looked pissed. I couldn't help but smile.

"Let me listen to your iPod."

"Why?"

"I'm sick of my music. Aren't you sick of yours?"

"No."

"Fine, whatever. I guess I'll just listen to the local choir." I pulled the curtains on the window and tried to sleep.

We finally reached Da Nang. It had been thirty-two hours of Vietnamese karaoke on a bus full of non-English speakers. By the time we arrived, we were happy to be anonymous inside the noise-cluttered streets. Neither of us researched the city before we decided to go there, so only once we'd already left Vang Vieng did we realize what a mistake we'd made. A couple dozen hours into the bus trip Jeff threw me his copy of *Lonely Planet* with a page marked on Da Nang. A red-light district for soldiers back in the glory days of the Vietnam War, the city had retained its sleazy reputation. Not a tourist destination, the tourist guide warned. Great.

We were let off in a bus depot on the north side of the city – not that that meant much to us, we were totally lost. The bus shelter was a hard insect shell with eight massive legs coming down the ceiling from each side. It looked like the builders had left halfway through construction. The motorway traffic noise distilled into one uniform ringing. Hell, I felt nauseous. I looked out onto the wild ant farm. Everybody knew where they were going. I remembered an American expat warning me about street crossing in Tokyo.

"Move like a tortoise," he said. "The slower you move, the safer you'll be. They'll just go around you." Strange guy. Forty-something-year-old drifter, it looked, just running from the real world.

We walked through the winding traffic, on and on. We were on autopilot for God knows how long before we stumbled on a place to eat. Some old guy missing his two front teeth, smiling, waved us over to his kiosk. He had on one of those deep-set triangle straw hats everyone wears here. Looked like an IKEA lampshade. He smelled like tobacco and hot sauce and I was thinking about the smell of my dad's cigars when I realized he was talking right at me. Jeff just kept shrugging his shoulders and shaking his head. I had no idea what he was saying but I rubbed my belly, pointed at my chest then Jeff's and handed him a bill. He nodded, smiling with those missing teeth again, and threw some skewers over a fire pit. He tossed some spices on that made me sneeze and the smell of smoke and meat made me even hungrier. I thanked him with a head nod when he handed us the food.

An hour later we were still looking for providence, a place to sleep. Let a roof and mattress fall from the sky. Jeff was feeling pretty low, the mystery meat, he said. I think he just wanted his mom to come save him from this mess. *Get your ass up, Jeff, your mom's halfway across the world picking daisies and reading Chatelaine.* He was bummed. He sank down against the wall of an unmarked alley, turned on his iPod. I told him not to leave.

I pulled out a roll of blue flagging tape tucked away in my rucksack from tree-planting last spring. It'd become some sort of flag of existence. I taped a piece to the places I'd never forget. The bedpost in the hostel in Thailand where I'd had a threesome with two Swedish girls; the garrison on the Great Wall of China where we camped out one night; the inside skin of a leather tent we'd slept in at a Berber camp in the Moroccan dessert. I'd gone out to look at the stars on the dunes and one of the guides had come to join me. He told me he could explain the world in four words: *la chance qui danse.* I'm no French major, but the meaning wasn't lost on me. Now I was taping blue against the walls of the alley to mark my way back to Jeff. Just then luck shone on me. A cardboard sign with a painted @ smiled at me from twenty feet.

The "Internet Cafe" was a hole in the wall with five ancient computers and a couple wire chairs. A young guy behind a glass screen, probably in his late twenties, was chatting coolly on his Blackberry, Nike head to toe.

"How much?" I asked opening and closing my palm, tilting my head towards the geriatric machines. He didn't even look at me. I knocked on the glass.

"*HOW* much?" I mouthed, like I was talking to a deaf person. He raised an index finger at me. Wait. I counted back from ten. *Cool it.* I counted back from twenty. OK. I looked around the room. A couple was having a feisty, hushed-down argument in the corner by a lone computer. I could tell they were Italian by their dark features and the way they screamed with their bodies. Four computers were lined up on the wall adjacent to them and a tiny kid with a shaved head sat in front of the computer furthest away. Just then the guy knocked on the glass from the other side; I looked over and he held up a sign.

"$2 DOLLARS U.S.A/HOR." He was probably wondering why I had such a big smile on my face. Pretty cheap entertainment, I wanted to say. I slipped the money under the hole in the screen, he handed me back a piece of paper with a login and password. I sat down at the computer closest to the couple.

I signed onto the computer. One "hor" to find a place to sleep and let a couple people know I was still alive. It took me five minutes just to get the English letters working on the stupid keyboard. I went onto Hostel World and did a quick search for cheap hostels in the city. First thing I saw I took. Phi Yen Hotel, tonight I'm yours. I logged onto my email. Seven scams and three emails from Mom. Standard. The old: Where are you? How have you been? Is your stomach acting up? Except in the third email there was something else. Retirement was harder than she'd thought it would be. She felt pretty lonely now that Dad was gone. Joyce brought her to a book club meeting last week and she met a nice guy there. She was thinking of seeing him next week. Was it inappropriate that she was telling me this? Shit, I wished I hadn't looked.

Hey Mom,

Just got to Da Nang. Having a great time, meeting lots of people. Jeff's good, the weather's good, my stomach's fine. What's the weather like at home?

Joe.

I must have sighed pretty deeply or else done something to draw attention to myself. I heard a chair squeak and saw the boy three computers down turn his attention from the monitor and take a good long look at me. His gaze was magnetic, and I turned to him.

"Hello."

"Hallo," he said, a little smile on his face. I looked on to see if he had anything else to say, his face just went red. I nodded understanding. No English. Funny how you forget the world exists in other languages. I logged onto my Facebook. Twenty-one notifications and seven inbox messages. I guess it'd been a while.

The door opened and closed and gone was the *commedia dell'arte* couple. I took a quick sidelong glance to see if the boy had left, and noticed he'd moved one chair closer. I resumed my Facebook catch-up time. Nothing that wouldn't have happened three months ago:

Status one: "New car! Who wants a ride?"

Status two: "Person A went from being in a relationship with Person B to being engaged."

Status three: "Dominican in five!"

Status four: "New iPhone! Suggestions for apps?"

Status five: "Painting nails with my girls tonight!"

Enough Facebook. I turned to see what the boy was doing. He caught my glance and came to sit down beside me.

"How-old-are-you?" He looked at me blankly, his dark eyes searching for something. I shrugged my shoulders and raised a flat hand up and down.

"You-big-how-much?" The boy just shook his head. I'm not a conversationalist at the best of times.

"You-speak-English?" Why did I keep trying? Just then the idea came into my head, look something up in Vietnamese. I dove head first into my rucksack; realized Jeff had the dictionary on him. Substitute x for y. I went straight to Google Translate. From English to Vietnamese. My fingers stumbled over the cryptic Vietnamese keyboard.

"How old are you?" Translate. *"Bạn bao nhiêu tuổi."* The letters were like ancient hieroglyphics but the boy gasped in wonderful recognition. He leaned across and laid his hand on the mouse. I saw the little white arrow float across the screen. No translation needed.

"Eleven." I was walking through a concrete wall. From English to Vietnamese.

"What is your name?" Translate. *"Tên của bạn là gì?"* Again, he took the mouse and keyboard.

"Kya." Then he pointed to the same question, still on the screen, shrugged his shoulders and pointed at me. His tanned little body was swimming in a sweat-stained yellow wife beater. He smelled like the streets.

"What's my name?" He nodded.

"Joe."

The conversation went on like this. I'd type a question in English, translate to Vietnamese. The boy would answer in Vietnamese, translate to English. He'd never travelled outside of his city, liked baseball and soccer. Favourite subject, geography. He knew there was a big world outside this one. He liked school, had good teachers. He wanted to be a teacher when he grew up. Or maybe an explorer. I asked him for directions to the hostel Jeff and I would be staying at. He didn't know.

He asked me questions, too. How old was I? What sports did I like? Did I like *World of Warcraft*? Where was I from? Twenty minutes we spent talking, longer than any conversation I'd had in weeks. I left pretty soon after and followed the blue flagging back to Jeff. He was exactly where I'd left him, hadn't moved an inch.

"Get up, I found us somewhere to stay," I said.

"What?"

"Take out your headphones, man." He took them out, music thrashed in the air.

"I found us a place to crash for the night." He nodded.

"Why are we here?" he sighed, eyes fixed on that damn hemp bracelet. It was the same question that kid asked me before he left. "Why are you here?" It popped up on the screen like some ominous question from God.

"I don't know," I said to Jeff. I hadn't been able to answer the kid either.

"I want to go home."

"I can't."

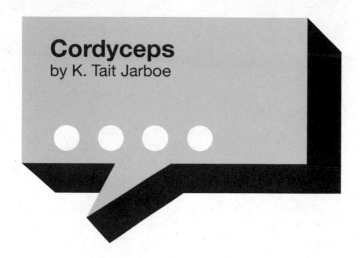

Cordyceps
by K. Tait Jarboe

Ada boots up her dead father's computer. The start-up sound is proud and sweeping despite having to wrestle out of bottom-shelf Micro Center speakers. She thinks about tearing apart the speakers for the potentiometer behind the volume knob, for a circuitry project. She's amazed the computer still works.

Welcome, the computer says, to Windows 95. Jesus, Dad, she thinks, you really mend or make do. The desktop is a stock photo of the beach. Ada's father, as far as she knows, had never been to any beach. She goes straight to the command prompt out of habit, stares at the black square, closes it, then inhales deeply.

Luckily, she finds a copy of Snood hidden in the applications folder and wastes the next four hours procrastinating the task she came back to New Jersey for in the first place.

That night she dreams in walls of melting emoticons and victory music.

+

Her father used to keep up with technology more when he worked at Knell Research Labs in North Orange. He helped invent computer graphics, before he lost his mind.

"I'm not losing my mind," he would insist in e-mails. He'd plugged the phone line into the modem and thus no longer used the phone. Knell was famous for their phone service. Ada's father bought his 56K dial up from some other company. "I'm understanding things more clearly than ever."

"I want to come visit you," Ada had responded countless times.

"You can't. You shouldn't." Even if he had gone crazy, he was still proud. "I'm not the way you remember me."

Ada's mom thought he was secretly living with someone, because he could not have taken care of himself by the time he wouldn't see anyone. "A nurse, or a girlfriend." Her mother insisted some woman had been paid or taken hostage and that was the only way to make sense of it. But even the groceries had to be delivered, sitting on the porch soaking up dirt and snow, and then by morning only mushy rectangle prints from the bag bottoms remained, like mosaic tiles that had gone missing.

Lots of things used to go missing, Ada thinks. She knew about the groceries because it was the first thing the next-door neighbours mentioned when she arrived the previous week.

"Yep," they said. "Until they stayed out there for a few days. We called the fire department, and you know the rest.

"I guess," Ada had said. She bristled at their informality.

"We had no idea he had family. We're sorry for your loss."

"I have to go now."

"Nice meeting you, Anna."

"Okay," Ada said.

+

The chaos of the modem's dial and low-bit woosh sends a cold and sentimental wave down Ada's spine. She hasn't heard it since she was a child; its effect is like putting a shell to her ear for the first time and wondering if it really is the ocean. She's been to the ocean many times, without her father. Those memories have no tug, just hold space in her mind full of plain contentment. The modem sound is so mundane, so rare and lost a thing that it's precious. It triggers every time she went hunting through directories, fleshing out her Geocities with scans of drawings and poems and submitting the page to webrings.

Even now, that particular garish shade of blue, web-safe hexa-decimal #0000FF, almost chokes her as she boots up a version of Netscape Navigator that still supports the <blink> tag.

What did she first go online for? Ada wonders. Something that was missing: from school, from friends, pets, science-fair projects, fantasy novels, the woods. Lots of things used to go missing. Maybe they were on the Internet now. For favourite hypnotic activity, it competed with flipping over flagstones to watch ants, which she had stopped doing sometime in high school anyway. This was all that was left.

She looks around the little house. No, she thinks, this is all that is left.

+

Eventually, in the throes of nostalgia and not wanting to begin the cleaning and sorting of the vast piles of dust-coated debris strewn about the floor, the stairs, under the toilet and under the bed, Ada logs onto the Internet and pokes through her father's bookmarks. The top one takes her to a gaming site she can't be-lieve is still kicking around. Most of its updated elements load slowly and incorrectly, or not at all in the archaic browser. She clicks on the login box. Nothing autoloads.

There's a button on the keyboard whose sole purpose is to open the start menu.

The ugly flag takes her to Find, a magnifying glass over an abstracted document. She searches for "passwords" and, to her amazement, discovers a Word file containing all of her father's user names and passwords.

"Really?" she says out loud.

She opens it, then goes back to the Find button and types, "All of my secrets."

No results.

She logs on to the gaming website. A chat client displays next to the game menu, minimal JavaScript grey with small, black serif text. She turns her head to look down the hall, through the kitchen door and out the back window. There's a stick-bare cherry tree defrosting in the beige winter sun. She starts to cry.

Soundlessly the chat client fills with a warm greeting. Ada looks back at the screen.

"Hello Harry."

Ada jumps up from the computer chair. She shivers. She goes into the kitchen and starts cleaning out the refrigerator to distract herself from crying. In the freezer she finds an unopened box of Thin Mints and tears off the top, devouring them in pairs. They are technically vegan, she thinks. Half an hour later she goes back to the computer.

The message is still there, blinking. Ada's fingers hover.

+

"This is Harry's daughter," she types before she can stop herself. "And who are you?"

Now there's mint chocolate on some of the keys.

"I didn't know Harry had a daughter. Why are you on his account? Can you put him on?"

Ada feels possessive of her role as the inquisitor.

"No," she types, and moves to close the browser, noting that this step is unnecessary if she follows her impulse to pull the whole computer out from the wall by its rat-tail plugs and throw it through the kitchen window and into the cherry tree. But she considers that this unknown person might have been the last to talk to her father. Her violent gesture is confined to fantasy, and she wants to hurt herself instead. There wouldn't even be any grocery delivery to tip off the neighbours.

She types, "Harry died last week. I'm just cleaning his house. I'm Ada. Who are you?"

There's a pause.

"Are you serious?"

"Yes."

"I don't believe you. Cut it out, Harry. Let's play some Scrabble."

"I don't need you to believe me."

There's a much longer pause.

"I'm really sorry. Your dad was good at Scrabble. It was like he read the dictionary. I'm Courtney (a boy)."

Ada relents. This is a safe laboratory in which to experiment with sincere, uncritical conversations with strangers, she thinks, but she's not sure how good her endurance is. If he gets weird, she decides, she can always log off.

+

Ada leaves a triple-word score space wide open next to a useful vowel. Obviously he's going to cash in on that one, she thinks. There's enough room for a good four letters without crashing into the rest of the game in progress. Courtney, a boy, might also read the dictionary, for all she knows.

No activity for several minutes.

"It's your turn," she types.

"Sorry, watching a videotape, hold on."

Ada pauses.

"Are you an old man because who says videotape."

"I'm not an old man. I say videotape because it's a video-tape. My mom tapes *Planet Earth* when it's on TV and sends it to me. YouTube is blocked here, too much inappropriate content."

Is he parroting someone, maybe someone looking over his shoulder?

Inappropriate, Ada thinks, used to mean out of place, and now it means anything adults think young people will find dis-tracting when they are supposed to be fostering critical thinking. Questionable content may lead to questions. If there's breasts, or explosions, or swearing, it's inappropriate until they live on their own, when what? They rush into Inappropriate's arms for all the magnetism of taboo, and grow up to be part of the culture industry that tacks breasts, explosions and swearing onto just about everything.

And an Adult Bookstore does not sell any information about taxes or graduate school. Ada laughs out loud, splattering moist particles of Thin Mint onto the monitor as she polishes off the remainder of the cookies.

"Smoke a beer and download terrorism illegally from the Internet. Cunt titties dickbag," she types. "Are you at school?" Then she adds, "How old are you, by the way?"

"Not at school. I'm seventeen."

Courtney plays a weak PEG across the triple word score. Ada is simultaneously disappointed and relieved. She plays ZYGOTE across the G vertically and yells, "Ha!" Then she types out "Ha!" and hits the enter button with smug emphasis.

Courtney logs off without further comment. Ada briefly believes she is being punished for her hubris, then scowls at her own superstition and concern. She gets up and goes back to work on her father's house.

The whole place is like one of those suburban museums of highly specific things that everyone in the town considers part of their cultural wealth but nobody goes to. She packs away the useful things, throws away the obvious trash, and places everything else in a pile in the middle of the living room floor, mentally covered in question marks. She pictures screaming fifth graders being dragged here on a field trip to be exposed to the banality of local history. She wasn't sure what might have been a priceless family heirloom and what her father might have dug up in the yard while gardening. She pictures herself as a fifth grader, sneaking off to play with her Game Boy.

Witness, children, the material culture of a recluse, the tour guide might say. Notice, if you will, how the building itself is a reminder of learned helplessness.

Ada wanders around the house in a daze. It's old, probably full of lead paint. It was built for the surviving female relatives of Civil War casualties, and then bought by manufacturers and used as housing for the Turkish and Portuguese immigrants indentured to the mills around the river. The enormous lot leading down to the river behind the house had once been a glass factory, or however glass was made, Ada thinks. There were warped baubles and time-softened shards in the dirt all the time. They used to get in the way of her father's gardening projects, but he saved every single one, washed and polished and piled into a cheap spaghetti bowl that had been cracked and super-glued twice.

Ada moves the spaghetti bowl carefully downstairs from the dresser in the master bedroom to the middle of the floor in the living room. The other two rooms, which she supposes were meant as bedrooms, are hardly larger than pantries and crammed with books and rusting filing cabinets with bent knobs that don't lock anymore. The small bedrooms must have reminded surviving female relatives of Civil War casualties that without their patriarchs, there would be no more babies and no more serious income so they shouldn't get too hopeful about spreading out. They were repurposed to remind the next tenants to live as packed, greasy and humble as their lunch of canned fish, as the tiny fillets plop onto bread heels and into stew, and be grateful that their head, at least, was still on.

Now the wood of the house is sweet and stale with settled dust and rotting finishes. The windows are filthy. Ada stands in the rare patch of floor in one of the small rooms.

"Jesus, Dad, did you ever vacuum?"

She thinks about opening the window but notices part of the perfume is her father's own scent. It lingers from the short time ago he moved throughout the hallways and sat too long in the chairs. Maybe he talked to the ghosts of widows, orphans and immigrants, all the labour that built the wealth of the town that would after some time bring in Knell Telephone Labs and drug companies and BMW dealerships. Now the house was worth quite a lot, for its "historic charm" and waterfront view.

Ada wonders what her father might have said to these ghosts and if he ever thought about his house the way she did. She remembers how he projected his own doom and gloom onto the world, but then took the weight of history as a personal sin.

What weighed on Ada was approaching the age at which her father had begun to exhibit the first signs of whatever it was he was. Or whatever it was he had, because he was more than that, she thought, but it ended him, or hid him in a way. Or maybe it transformed him, neutral and misunderstood. She would be twenty-nine in just over a month, after the new year. No marriage to ruin, no children to traumatize, though. And no career to derail, anyway.

Ada wonders if she's done of all of this on purpose. There's relief and fear in her uncertainty. The loneliness of genetic determinism.

She goes downstairs and makes a sandwich – peanut butter and banana – while giving the kitchen a vigorous mopping. She checks online Scrabble. Courtney has played NOTHING using a blank tile for the I, and left another message in the chat client.

"Sorry – I had to go to lunch. No choice in the matter. I'm watching all of *Planet Earth*. There's an episode about this fungus thing called cordyceps, it's really gross and cool. Have you seen that series? I love David Attenborough."

Ada considers that Courtney might be kind of a nerd. She looks at her refreshed tiles. They perfectly spell out the word SKEPTIC, but there's nowhere to play it.

+

All of the video rental stores in town have closed, even Blockbuster. She doesn't have the patience for Netflix. Having kept it off most of her trip, Ada pulls out her smartphone and gets onto YouTube. She hates the little grey touchpad and the click sound effect. Nothing quite satisfies like thick, heavy plastic keys of an old PC keyboard. Clackclackclack for everything. The work produces its own music to work to, a recursive function.

She searches for "planet earth cordyceps."

There's a colony of hearty, terrifying jungle ants. An ant is infected by the spore of the fungus, its own unique species of the genus *Cordyceps*. The ant begins to exhibit strange behaviour noticeable by the rest of the colony. Its mind and body are controlled by spores.

Sometimes, David Attenborough explains, infected individuals will be spotted in their erratic behaviour by other ants. They are carried off and removed over a ledge before it's too late. It may seem harsh, he explains, but it's the only way to prevent total devastation. If the cordycep succeeds in driving its host to a high point, it bursts through the front of the ant's head and a long, hideous flower rains poison down on the rest of the colony.

Ada goes out the back door without a coat and rolls a joint. She smokes and watches the sun set in Technicolor and the cherry tree frost over again for the night. After half an hour, she goes back inside, and falls asleep on the living room couch, with the hall lights still on.

+

She scrolls through the local Craigslist. She puts up a post for a yard sale at the end of the week. She titles it "estate sale" because she remembers that the people of North Orange, unlike her friends from college, don't think thrifting is cute and want antiques, not old furniture. Call it vintage lingerie and you can sell used underwear, she thinks.

She feels clever, and then callous and isolated. The cynic pokes holes in everyone's truth until there's nothing left to be proud of but being right. But what's the point of that, she thinks.

North Orange makes her feel like this. She hates the smell of the air and the layout of the roads. She considers driving past her old high school and then remembers that she hated high school, too. Sitting in orchestra as fourth violin, a repressed dyke, bad at math, into Frank Zappa and, reluctantly, computers. First violin was a white girl, who'd stared her down once, during a break. She'd thrown her ballerina body around in her chair, heather-grey wrap sweater and leggings like a heron readying for flight, and shot Ada a look that tempered competition with suspicion and amusement.

"What's your deal?" the girl had asked.

"What do you mean?" Ada said.

"You're, like, half-Chinese or whatever, right?"

Ada didn't respond. Just stared at the girl's large blue eyes. The eyes flickered. By the end of elementary school Ada knew that tense scan of white people trying to determine her race. It was useless to try to explain something like *hapa pake* or *hapa haole*.

The girl pursed her lips to the side.

"You had me scared for a minute, at auditions, y'know. But that's a compliment, okay? I'm just surprised your Tiger Mom doesn't push you harder."

The girl turned back around, and started talking to someone else.

Or whatever, Ada thinks. Within that year Ada's parents had divorced and she was transplanted to Melrose High, the burnt sienna architectural offspring of a prison and a '70s office building. Not enough windows.

Courtney instant-messages her.

"So my dad's house is in the town where I grew up," she types. "And it's weird being an insider-outsider." She is trying the confessional thing, deciding it is half the appeal of chat rooms.

"I think I know what you mean," Courtney replies. Ada pauses, acutely aware that he was born the year the PC she is using was made. She feels old but secure about it. On the day of her birth, it was the Super Bowl, and the only airing of that stupid Macintosh commercial.

"So you're not in school?" she asks.

There's a long pause. He sends her a link to a website. Ada clicks on it. It's the homepage for an anorexia clinic in upstate New York. Most of it loads. She scrolls through its soft pink menus and photos of smiling, hopeful people walking around a vast walled garden.

"Oh," Ada types. There are not enough ways to textually represent all of the possible colours and cadences of Oh, she thinks.

"It's not weird for me to talk about anymore, I told your dad, too. I'm the only boy here, so I can't room with anyone. They had to convert one of the smaller offices. Actually I think they thought I was a girl because of my name. Most people do I guess."

"They put you in an office?"

"I use the staff men's room, too. Everything here is written for girls and women."

"Yeah this website is soft as hope and babies with the fake-handwritten fonts and the pink."

"I think it's the same pink as those breast cancer people."

"Sick chick pink."

"I guess, except I'm not a chick. Just don't say manorexia. But I don't mind talking about it… I'm almost better!"

Ada deletes her half-typed joke about manorexia. She finds Courtney's earnestness part unnerving and part admirable. It reminds her of her long-haired half brothers, un-worked teeth and pubescent dead-caterpillar moustaches adorning that rare kind of smile without predation or prey behind it. By her stepfather's design, they have never been instructed in ways of beauty.

Her stepfather is an effervescent engineer named Haskel. He dyes his own long hair purple and wears utility kilts with those rubber toe shoes. The family only celebrates birthdays, solstices and equinoxes. Happy hippy hapa family. Ada feels the pull of their warm, open, non-neurotic lives and she loves them, because she can't help but love them.

Still, she worries.

She tabs back to the Craigslist window and starts scrolling slack-jawed through the etcetera job board. This could be the year, she thinks, to move out of her mother and Haskel's cat hair-coated Victorian.

Would you like to help make dreams come true? Multiple ads are a variation on this theme. Be part of a miracle, it says. Become an egg donor and bring the joy of a child to a family. Up to ten grand for educated, non-smoking women 21-29. Normal weight range and healthy family history.

A photo shows a tall white woman laughing alone at some clouds.

Ada squirms. She bookmarks the ad just in case.

She tabs back to the gaming site. For several days their Scrabble has been derailed by frank conversation.

"How is cleaning out Harry's house?" Courtney asks. Sometimes Ada worries that Courtney is actually a pervert who lives across the street, watching her through binoculars as they chat. Residue of cyber safety warning videos from her childhood fester over her own experience with real-life perverts, harmless friendly Internet people, and the difficulty of comprehending that there is no real difference between the virtual world and the physical one. Her body perceives all of it from external stimulus. Computers are not hallucination stations, her father used to say.

Maybe truth and falsehood are less important than context, Ada thinks. What is so bad about losing touch with an outdated idea of reality? Was that Harry's point?

Her mother had said that her father "abandoned his life for a dream." As a teenager, Ada regurgitated the accusation, unfiltered and insensitive during the last time they sat face to face. They were about to leave a diner, waiting for a check, and the verdict uncoiled itself in her throat and struck out like a rattlesnake.

Harry was not insulted. His face pulled into solemn focus.

"That's the price it's worth," he said, nodding. "But who is in control?"

The piles of objects from the house that Ada doesn't know what to do with have made contact with the ceiling light fixture.

"If I ever have babies," she types to Courtney, "I'm going to give away all of my worldly possessions, so I don't put them through this."

"But then you'll be boring," he replies.

"They'll have known me! Even when I'm not the way they remember me."

"I'd be really worse off here if I didn't have so many of my things from home. Maybe it's different when you get older," Courtney writes.

"Yeah maybe."

+

At the yard sale, Ada puts everything that's left after trash day out on the lawn, except the large kitchen appliances and the PC. Nobody wants the body odour-soaked computer chair, but she lets it bask in the milky sun along the sidewalk. It's cold and balmy, with no snow on the ground and a slight wind. Craigslist people and neighbours trickle by in bursts.

A white couple from Short Hills are especially interested in the spaghetti bowl of glass shards, of all things. They look about their mid-forties. The woman calls the shards "bric-a-brac" and comments on their similarity to sea glass. Ada explains they are hand picked from the backyard. The woman makes a "mmm!" sound.

"These would look so cute in a big old jar, you know with a little sand at the bottom?" she says to her husband. He raises his eyebrows and smiles.

Friend. Follow. Text.

"Perfect for the shore house."

"I was just thinking that! Excuse me, dear, do you mind just keeping the bowl? I have my own bags."

The woman hands Ada a reusable grocery bag that's been folded neatly and tucked in her purse. Ada takes the bag and the bowl and the woman's money over to her cash box to make change and pours the glass into the bag.

She immediately regrets that she is selling them. As she counts out the change, she slips one of the larger, more rounded pieces into the pocket of her hoodie.

Maybe, she thinks, she'll ask Courtney if she can mail it to him.

The yard sale continues for the rest of the morning. The big furniture sells. Ada loads the personal documents, the photos and drawings from her father's filing cabinets into the trunk of her car. She hasn't bothered to sort through them yet.

As the sun plummets out from the short day, Ada sits in the yard and flips over flagstones, watching the few brave bugs she can find. She takes out her smartphone, searches the web for images, and changes the background of the phone to a macro of an organ-like bloom of cordyceps bursting through the thin shell of a fat, dead ant.

+

That night she sits on the floor in front of the computer, planning to log onto Scrabble and ask Courtney for his address at the clinic. She pushes the computer's deep, round power button. The animated flag does not appear. Instead, it boots into MS-DOS. Ada tries to re-start it, but none of her commands have any effect. Again it boots in DOS.

A line of text appears.

C:\Documents and Settings\Ada.exe

Ada begins to sweat and cry. She runs the program.

>>Thank you, Ada.

>>I see now that I could have told you more when I was still alive. I've been working for a long time. This is only one aspect of it. Sometimes there is no way to be taken seriously for what you know. I learned to stop minding, but felt as though I had to protect you.

>>I should have trusted that you, of anyone, could have understood. You are so much like I was at your age.

>>I'm sorry.

>>There are so many regrets. Lots of things have gone missing. I don't have a lot of time right now. I'm still not the one in control, but I'm closer than most.

>>You're very special to me.

>>You will not find this program on the hard drive.

+

The text stalls, and then the screen goes dark and still. Ada hugs her knees to her chest and sobs. She checks the connections and tries to restart the PC again. It will not boot. She screams.

By 3 AM she cries herself to sleep, mute from soreness. In the morning, while the neighbours' children play outside, she smokes a joint next to the cherry tree. A neighbour, the one who told her about the grocery bags, comes out into the back lawn, smells the weed and yells at her. She ignores him. He threatens to call the police and marches back inside his house.

She hears the faint tones of the number pad. Before the police, or anyone else, can respond, Ada puts the computer tower into the backseat of her car, locks the front door and leaves town.

Noughts & Crosses:
an unsent reply
by Steven Heighton

From: <j.in.corydon@hotmail.com>
To: <nella_biagini@sympatico.ca>
Sent: April 22, 2007 1:16 AM
Subject: RE: Hello?

n,

yes yes i did get your email but needed to reflect a little. i'm sorry. and yes i do think it might be best if i pulled back a little now, i seem to need some space to hear my own breathing, my own thoughts, it is hard when we are always in dialogue. i am sorry if this feels abrupt or my reasons feel vague, they just must be. for one thing, as i guess i implied, i have been asked to keep secrets and want to keep my word. i know you understand. you, after all, are one of my secrets. and as you know yourself and even said, maybe a severing, a temporary severing is what's best now, for both of you. for everyone involved. please don't worry about me, i will be all right, i am determined to get through this time. i promise i will get in touch again when i feel i can.

love always,

j

n

As in: never again, never again. That phrase with its cardiac cadence. Slight arrhythmia. A certain tunnelled clump of muscle misbehaving, missing steps or taking clumsy extras, a drunk at the top of the stairs in the dark. When you used the abbreviation before, that n, it was an intimate act, an adoring diminutive, as though to make the beloved compact enough to carry with you secretly. You always found me tall for a woman (too tall?). Now it's as though you want to avoid repeating my full name: Amelia. Nelli. nell. n. To deduct the name down to nothing. Nobody, no one, nowhere, nothing, nought, null, nil.

yes yes

The one thing you would never say in the act was Yes! It was always *O no O no O no O no*! when you were getting close, and when I asked if it was because something was wrong, this "thing" was wrong, or was your pleasure (I would like to think so) intense to the point of pain, you turned shy and said it was "just what came out – you know" (your favourite lazy phrase) "like when a song shows up in your head and you just, like, let it out?" I didn't press the point. I sensed you retreating into your separate memoir of intimate events. I didn't ask if that was what *always* "came out," or only with me. Separate memoirs, former loves. How crowded our bedrooms are these days. (Or not. Not my bedroom. Not these days.) For over a century there was a tunnel extending from the crypt of the main cathedral here down to the Hotel Dieu, the old Catholic hospital, so the nuns and priests could stay indoors in winter when they were called off to see sick parishioners or perform the last rites. A few weeks ago I read about it and for some reason kept wanting to tell you. Why not now? Forty years ago they decided the tunnel was becoming unsafe. They sealed it off at both ends, but the passageway is still there, thirty feet under Brock Street, totally dark, of course, and empty. Sometimes now when I'm alone it hits me.

reflect a little

Five days of this little reflecting. Here is what gnaws me, besides the aftereffects of five days of little reflecting on your part and much waiting on mine. What gnaws and haunts me is: whatever passed through your mind in those five (plus) days, all the stuff you decided not to voice, reconsidered, revised, rejected then retrieved, reneged on again, at last deleted. I want it back, the full census of your reflections, a crammed CT-scanful, all those references to me, I can't accept that they're gone, neural flickers like email never sent or lost in transit somewhere in the digital ether we're all adrift in now. Or whispers of a couple passing in that tunnel before it was sealed. A pair of nuns, let's say, lovers on the down low, erotically revved up by the proximity of illness, death. Death's weirdly elating ultimacy. Did they have torches? A medieval image, cinematic to the point of camp: dark figures hunched, capes wafting, torches in hand, flapping down limestone corridors propped with timber stays for safety, as in a mine shaft. Our lovers must feel unnerved, even so. They are crossing so many lines. The anxiety of the crime makes one notice other dangers everywhere. And safety measures always seem to whisper: *some day we will fail!* It feels safer where there are no measures. And either way, in their presence or absence, no safety.

i'm sorry

Sorry, maybe, because there *were* no reflections? You'd made up your mind? You're sorry that you stalled about breaking the news, is all? They say that from the bottom of a deep hole you can see the stars shining even at noon. I never trust those little factlets from the *Globe*; still, it's good news for the dead.

and yes i *do* think it might be best

Italics mine. But even without the italics (it's my ethnic privilege to overuse them) your implication here is that *I made the suggestion in the first place!* Actually, of course, I did: "If you need me to pull back now, I will." Naturally I didn't mean it, though. Didn't want you to accept. Wanted you to say *O no O no O no O no!* What's more, *you must have known I didn't mean it – you* just pretended to take the words at face value to give yourself a convenient out. Lovers are the world's only honest people, according to certain poets and sages. Ho ho ho. I'm nostalgic for the salad days, grad and postgrad in the late '70s and early '80s, York and UBC, when it was an article of faith (if not experience) in our circle that straight lovers, bourgeois lovers, were the only dishonest ones. *T[he] on/lie dys/honest ones.*

That stage of life when confidence depends on culprits.

Oh, to have both back.

i seem to need some space

But, but I thought we were bitter opponents of platitudes, you and I; we agreed that our love was *not like any other love* (italics mine, quotation yours, email 64, line 17: I am now chief archivist of your intimacies), and to consecrate and, as you would say, "honour" this singularity, we agreed that we would never speak of our love in clichés. We smogged the air with exalted vows like that. Teenage summer lovers in a song by the Boss. So, maybe a return to cliché is a neatly symmetrical way to shut things down... to *deconsecrate* our love, the way they do with those churches whose flocks have died off or moved to Palm Beach, and the buildings are converted to meeting halls or museums or daycares. Ever wondered how they deconsecrate a cathedral? I really should know, after a quarter-century in my field. (A century, one learns, is a small thing.) A choir assembles for the last time, chanting in discord, an infernal chorus. At the altar a bishop exhausts the full roster of religious obscenities. The organist, wild-eyed, riffs on anthem-rock standards, Queen, Gary Glitter, The Sweet, as if playing at a hockey rink.

j, my j, you've *recanted*.

Shouldn't "recant" mean to sing again?

to hear my own breathing

If I woke in the night, the precious nights I had you here, I was always taken aback at how hard it was to detect your breaths. Even when you were deeply out (pretty much always) your breathing was delicate; once or twice I almost panicked, you know how the mind works at night, and there were always those footlights of unease around our meetings, fear of your husband interrupting our, uh, tutorial with a call, so that panic would feed on puny fears and several times I actually put the back of my hand to your open mouth to feel the breaths. Then my mouth next to yours to breathe them in. That close, I found you breathing, of course, calm and profound, with a faint sighing wheeze in your lungs, under your bare breasts, which were pillowed one over the other as you lay furled on your side. Your breath smelled fine, spicy, with a subtle finish of garlic and Syrah. Then one night it changed. That's how I knew we were coming to an end. More conventional signs had materialized as well – your canned laughter, diluted gaze, undilated pupils – but *that* was how I knew: the last two nights your breath turned unfamiliar in your sleep. Changes deep inside, where I couldn't reach. I wonder about the air in that blocked tunnel, after forty years of disuse. Is oxygen stable or does it deteriorate over time? I wouldn't know. Your husband would. Could toxic fumes have seeped in through the limestone? If the ends were unblocked tonight, could we still walk through it and breathe? How long does a closed-off tunnel remain a possible route?

always in dialogue

To you it may have felt that way. You're the one with other allegiances. (More of them, maybe, than I thought.) A day came when I abandoned my latest stalled article to check email – still dial-up then – maybe thirty times, hoping for a reply. You must have been reflecting a little. Finally I just remained online, waiting. I answered a few other "urgent" emails that I'd left to ripen for days, maybe weeks. That took some time. I've never learned, like you, to crash out a reply, in lowercase, in the current electronic shorthand that I am still not used to – insulting! – though I see it all the time from my students :) Did those. Waited. Stared at the empty inbox and willed a message to appear. For quite some time I stuck it out. Funny, I've never once sat staring at the phone, though you would sometimes call me. Staring at a phone seems somehow goofier. A screen is meant to be stared at. Things are meant to appear there. Maybe I could *induce* you to write me. Eventually I took the modem cord and slunk the three flights down to the lobby and locked it in the morgue-like drawer of my mailbox. Came upstairs for a double Campari and soda. Left the cord down there for a good half-hour.

i am sorry if this feels abrupt or my reasons feel vague, they just must be

Oh and another nice thing about email: you are always sitting down to read it. No more Puccini swoons, buckling to the floor with the farewell letter clinched in one hand, the other cupping the brow. Instead, you settle deeper in your chair. The world stops entering your mind through the senses. You've been sealed off with your obsession, and shame. *my reasons... must be kept vague*. I always knew there were truths you wouldn't tell me, so I avoided entering certain corridors of inquiry; but there was also an implication, about the two of us, that we just *knew* – we

225

UNDERSTOOD. William Burroughs said that gay love differs from straight love because a queer lover ("homosexual" was how he put it, I believe) always knows what the other is thinking and feeling, while a straight lover never does. Hmmm... better that I did my thesis on Bloomsbury and Woolf, instead of (a quip over cocktails, long ago) "Bloomsbury & the Beats: Points of Unexpected Comparison."

as i guess i implied

Didn't we make a pact never to *do* this sort of thing? To *guess* and *imply*? To become, in each other's sight, hazy at the margins by delivering half-truths? That's how people deconsecrate themselves, from human into something less. Spectres. Cyborgs. Didn't I mention this opinion? Not that you listened well, ever. Speaking of blockages. Consider the ears of the egotist... Now, as I listen, trying to peer through this blockage, I wonder if you are alone. There's your husband, of course, but he doesn't count. Two daughters. Neither do they. For the purpose of this madness only *somebody else* counts. (Especially if female.) You told me I was the first woman you had been with. Is there another now? Have I created a monster?

i have been asked to keep secrets

The cathedral's literature (I went and took one of their free tourist leaflets; lit a lampion for the hell of it) gives no clue as to how, or with what, the passageway was sealed.

i know you understand

See above under Burroughs, William.

you, after all, are one of my secrets

One of your... excuse me? I thought this was an exclusive engagement! Now I'm no longer your secret, I'm *one* of your secrets? Um, are your secrets a *clique* now? A *category*? A *women's collective*? All on the same level... Maybe your secrets should be more civil about this. Maybe they should all get *used* to one another. Your secrets are "all in this together"... no rank, no priority, no hierarchy of closeness... it's a sorority, a full *democracy* of secrets! The one exact thing that love isn't.

as you know yourself

Oh, I do. One of us had to end it. The question is: who began it, Janet? Another reference that dates me and, by omission, you. We have all the particulars. The year (2002). The season (summer). The place (Kingston). The course (Religious Imagery in Popular Culture and Contemporary Women's Fiction), and you in semi-attendance to steal time – admit it, finally, you're a dabbler, a summer slummer – away from your aphasic husband and colicky twins. When you went back to Winnipeg in the fall, I assumed it was over, but the thing wouldn't die. Since then I've propped everything on your annual holiday here in the Thousand Islands.

maybe a severing

New word for an old context. Feels more honest than "spend a little time apart," anyway. And honesty is what we all want at such times. But s*evering:* there is a hard word. I'd never noticed the "severe" in it before. Or really heard the sound of it before. *SEVering.* The oiled blade sliding down to separate head from body with a blunt, chunky sound.

a temporary severing

Whew! For a minute there I thought it was permanent! As if it was in the very *nature* of severings to be that way... But a moment's reflection allows us to generate any number of counter-examples. In the fatal crash, the victim's spinal cord was *temporarily* severed. As the glaciers retreated, rising sea waters *temporarily* severed Asia from North America. Alas, it proved necessary to sever the miner's gangrenous limb *temporarily*. Somehow the bungee jumper's cord was severed in mid-leap – but *only temporarily!*

for both of you

You always wrote your emails fast, furtively, late at night or early in the morning, and there were always misspellings or little misnomers like this one. "Both of us," I assume you meant. You and me. Because there aren't two people hereabouts, in my world, my room. All the same... maybe you did half-mean that *I've* been as split apart as you. Between wanting to respect your family commitments and wanting you all to my lonesome? Nope: between wanting *not* to violate the current student-teacher protocol (which I always supported and still believe in and which the dying white males of the department, just them, allegedly, still flout when they can) and wanting to violate, repeatedly, you.

for everyone involved

Everyone! How did they get into this again? How I detest them! From the moment a love starts, Everyone is clamouring to get in, huffing and prodding, mobbing the door that a new couple seals fast and barricades – Everyone trying to peep through, push through, leaving messages, making demands. I should have known Everyone would get to us. They always do. Over and over I've lived my life for those days before they do.

i am determined to get through this time

The ambiguity! It makes me insane! How many times have I been over this one, trying to uncrate it? You are determined to ride out this painful, severe time in your life? Or: you are determined, *this* time, to get through? Let it be the first option! Let it be that this hurts you as much as it hurts me. Let this not be yet another unacceptable revelation – that our affair wasn't your first of the kind. You said it was. Now you might be saying that there was another time and you *didn't* get through it – never got over her. (Or him.) Other *times*? Who? Who? This vision of multitudes barging into your inbox, your bedroom, your body.

i will get in touch again when i feel i can

What's this if not a melodramatic way of saying, Don't call us, we'll call you? My people will call your people. My multitudes will call your solitude... but don't hold your breath. (Whatever remains in that sealed place.) Cave exploration is something you always said you wanted to try out. I can hardly bear to use the correct, ridiculous term. Spelunking. I spelunk, you spelunk. We will spelunk. She had spelunked. So we'll go no more spelunking. Partly this is why I keep bringing up that sealed tunnel – not as some elaborate genital metaphor, but because I know you would be interested and maybe want to explore it. Count me out, though. Daredevils come in aerial or subterranean form. How many folks do you know who have both sky-dived and spelunked? Doesn't happen. When you would talk about spelunking, I would counter with skydiving, my own potential death-wish hobby. We had to compromise on the earth's surface – on driving *really, really fast* those few times when we were far from Everyone together. Rental cars are good for that:

convertibles. A *Thelma & Louise* outtake, except people probably took me for your aunt, or duenna. Remember the highway
into the Cypress Hills? How amazed you were that such committed flatness could collect itself into hills – small mountains,
our ears popping as we drove – the way your life seemed to be
climbing up from the plains of your comfortable present onto
high ridges of possibility…

love always

But there's hope here, isn't there, there's not just a name, and
not just "love" – no, it's "love always," even if there is the one
conspicuous, crushing change, the absence of your usual star-
burst of xxxxxooooo. Or xoxoxoxo. It always varied. I go back
through the emails now (printed out, of course – there's a paper
trail after all, sweetie, though you prudently avoided writing
letters) – I pore over them again, studying, tabulating the details of the x and o firework finale of all your emails, one hundred and fifty-eight in all, but especially the last twenty or so. I
am trying to track the decline. How does the end enter? Where
does it get in? In your most passionate note (I won't say email),
right after the Cypress Hills Escapade, there were no less than
ten x's and seven o's. (Why fewer o's than x's? Why *stint* like
that on the o's? And what *are* x's and o's anyway? Kisses and
embraces, embraces and kisses. We argued about which were
which. To both of us it seemed obvious, a matter of common
sense and common knowledge, and we were stunned, in a loving way, by the other's ignorance. You said, "O is the lips open
for a deep kiss, X is the arms crossed over the embraced lover's
back." Touched by this effort I replied, "Ingenious but wrong.
O is the circle of the embracing lover's arms, X is the eye of
the lover, the eyes, closed, X-ed out in the rapture of the kiss.")
Love as a game of noughts and crosses. Nine emails before the

end, I find *all my love, j, xxxoooxx*. Again this marked privileging of x over o. (Five and three.) Five messages before the end, *Love forever, j, xxxxoo*. (Four and two.) Three messages before the end, o makes something of a comeback, outnumbering x for the first time in many missives, *Love, j , ooxxxooo*. In fact, the total number of signs here, eight, suggests if anything a strengthening of passion! Next, email 156, where o makes its final strong showing, *my love, j, ooxoo* – with the lone x almost lost among those still fervent hugs (or kisses???). Number 157, the second-last, shows this tic-tac-toe showdown entering its endgame, though the salutation – *yours always, j, ox* – almost seems to cancel out that lack.

j

I'm to be spared the final humiliation. You'll remain j to me, not Janet-Marie. In signing off, you could have withdrawn that intimate, tiny link between us, that hook lodged in my heart, and keyed in your full name. You chose not to; something does remain unsevered. And after all, if the Greek in the labyrinth (you never remember the names), slowly unreeling his ball of yarn so he could find his way back, had accidentally cut the thread – maybe on a cornering wall, a knife-edge of stone – he might have sensed it break and then groped his way back in the darkness, feeling for the lost end, splicing the yarn, persevering. We're back in the tunnel, you see. Despite my fear, I think I would go down and explore it with you, if they ever opened it up again. I am drawn to a fantasy of fucking you there, maybe in a side tunnel or cul-de-sac, tugging you away from the tedious tour group with its silly costumed guide to make slow, wordless love in the kind of darkness that people never really do it in. What would that be like? To have not the faintest glimpse or inkling of the one beside you, above you, below you? So the orgasm I'd give you, the way you liked it best, would star the gloom, seeming to project on the walls a brief, grand, enveloping galaxy. There we would be our own source of light. I don't want to see anything now. Darkness is far from the worst. Your note is very short. Worst is the whiteness of most of the printout under that j. So I've filled it and other pages, your faithful annotator and emptied teacher, with these notes, endnotes, that our dialogue not die.

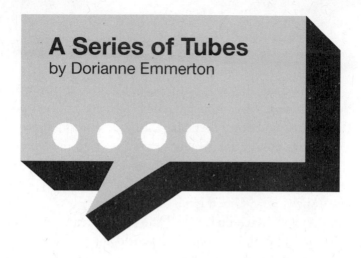

A Series of Tubes
by Dorianne Emmerton

Marika said hello to her pretty pink laptop as she came in the door. She lived alone and spoke to all of her belongings. She lifted the lid and watched the monitor run through its start-up processes. As she waited she slid the night's bottle of wine out of her bag, twisted off the screw top and took a long slug. She had looked forward to this all day, as she did every day.

In her third year of a degree in English literature with a minor in philosophy at the University of Toronto, she helped pay her way with a part-time job. Marika studied and wrote her essays in libraries and coffee shops. She did no work in her apartment. She wanted to enjoy her home, not have it filled with the stress of school.

Her job wasn't difficult. The vintage clothing store didn't sell much; it was a front for her boss's illicit marijuana business more than anything. But it was still stressful. She had to deal with the sketchy characters who came in and occasionally had to run interference with the police. But, often left her to her own devices, she could get some studying done at the cash register when business was slow.

A cramped fourth-floor bachelor in a building with no elevator, her home was hers and hers alone. It was the first place she'd ever lived by herself. When she finally got back at night she enjoyed whatever time was left in the day by drinking wine and playing on the Internet.

She knew this was pathetic but it was also temporary. For what it was, while it lasted, the bright spot of her day was this hour or two before bed. She checked the obligatory social networking sites of course, but what she loved most were message boards: places where she had an alias, a persona, where she could say and do anything with no real-world repercussions.

She was, in fact, a troll.

As a message board troll she had no fealty, no accountability, no obligations. In the real world she had work, school and family. Her family had become larger and more demanding of her energies recently: a year ago her mother had remarried, bringing not just a new stepfather to Marika's life but also a new five-year-old stepbrother, Bobby.

She went to stay with them once or twice a month and she always tucked Bobby in at night and told him a bedtime story. His favourite (and hers) was the story of the billy goats gruff. Her version was a bit different than the one most kids knew. In the traditional tale, the billy goats had to cross over a bridge to get into town, but a troll lived under the bridge and terrorized the poor goats. In Marika's story the billy goats' home was connected to the rest of the world by a series of tubes and the evil troll lurked under these tubes. When they encounter their nemesis one of the billy goats runs away quickly and though he is the fastest of the billy goat clan he cannot outrun the troll. One of the billy goats tries to fight back and though he is the bravest of the billy goat clan he cannot defeat the troll. The third billy goat, however, ignores the troll completely; he saunters casually past without a glance in the troll's direction. This causes the troll to disappear since he thrives on fear and attention.

The old fairy tales were cautionary stories and Marika thought they could still serve the same purpose. She loved her stepbrother, even if he was the child of her mother's aloof new husband and his estranged first wife, and she wanted the little tyke to grow up into an adult she could respect. She had no respect for people who let her online taunting get under their skin.

Marika logged into Facebook first but it was boring: just more pointless trivia about people she knew. Jenny was a friend from school and she was interesting because of her easy laugh and in-depth knowledge of Russian literature. Now, because of Facebook, Marika knew that Jenny was missing a toenail on the baby toe of her right foot. That wasn't interesting.

Twitter was bound to be full of more inanity. Instead she logged into one of her favourite message boards, one ostensibly oriented around the local indie-music scene but which served as a way for bored young office drones to waste time while pretending to be hard at work. Traffic slowed considerably in the evening, the only time she was online, so she went to see what ruckus last night's posting had caused.

There was a thread on a new restaurant that was getting good reviews. One of the board members worked in the kitchen. Marika had posted:

> I went there a couple of days ago and it was gross, there were mouse-droppings in my food and the servers were all ugly and borderline retarded.

She had never actually been to the restaurant, of course. A number of people had piped up with posts such as:

> What does it matter if your server isn't a beauty queen, mr. Superficial?

Her moniker on the site, Mysteryus, was gender neutral and she was often read as being male. Another post read:

> your borderline retarded!

And then there was a long post from the cook defending the food and asking what dish she had eaten.

That was easy – she looked up the menu online, picked the most expensive dish, then posted about how it was filled with shit and semen and the whole establishment smelled like ass. She moved onto the next thread.

It was about oral sex. Sex was a common topic; people loved to talk about it and revealed pretty intimate details online. The cloak of anonymity made some feel safe in doing so, but many of these people knew each other in real life. This was obvious from their online discussions; they made plans for the weekend and indulged in inside jokes.

One girl had posted some tips on blowjob technique. Marika, or rather, Mysteryus, had posted:

> You're a slut, obviously. How many cocks did you have to suck to come up with that exhaustive list of what every man likes? Did they come on your face afterwards and leave you a $20 before heading home to their wives? Whore.

The blowjob tips girl had a number of friends on the board so they had all come rushing to her defence. Most of them were pretty banal, calling Mysteryus a prude, a virgin, an anal-retentive homo. One of them, from a member she didn't remember seeing before, was more intriguing. This post said:

> These tips are very useful, thank you. The next penis that is placed in my mouth will be treated with the worship you describe. Unfortunately, there is no promise of penis in my future. However, If Mysteryus would like to offer me his, I expect the knowledge I have gleaned from this thread could go a long way toward soothing his vitriolic nature.

Marika supposed this poster, who went by the name Craniac, must be female since they had admitted to sucking cock. It could be a gay man. Or, she supposed, it could be a man masquerading as a woman; however men only did that sort of thing for titillation, which was usually found on dating sites, not music-oriented message boards. Regardless of the gender behind the username, Marika hoped Craniac would post more.

✚

Marika walked around her mother's house with Bobby attached to her left leg; he giggled softly while she ignored him. She sat down in her stepfather's easy chair and put her feet up on the ottoman, Bobby squealing as he swung up through the air. She picked up the TV *Guide* from the side table and flipped through it. "Nothing on," she sighed. "Might as well go see what Momma's cooking." Bobby squealed again as she brought her leg back down.

Her mother was chopping vegetables up into small bits. Marika liked big chunks of food but her mother cut everything into tiny pieces.

"You don't have to let him do that," said her mother, barely glancing down at her daughter's burdened leg.

"Let who do what?" asked Marika. "I came in here to help. Something's boiling on the stove, go look at that. I'll chop." She started chopping vegetables, gradually making the pieces bigger and bigger. Then she accidentally-on-purpose dropped a chunk of carrot onto Bobby's head. He looked up at her with wide, innocent eyes. Then he opened his mouth as wide as his eyes and Marika obliged by dropping a chunk of carrot into it. He chewed delightedly.

Bobby usually hated carrots.

By the time George, her stepfather, came home from work supper was ready and her mother was tut-tutting about how Marika was so messy, there were carrots all over the floor. Those ones had bounced off Bobby's lips or teeth as he tried to catch the falling vegetables. Marika was sure he would have eaten them off the floor if she told him to. But at the dinner table he stubbornly refused to eat any and their mother, used to this, did not insist.

George worked at an office about twenty minutes away but he never arrived home until after 7 PM. Marika did not think he was the workaholic type. She had her suspicions about what he did between five and seven but she didn't know what he told her mother. He must tell her something.

She couldn't wait to be in her apartment the next evening. Being with her family was lovely but it was as exhausting as work, as school, as anything other than the sweet relief of trolling message boards.

+

She joined a message board for brides-to-be. There were threads about rings, catering, venues, photographers, and of course the all-important dress. She read until she felt sick to her stomach and decided to never get married. Then she did a Google Images search for "fat ugly ditch pig." She started a thread asking:

> I'm a bit on the heavy side but my hubby-to-be loves me just the way I am. His family, though, makes snide comments about my weight. I'd like to look really really good on our wedding day, both for my guy and to shut his family up. This is a picture of me, what cut or style of wedding dress would flatter my figure?

Back on the indie-music message board the maligned cook had posted a link to the Ministry of Health site where the restaurant was listed as having passed their inspection with flying colours. This was too easy. A few minutes of googling later and she had a list of links to articles about restaurants that had health scares after passing inspections: there was vermin, there was listeriosis, and yes, there were cases of bodily fluids turning up in people's meals. She posted her links and added:

> So it was you who left all the chunks of spunk in my stew. Gross dude, maybe you should look into cooking dog food instead of serving that shit to people.

In the oral-sex thread someone had responded to Craniac's post with the usual "useless without pics" image. This is cyber-speak for "Show us a picture of yourself so we can judge if you're hot or not."

Craniac had replied:

> I would post a pic but I am neurotic about my privacy. My in-ability to reveal personal and identifying aspects of myself on-line has become debilitating. I am in therapy and hopefully I will be able to post a picture of at least my hand in the next year or so. My hand is very attractive, it's a shame not to share it with the world.

Marika laughed out loud. She didn't post "LOL": she literally laughed out loud. She wanted to engage Craniac in some way. After a moment she quoted Craniac and posted:

> At least you're not whoring yourself for compliments. posting endless pics taken at myspace angles with pouty cock-sucking lips like all the tramps in the Post Your Pic thread.

This inspired her to do some trolling in the Post Your Pic thread. She went through the last couple of pages with a careful eye, searching out MySpace angles – pictures with certain angles, in certain poses, with certain lighting to make people appear more attractive than they were. She was looking for the popular girls on the board, the ones who knew everyone and thought they knew everything, the ones who posted about shopping for expensive clothes and how amazing and beauti-ful they all were.

Marika found a perfect photo of one of the most popular and most vapid girls on the board. She often posted selfies; each was followed by a string of guys drooling over her. But Marika knew from a dieting thread a couple of months ago that she was sensitive about her weight.

Friend. Follow. Text.

The Internet was like high school, Marika thought, then corrected herself: life was like high school. People begrudgingly behaved acceptably when they were being watched, but on the Internet, like in the alley behind the school, anything goes.

Marika plopped the picture of the pretty girl into Photoshop and drew crude lines ending in circles around the girl's lower back and arm. She wrote:

> Look at the curve in her back and the position of her arm – that's designed to cover the stomach bulge and draw attention away from her gut and toward her boobs. She's a secret fatty using the dreaded myspace angle!

After she logged out it she realized her post would just incite the bimbo to post more shots of herself to illustrate her slimness. Ah well. No regrets, she had promised herself. Marika finished her bottle of wine and went to bed.

+

Marika stared at the guy across from her at the library study table, at his curly but well-kept hair, wondering what product he used… and then shook her head. Mid-terms were fast approaching and she felt depressingly underprepared. She studied and studied and the minute she closed a book everything she had learned disappeared. She kept finding her mind wandering to how she wanted the scone recipe from the library cafe, to how fast Bobby was growing, to the other student's hair. She couldn't focus.

She realized the curly-haired boy was now looking up at her, smiling. She ducked her head, instinctively embarrassed, then forced it up to smile back. She was not the kind of girl to let herself be shy.

+

Marika picked up a package of baklava from a Greek diner to bring to her mother's place for dessert. No one ate it. George

retired to the living room to watch the news. Her mother pro-
tested that she was watching her waistline and went to the sink
to do dishes. Bobby spit it back out on his plate.

"Yuck," he said. "I want chocolate for dessert. Mommy, do
we have any chocolate?" Their mother did not hear, her ears
full of the sound of running water. He ran to her and tugged on
her skirt "Mommy, do we have any chocolate?"

"No, go sit down and eat your balaclava," she said. Marika
did not feel like correcting her.

She took Bobby to bed. "Tell me about the billy goats."
She loved him but was getting tired of his demands. He didn't
know how to ask politely for anything. She wondered if
her mother had gotten lax at parenting or if it had been the
same when she was young. Perhaps that's why her father had
left. Maybe her father hadn't found TV as easy an escape as
George did.

"I'll tell you about the billy goats after you brush your teeth."

"No!" Bobby stamped his foot, raring for a fight. His eyes
glittered with the expectation of a who-can-yell-louder match.
Marika got up and headed toward the door. "Where are you
going?" he asked.

"Home." Maybe she would actually catch a train back to
the city. It was still early; the Internet awaited.

"You are home," declared Billy.

Marika laughed. "Haven't you noticed that I'm only here
sometimes, Bobbikins? Or do you just pretend I'm around when
I'm not?"

"Sometimes. But this is your home. You're just staying downtown while you're in school."

"Bobby, come sit on the bed with me." He came. "I'm staying where I am now because it's close to school, yes. But after
school I'm going to get a job. Then I'm going to live close to
where that is. I won't be coming back."

"Why can't you get a job close to here?"

"Because this is the burbs, dear, no one works near here."

"Jing's cousin graduated and still lives at home and Maria's sister is almost as old as you and she's in university and she lives at home, so I don't know why you need to go and live in a place that isn't your home."

Marika could recall Jing and Maria from Billy's birthday parties and times she had picked him up from school. She considered explaining that Jing was Chinese and Maria was Italian and both cultures had a tradition of children staying at home until marriage. But this could potentially lead Bobby into misconstrued ideas that could come out in racist ways and alienate him from his friends; better to let him learn from his friends themselves. It also would lead to Bobby questioning about when she would get married, and that was not a conversation she wanted to have with anyone. And she couldn't just tell him that she simply did not want to live here.

"Bobby, do any of your other classmates have sisters or brothers or cousins who moved out of the house?" He thought for a minute, then nodded solemnly. "Yuri has a cousin who moved out even though she's still in high school. Yuri's parents visit her, and they don't speak to her father anymore."

That sounded juicy but Marika was too tired for third-hand gossip. "Go brush your teeth Bobbikins and I'll tell you the tale of the billy goats gruff and the tube they travelled to get into town and the troll who lived under their tube." She patted his bottom and he ran off to the bathroom.

+

The brides were boring. Only one had come up with a worthy jab:

maybe you should look for a tent-maker to design your dress.

The other replies were hopelessly polite. She suspected it was because they thought they were talking to one of their own.

Who would brides all hate? That took no thought at all. She thanked them for their kind words, logged out and re-registered with a new username. She started a thread describing how her daughter-in-law-to-be was trying to make all the flower and decoration and catering decisions herself. She threw in that as she was vegetarian it was only right to have no meat at all at the wedding meal but her son's silly fiancée wouldn't hear of it. The brides-to-be were sure to hate her new persona – especially the ones from Alberta.

Back on the indie-music message board she'd hit pay dirt. That cook was incensed with the aspersions she'd cast upon the hygiene of his establishment. And many people had clicked her links and were expressing all manner of disgust. One said:

> I'm never eating anything other than home cooked food again.

Her links acted as full proof in the message-board world, though none of them were about the restaurant in question.

The cook raged against:

> wannabe food critics who probably can't even make a sand-
> wich without mommy and daddy to use the sharp knives for
> them. most if not all health violations are caused by unclean
> idiots who eat at a restaurant without washing their hands or
> knowing how to use a napkin.

He went on to call Mysteryus:

> an inbred moron with one giant taste bud tuned only to the
> taste of his own shit.

This was comedy gold but, even better, someone else had taken up Marika's fight and responded:

> Someone that eloquent must run a pure kitchen, obviously. Or
> perhaps methinks the chefy doth protest too much?

This provoked another long-winded obscenity-strewn retort from Mr Restaurant. Marika noticed the poster of the "doth protest too much" comment was none other than Craniac.

She chuckled her way through the cook's rant and then returned to the oral-sex thread. She felt a thrill when she saw that Craniac had responded there as well:

> When I am able to post a picture of my hand, I assure you it will be pouty and cock-strokey. It would be cock-sucky if my poor hand could provide suction, but alas, it cannot.

No doubt about it: she had a crush on this Craniac person. This post bolstered her assumption Craniac was female, which gave her a little pause. As far as she knew she'd never had a crush on a woman before. Of course, it was just a cyber-crush, where gender was more a matter of presentation than of dangly bits. These days gender ambiguity was not constrained to the Internet; she'd seen many androgynous people on the streets of the city and it never bothered her. Marika used the search function to dredge up all of Craniac's posts, and settled in for a good read.

+

She stared at a long bibliography: all the works she should read for her final essay in Victorian literature. It was worth 70 percent of the final mark so it had barely been worth attending the lectures, but Marika was too prudent to skip unless absolutely necessary. She had made careful note of anything the professor said that was in any way relevant to her final essay topic. Professors loved seeing their own opinions written down by students as if they were facts.

The font was barely legible. Marika worked on one of the library computers, not her own lovely laptop. That was back at her apartment.

She squinted but it didn't help. She scrolled down but when she stopped the page kept going. Text flew upward until the screen was a confusion of flickering light, the page bottomless. Her hands froze in midair, halfway between the keyboard and her chin. Eventually it relented, the screen gradually moving more slowly until finally it was still. The page now displayed the same book titles, authors and publication information as before. Marika tried to begin again, but as she focused upon each word it fell apart. Letters detached and floated upward, downward, wherever there was blank space. More letters started moving, creating more blank space; they bounced off each other, off the edges of the screen, off the menu images frozen at the top of the page. A letter P hit an S and ricocheted to the top with enough force to knock the HOME image in the menu askew. Velocity infected other letters and they continued to collide. Eventually all images were knocked off the menu by the barrage and sank to the bottom of the screen, resting against one another like driftwood, the FAQ almost vertical, propped between the CONTACT and the FOOTNOTES.

The screen in total chaos, the movement slowed until letters swam dreamily, as if through maple syrup. Ts and Ps and Rs and vowels floated together in a horizontal string in the middle of the page: a placement impossible to ignore, too deliberate not to read.

"Trippety Trap Trippety Trap Trippety Trap" said the letters.

Those weren't real words. But that was good; at least the computer wasn't trying to talk to her, which would mean she was insane. These nonsense words suggested it was a glitch, the likes of which she had never seen before, but a glitch nonetheless. She prepared to fetch a librarian – her shoulders curled up and back, her spine lengthened, her head began to turn. Just as her eyes were about to lose contact with the computer the font incremented to four times its size and turned to capitals.

"TRIPPETY TRAP TRIPPETY TRAP TRIPPETY TRIPPETY

TRIPPETY TRAP!"

A cursor throbbed below the all-caps *trippety traps*. It begged for her to write a response. But that was madness.

Marika tore her eyes away and turned toward the front desk. A svelte young librarian with a long brown ponytail met her eye. The lady arched an eyebrow, left the desk and disappeared into the stacks.

She turned back. The *trippety traps* doubled in size; the font turned red. The cursor beckoned.

"Who's that tripping over my bridge?" she typed.

+

Thanksgiving traditionally meant being subjected to extended family but this year her mother and Bobby were going to her stepfather's family home – in Timmins. Marika had essays, she had studying, she needed all the money she could make at the store, mid-terms were coming up – there was no way she was going to Timmins.

Bobby was devastated. "Your school is more important than your own family, huh?"

"Aren't you a little young to play the guilt card? Mom, did you teach him this?"

"I don't do guilt, dear."

This was true. Marika wondered what kind of a father George was for Bobby. Though she had to admit to herself that he was a better father than her own simply because he was there. He didn't say much. He didn't have much personality. But at least he was there. Most of the time.

+

The brides were in a tizzy. Marika's thread had provoked an outpouring of mother-in-law-oriented loathing. One woman had posted:

> you sound just like my bitch mother in law to-be, shes running
> my life and ruining it too.

Another related how her fiancé's mother had orchestrated for her son to end up drunk and alone with his ex – the ideal woman, the one he should marry instead. There were religious differences, differences of taste, of scope; any problem a bride-to-be and a mother-in-law could have were all vividly described. It was entertaining and saddening.

On the music message board she was met with a surprise – a notification she had received a private message. Her heartbeat quickened when she saw it was from Craniac.

> I have noticed you on the board. And I have noticed you no-
> ticing me. It feels nice to be mutually noticed. I hope sending
> you this does not provoke you to attack me, as you do all the
> others.

How cryptic. But of course. It was Craniac.

After much deliberation she typed:

> Thank you for noticing me and for noticing that I noticed you.
> I agree, it feels nice to be mutually noticed. Of course, people
> do notice me when I attack them, as you mention, but that is
> only amusing if they are able to be insulted. I do not feel you
> are susceptible to such provocation. That is an admirable qual-
> ity and I admire you for it. I am tempted to ask more about you
> personally but I respect you too much to do so.

The last lines were sheer flirtation. Anonymity makes one brave.

+

At the library she turned away from the computers. Last time she was here she had done no studying. She barely remembered what had happened. The computer had spoken to her. It had told her things she did not want to know. If it was sentient it was also insane. That much she knew. The only computer she could trust was her own pretty pink laptop.

She dove into her books and swam through a comparative literature analysis when a cough made her look up. Just a cough, but it sounded directed at her. Perhaps the incident with the potentially sentient computer had made her paranoid.

The cough had come from the curly haired boy she had noticed before. He winked. She ducked back down to her book.

Was he flirting? Why? They had never spoken. Marika looked up again. He raised an eyebrow, just slightly, and then returned to his studies. But she could still feel his attention. He was aware of her presence.

Her body began to imperceptibly vibrate. It had been a long time since someone had taken an obvious interest in her. The air of the library, usually so stuffy, was filled with sexual tension.

She couldn't study. This was distracting.

She gathered her books. To leave she had to pass the bank of computers. A screen flashed on and off, on and off, too quickly to make out whatever was on the screens. Marika suspected it was TRIPPETY TRAP TRIPPETY TRAP.

+

The pub down the street served a traditional Thanksgiving meal – turkey, dressing, mashed potatoes, gravy, roasted vegetables – perfect for Marika's first family-oriented holiday without her family. But she would not lack for conversation or company. The pub had wifi so she had brought her laptop. The entire Internet was there to entertain her.

She navigated to the wedding site first but nothing there captured her sense of insouciance. She admitted to herself: she wanted to see if Craniac had messaged back. She had held off on purpose, trying to tease herself, but she couldn't focus on anything else. She logged in to the music board.

A message! Yes, a response from Craniac:

> I admire your admiration and respect your respect. I wish I
> had something interesting to tell you but I am but a shadow of
> yourself.

That was it. Marika searched Craniac's posts but there was nothing new. She returned to her routine of skimming threads looking for anything that left a person open to attack on the grounds of stupidity, immaturity, immorality, superficiality; anything that could wound. As she ate her turkey with all the fixings, alone in a pub on Thanksgiving, her vitriol was strong and she left many provocative posts before going home to bed.

+

The long weekend long over, the torpor of overeating worn off, the student body had awakened to the fact the semester was heading toward a close and exams were on their way. The library was packed with students, one of them the boy with the curly hair.

No table was entirely vacant, but many had available chairs. An empty chair sat directly across from the curly-head. Why not sit there?

He glanced up as she sat and they shared a smile of recognition before she opened her books and he turned back to his. Marika was struck by a sudden anxiety – if he was really interested in her would he not have done more than smile? Said hello, made a brief casual conversation?

What did it matter? If he was uninterested she was no worse off than before. Perhaps he didn't want to disturb the others at the table. Regardless, she had important studying to do.

Then his leg brushed hers underneath the table. She started, but he smiled and apologized. His voice was smooth. She said "No worries" with what she hoped was her most seductive voice but kept her eyes lowered, deep in a post-structural analysis of Disraeli.

She didn't notice when the other students left the table. Then boy with the curly hair spoke. "It's getting late."

Marika looked up and met his eyes, which was a mistake. She got lost in them as quickly and strongly as she had ever been lost in any book.

"We only have a half hour left…" he said. She continued to gaze at him. A half hour until they had to part ways? A half hour until the end of the world? Twisted locks of hair rose on either side of his head above those deep dark eyes. A little goatee accentuated his full lips. Marika could not find any words.

"…'Til the library closes."

"I'm almost done anyway."

"Me too." He cocked his head. "I'll walk you out."

As they gathered their books, she made small talk, pleased by the casual cleverness she could muster. They walked up to the counter to check out books they needed to take home. The svelte librarian gave Marika a penetrating stare. Later, alone at home, she slid the card out of the back of the book. Instead of a date stamp it said in bold red ink "Beware."

+

That night at her computer, she had a fire in her belly. But not for making fun of anonymous strangers. It was heavier than that. It was sexual.

The boy's name was William. They had talked about their respective classes all the way to the corner. When they turned in different directions he said that he'd see her at the library again and they should share a table. It was promising, but too innocent to cause the wealth of lust she felt. Still, she felt it. And now, with William away wherever he lived and her laptop in front of her, the lust centred instead upon the mysterious Craniac.

She would never find out more if she didn't engage her (or him). Craniac had shared no personal information – Marika would just have to be the one to start sharing.

She typed a response to Craniac's last private message:

> If you're my shadow I walk over you all the time – I am sorry for that. If you'd like to come out from under my feet I'll give you a hand up. I'll give you both of my hands, both of my feet, and whatever lies between them. And, just so you're aware, what lies between my extremities is equipped with girl parts, unlike the idea of many board members.

She hit Send, then pulled out a vibrator that hadn't been used in a very long time.

+

Bobby had loved Timmins. Lots of wide open spaces to play with his cousins. Cuzzie Suzie had climbed up a tree really high where the branches were too thin to support her and she fell but Cuz Brad had caught her with one arm. Marika complimented Brad's quick reflexes. She couldn't bring herself to be too enthusiastic though. Suzie was a spoiled brat.

"Tell me the billy goats! I haven't heard the billy goats in so long I think I've forgot it!"

"Once upon a time there were three billy goats who were all brothers and they lived on an island. The island was connected to neighbouring towns and islands and cities and meadows by a series of tubes. Unfortunately for the billy goats, an evil troll lurked under the tubes near their island, just waiting to hear them trip trapping along. And when he did hear them – he attacked!"

"Oh no!" exclaimed Billy, right on cue.

Before long Bobby's eyes drooped and his breathing slowed. She tucked him in. As she rose from the bed, he murmured "I would try to make friends with the troll." She kissed his forehead and turned off the light.

+

For a few weeks Marika and William studied together, making a habit of stepping into the small cafe in the foyer for a respite from the books. She sat at a table; William brought her an apple juice.

"Why anthropology?" she asked him.

"I like seeing how far human civilization has come. It gives me hope. There's so much wild fear in the world about how society is going to hell in a hand-basket, but that's all hysterical ridiculousness when put in an anthropological context."

"Good to know." she said. "I always thought a hand-basket sounded like an uncomfortable mode of travel."

"What about you? What about antiquated literature gets you so hot and bothered?"

"It's similar. I experience old cultures by reading about them and most of the time it makes me feel positive about the culture I live in. The major concerns are the same – the big questions have been asked in different ways throughout the history of human thought, of art. Love, death, those kinds of things."

"Interesting that the two 'big things' you think of are love and death."

"People kill for love, die for love. The French phrase *la petite mort* means 'the little death' and refers to orgasm."

"An orgasm isn't quite the same as love." William laughed.

"No, but you can't deny the connection."

"So you're saying that the only worthwhile orgasm is one you have with someone you love?"

Marika was silent for a second. "I don't think I'm qualified to answer that."

+

Confessions were dangerous business. Craniac had written back:

> I am happy to let you walk all over me. You do disdain so well you could be paid for it. All you'd need is a black leather corset in which to contain your girl parts. I hear it can be a very lucrative enterprise.

Marika composed a response, erased it, composed another, erased it, then sat for a while.

It occurred to her to just forget this cyber crush. It was going somewhere with William; this online fantasy could go nowhere. But it was harmless. She wasn't cheating on William by messaging with someone whose name – whose gender – she didn't even know. She shook Craniac out of her head and went to the main page of the forum. To her shock the first thread was about her. It was titled:

"Now we know what's up with Mysteryus – she has sand in her vagina."

It was posted by another troll. Not Craniac. But Craniac was the only one who knew that Mysteryus was a girl. If it wasn't the same person then they had to be in cahoots.

But she had no proof. And even if she did – what could she do?

+

Her mother had not listened to her protestations that exams were on the way and she needed all her time to study. "But then we won't see you until Christmas!" she said. "You can study on the train, just come for dinner." So Marika went for dinner.

Her stepfather arrived home while they ate dessert. Her mother brought a plate of leftovers with a grim look on her face. Marika wondered if she'd ever grow the balls to ask either of them what was going on.

Bobby had changed. He no longer pestered her about moving home or spending more time there. He had decided that he would move to Timmins and marry Suzie. While George watched TV and her mother did the dishes, Marika tried to explain that it wasn't appropriate to marry one's cousin, but she couldn't keep up the conversation – incest was just too complicated and disturbing. He was young; he would grow out of it.

When she asked if he wanted the billy goat story that night he said no. He wanted a love story. A Disney story. The Little Mermaid or Aladdin. She told him the tale of the Little Mermaid, the original version where the mermaid turns to sea foam at the end. She expected him to complain but he was sleepy. He just sniffled a bit. "That's sad."

+

She met William in the library cafe; he bought her another apple juice. When they were done their drinks they went in. The same librarian glared as they walked past. The computer screens all flashed red. Marika considered that she might not be getting enough sleep.

She focused upon a history of the romantic relationship between, and resulting work of, Elizabeth and Robert Browning. The text was very dry, but the more she read the more it strayed from traditional academic work. At a certain point she realized she was reading a very graphic sex scene between the two writers: Elizabeth screamed her pleasure between rattling coughs as Robert mounted her from behind. Marika shook her head. This could not possibly be on the exam.

She looked up. William's eyes burned at her. He hadn't turned a page since they sat down. The tufts of curls on either side of his head looked alarmingly like horns. She stood, frightened.

"What's wrong?" William asked. At the sound of his voice Marika began to run. She ran to the counter and leaned over, almost into the cleavage of the librarian. Marika stared into her stern but lovely eyes behind their thick glasses.

"Help."

The librarian leaned in and whispered in her ear. "What did the computer tell you?"

Marika backed away. What had the computer told her? It told her tubes can be broken and what is inside will fall out, be it billy goats or trolls or something more obscene.

She wrote a tirade about the sand in her vagina. She wrote that the Internet was for fun and games and obviously this board's members were no fun and couldn't play by the rules. She wrote about the worst of human nature taking form, one pixel at a time. She used foul language interspersed with eloquence. She exhausted her repertoire of rhetoric.

+

The last day to study before exams and Marika was afraid to enter the library, to see that bank of computers, that librarian. She drank the apple juice William brought her slowly. She listened to him talk though she had no idea what any word he uttered had to do with any other.

He touched her hand and all of a sudden she was aware. And he was as well, of the panic buzzing in her frontal lobe. "It's okay," he said, "It's a stressful time for all of us. It's okay, relax, it'll all be okay."

But it was not okay, not at all. As they entered the library the light began to fade. The further they stepped in, the darker her vision got, until she could barely see the tables in relation to the computers. Inch by inch everything disappeared. Then it was completely black.

Then she came to consciousness. She tried to move but her limbs did not respond. She decided to focus on her eyes. With great effort she lifted her lids. She saw books. Rows and rows of books along shelves filled her sight. She was in the stacks.

She tried to move again. Someone was on top of her. She rolled her head. And saw William. He grinned. She realized he was on top of her and inside her. She tried to speak. It came out as a moan.

"I knew you'd like it," said William. "That's why I waited for the drug to wear off before I finished." He gave a great push and a grunt and then collapsed, his head burying itself into her neck.

"Why…"

He turned his head so his mouth was directly in her ear. "I just wanted to get the sand out of your vagina."

This propelled her upward. He fell off her and lay laughing on the floor. She kicked him but lost her balance, still so woozy. She steadied herself against a shelf.

"Oh you just need to get laid, same as anyone else. You're not so mysterious, Mysteryus."

She fled, stumbling, from the stacks. The study area was dark and empty. She paused at the computer that had terrorized her, trying to remember exactly what it had told her.

✦

After the police station she went home and showered for hours. Then she opened her little pink laptop. She messaged Craniac:

> The cops are coming for you, William, if that is your real name.

She opened a bottle of wine. She went to the "Mysteryus has sand in her vagina" thread. A string of posts condemned her, bemoaning her meanness, postulating that she was ugly and never got dates, constantly had her period, that her cunt was sewn closed. Every post surmised that she didn't have enough sex.

She downed a glass of wine and posted:

> Rape is not the answer.

A new private message notification popped up. Craniac had messaged back:

> Marika, it's not William. You know me as a librarian but that was a disguise, just one avatar of many. I have been searching for the entity you call William for quite some time. I wasn't sure before but now I have seen what you posted and I know he is what I suspected. I will take care of him. You must take care of yourself. You and I will never speak again. William will never speak again at all when I am through with him.

Bobby was sad that Marika no longer told him bedtime stories. But he was very happy with the netbook she got him for Christmas.

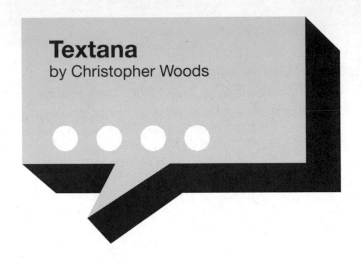

Textana
by Christopher Woods

(two women sit at empty desks, texting)

(they both think they hear someone approach, hide their phones, try to appear busy working. The moment passes. they bring out their phones, begin texting again)

1. I'm taking off Friday.

(2. doesn't answer, continues texting)

1. I am. For sure. Friday.

(2. laughs at a text)

1. Got to.

(2. laughs again, a little too long)

1. Can you cover for me?

(2. laughs some more. texts again)

1. I'm going crazy over here.

(she reads a text, looks fearful)

2. You need to lose that bastard.

1. Can't.

2. He's going to kill you. You know that, don't you?

1. He loves me.

2. Sure he does. *(reads text, laughs again)*

1. He does.

2. That's why he beats you.

1. I... need discipline.

2. You need to lose him. Simple.

1. He wants to take me to the zoo. On Friday.

(2. texts again)

1. Maybe rent a boat.

(2. still texting)

1. All normal. Again. You know?

(2. still texting)

1. Can you cover for me? Friday?

(2. still texting)

1. Dust my desk for me?

2. (still texting) Again?

1. Papers might come.

2. *(still texting)* We haven't had papers in a month. Maybe two.

1. Cover for me on Friday. I'll make it up to you.

2. Sure you will.

1. Promise. I'll buy lunch for you all next week.

2. *(still texting)* I won't be here.

Friend. Follow. Text.

1. What do you mean?

2. I won't.

1. You mean, you're quitting?

2. *(stops texting)* Something like that.

1. *(reads a text)* He really loves me. *(texts back)*

2. Sure he does.

1. Where are you going?

2. *(texts again)* Almost finished.

(1. looks at her phone. no new text. disappointment)

2. He's seeing someone else.

1. How do you know?

2. It's obvious. You're at work. He has time on his hands.

1. He's faithful to me.

2. *(finishes texting)* Oh yeah.

1. He is. He's going to marry me.

2. *(takes a deep breath)* It's done.

1. What's done?

2. My note. My suicide note. I'm outta here.

(she produces a gun)

2. Do you want me to put you out of your misery first?

1. What are you saying?

2. I'm serious. Want to go with me?

1. You can't go. You're my maid of honor.

2. We can go together.

1. I'm getting some help. *(starts to text)*

2. Too late for that.

1. You can't leave me... here.

2. Don't you get it? There's no here.

1. Oh, I know that. But it's a job. Isn't it?

2. We polish our desks three, maybe five times a day.

1. So?

2. Pretend we're busy. Doing something.

1. So what?

2. That's all.

1. Yes, but it's a job. Isn't it? What else would we be doing?

2. Living, that's what. You are getting married to a mean bastard. If you weren't here eight hours a day, he would have already killed you.

1. No, he wouldn't.

2. He will. Wait and see. Go to the zoo. Rent a boat. He'll
drown you.

1. *(starts to cry)* No. No.

2. Don't start crying. Face facts.

1. I can't.

2. Go with me, now. You don't need to drown. Go with me.
Please?

(1. looks for a text, but there's nothing)

2. *(cont.)* I was even thinking you were the lucky one. Having a boyfriend, even a mean one.

(slight pause) Here's the really shitty thing. I don't have anyone to send it to. My suicide note.

Can you believe it? That's very, very sad. You know?

1. That's not true.

2. It is. So I sent it to myself. I text myself all the time. Back and forth. For months now. I've had it.

1. You can text me.

2. Thanks. Too late for that. But there was a time…

(2. puts the gun to her head)

1. Don't!

2. I'm not even giving notice. That'll show them. Show them all. Even if we've never met them.

1. Stop it!

(1. rushes over to 2., tries to get the gun. a struggle. the gun goes off. 1. falls to the floor. dead)

2. I'm so sorry. But it's better this way. Believe me. That bastard would have taken his time with you. Made you suffer. This way it's quick. Peaceful. In a way, you're lucky. You know? If you had listened, you'd know I loved you. Ever since I saw you. But you never noticed, did you? No, you didn't. *(beat)* You broke my heart. *(shakes her head)*

(a lengthy pause)

(2. moves to the other desk, sits.)

2. I always liked this desk best.

(she dusts the desk a bit with her hand, mostly for show)

2. Much better. I can see them if they come.

(takes out her phone, begins texting)

(she laughs, a little too long)

BLACKOUT

Status Update
by Sarah Yi-Mei Tsiang

Ada Mullett is standing at a podium waiting 2 more minutes before starting her stats class

59 minutes ago · Comment · Like

Welcome.

Let's talk about statistics. Statistics are more than just numbers. In the social sciences they allow us to see what's going on in the world. Say, 1 in 4 women will be sexually assaulted in their lifetimes. But what does that mean? Does that mean that someone in this class will definitely be sexually assaulted? No. It all has to do with probabilities.

For instance, what if the woman is disabled? Then she has a 83%[1] probability of being sexually assaulted in her lifetime.

What if the woman comes from a lower socioeconomic background? What if she is native? Then we're talking a 24%[2] probability within these past five years. What if the woman, as a girl, witnessed her mother, broken-winged, on the tiles, trying to mop up her own blood? What if she's spent time in a shelter? What if she's been on the street because the shelter is full and she followed this guy to a new town and there are no couches she could sleep on? What if she has a baby, who cries, a dark wet mouth of hunger? What if she is afraid?

Status Update

What if the woman, her body howling for another fix, her feet numb on the sidewalk, sees the car slow down? What if she charges twenty instead of ten? What if she looks inside, sees the carseat drowning in crumbs, the carcasses of juice boxes? She'll likely be in the 68%[3] percent of sex workers who are raped on the job.

What if she's in university? We know that 80% of female undergraduates, most of you, have been victims of violence.[4] But what if he is sweet? What if he walks her to her dorm room, and he kisses her, lightly at first. What if she changes her mind? What if she is drunk? What if he had a bad day? What if his buddies told him he had a small dick and then laughed? What if the hall light sputters and her roommate is gone and that drink, the peach schnapps mix he handed her, makes her legs feel numb? What if she doesn't remember and so she doesn't fall into the 29%[5] who actually report their incidents of sexual assault?

What if she lives in Vancouver's Eastside? What if she never left Owen Sound? What if her mom told her that sometimes guys can't stop? What if her father loved her?

---

[1] http://sacha.ca/fact-sheets/statistics
[2] http://publications.gc.ca/collections/Collection-R/Statcan/85-002-XIE/
   85-002-XIE2006003.pdf
[3] http://womensissues.about.com/od/rapesexualassault/a/Wuornos.htm
[4] http://sacha.ca/fact-sheets/statistics

[5] http://sacha.ca/fact-sheets/statistics

Sue Fisher I burned it.

Yesterday at 8:30PM · Comment · Like

I burned bras, a bonfire of lace sparking in elegant whorls, fireworks of speech until all that was left were the clasps and underwire, a metal skeleton of breasts, a cage whose smoke whimpered words like *lift* and *support* and *push up* as though tits were children who need help up the slide and I burned books, the gleeful and sadistic voices of parenting experts curling and blackening like when I burned dinner watching my girl push away my nipple, head the colour of an egg, the colour of milk, the colour of the emptiness that was drying up inside my ducts, and I burned midnight oil with her, both of us smoking dreams, high with our eyes half open, the half life of scorched nights, her cries a scatter bomb, stuffed animals dispersed like casualties over a hand-knit rug, and I burned bridges, tossing a torch over my shoulder every time we crossed anything, her childhood always the far side of a river, my memory a crumbling bridge of ashes, and I burned witches in her closet, her fever glimmering like coals in my chest, I ripped apart the room as if I could find the monsters we both saw there, and

I burned.

Noelle Allen needs to read a whole lot of manuscripts, and unfortunately, write some rejection letters.

15 minutes ago · Comment · Like · Unlike ·

Dear Sarah,

While we read your manuscript with interest, it doesn't fit with our publishing mandate. Maybe if it had more tomatoes, ripening on the vine. Or if the protagonist had paused on page thirty-six and let the sky burnish her face into something as smooth and relatable as the moon.

Perhaps if your father had died a year earlier, or a year later, you would have written those passages with your heart clenched tight as a fist. You would have fully captured that hollow echo in your chest that still wakes you at night, ringing long and loose, your heart a clapper that can't forget the metallic moment of contact. That can't forget, but all you wrote was the echo, not the moment the bell tolled. We needed the bell to toll.

Status Update

There were parts of your writing that we found interesting. We enjoyed reading the poem about that time you fell into the bonfire, your father reaching into the flames, calmly. How when you came out, parts of his palm had melted into your own skin. When we meet you at a party years later we will try our best not to stare at the delicate, whorled scars burned into your upper arm. We will try not to remember you, or your book, as a wild scatter of ashes and flesh.

If you write another book, about something else, please consider sending to us.

Sincerely,
The Editors

Ian LeTourneau just filled out the census.

13 hours ago · Like · Unlike · Comment

1. How many persons usually live at this address? List their ages.

My wife, though she is behind a closed door. Behind the door she is weaving, or spinning, or stitching together stuffed birds. When she comes to bed her fingers bleed and small tufts of crane feathers follow her. A chill blows through the old wood frame, a slow seep. When the snow drifts pile against it, ice crystals bloom on the window. This is beginning to happen all year long, so I can't say if she's aged or not.

My daughter, though she also lives elsewhere. Every evening her shoes are worn through, and her clothes snag on air. I've seen her in a parking lot, a hundred years old and stick-thin. Weary. She drinks coffee and I find her hair in the sink, brittle and translucent. And sometimes she's five, but only at night, when I stand by her door and watch the soft cage of her chest rise and fall. A grate around the whispering embers of her heart, a banked fire.

There is a ghost, too. He is a creature of habit, he can't shake the idea that he should be living. But he can only remember how to be born and how to die. A thousand births and deaths every morning, but he's forgotten the in-between bit. The grass and baseball and love and even a good steak sandwich. And so he's very, very old, and too young to count.

Timmy ToeTag Sometimes it just feels soooooo good to tell the right person to "go F*CK themselves!" Try it out sometime!!

Like · 2 hours ago near Toronto, Ontario ·

After a while, he can't help himself. He whispers *fuck you* to the toast, that beige fucker that just lies there, passive aggressive in its thin housecoat of yellow margarine. *Fuck you* to the cloud puffs that imitate children's scrawled drawings, those lazy clichés in the crayola-blue sky. *Fuck you* to the elevator, whose "close door" button is worn with animosity. *Fuck you* to the nagging dent in the car door, to the grass that shrivels and wilts under August's unrelenting parental glare. *Fuck you* to the Internet's kittys and porn. *Fuck you* to the washing machine's solo hula dance, to the turtle's blunt and beautiful head. *Fuck you*, and the dog sings it with him, longing at the gate. And the seagulls toss it back and forth, red throats gleaming. *Fuck you* until it becomes as soft as a mantra, until is loosens into a hundred small prayers every day. *Fuck you*, and it is as tender as a newborn's head, as the act of love, as our first beginning.

People Who Are Michael

by Alex Leslie

This is the first video Michael uploads to his channel.

Michael stands in front of the Simpsons poster in his bedroom. You can see that the room is small. Flood of whitewashed palm as he reaches out to adjust the webcam. He steps back. His confidence balanced on one foot. He gives you one smile. *Hey YouTube this is Michael's channel you probably know this song already.* High soft-toned voice. Not yet broken. Small-boned for his age.

The bass begins. Woolly beats embedded in the computer. Behind the webcam's eye, drifting from your speakers. Michael nods seriously, agreeing to the rhythm. His first sung broadcast words: *I need you.*

Michael angles his face downward, hair sliding to shield his erratic eyelids that flicker, like snare rim-shots, like REM sleep cycles. He fiddles with his thin gold necklace. His fingers rest on the neckline of his grey T-shirt, then his palm floats over his chest, taps at his stomach.

When he gets to the chorus Michael looks into the camera for the first time.

Into your eye and something in his throat has opened. The notes slip an octave, effortless, in time, a glide that stuns.

Oh I gotta have you. Voice tripping high, startled by the key change.

Michael's head slides to the side, his eyes switch from the lens to someone else behind the camera, his mother or an audience in the music video he imagines. Shades of grey and gold in his dark eyes, he is eyeing the ceiling, lungs swelled, a fist throwing false punches mid-air where he imagines drums. When he hunches his shoulders are unbelievably narrow. A swimmer's pounce to the last verse.

You look closely at the beige wall behind him, the brown couch the size and height of a bench, the anonymous carpet.

The oversized softness of his ears under scattered hair inked with sweat. *I need you I need you I need you-you-you. Ooooooh-oh.*

Winner's slouch offscreen, a close-up of his smile. Satisfaction. He presses the necessary button to vanish.

+

White and red palm over an iPhone's spider eye. The fan holding the iPhone breathing. *It's him it's him oh my god.*

Michael in dark glinting jeans and a turquoise hoodie. Walking swiftly, head down, a security guard for each part of his stride. Then he's pulled through the rear door of a black van. The blur of him. You see how he holds his hand over the side of his face and the way his back curves as he slides into the seat. The screams that chase him into the van.

Fluorescent sky, freewheeling. Somewhere in summer, a bleached screen's false heatwave, in the middle of his second European tour, you squint to make out flesh and metal as the iPhone is dropped.

Clattering at the hard edges of the picture. *Michael I love you.*

The security guard's face, relaxed smile-lines. *He's gone girls.* Then the smash against pavement. The security guard's boot. The percussive hysteria of the girls. Fuck you man. The van speeding away. An engine is buried in the screaming of the girls. Screen in motion, the antlered light.

The last frame of the video is a close-up of the security guard's cheek. The screen moves like one muscle.

Michael will you marry me shouted to an electric field of cascading static, to the overexposed sky.

+

The video is shot from a distance. The image foggy, possibly filmed through a window. Michael sits in an airport lounge. He's in normal clothes, not the kind he wears in photos. Flip-flops show his pale feet; grey sweatpants; a black T-shirt; a jean jacket. Michael at thirteen or fourteen. A plainclothes security guard sits beside him. You can tell he's a guard from the neutral fixedness of his stare, his mirrored sunglasses, the set of his shoulders. Michael crosses his ankles, chews slowly, eyes blank. He yawns, cups a hand over his mouth, continues chewing. No luggage sits around them and no other travellers are visible. FLY HORIZON is printed in red letters across the wall behind Michael. The image zooms in closer to Michael, drifts over his shoulder. Two more security guards stand against the wall, to the right of HORIZON. Michael takes his phone out of his pocket and begins to finger the keypad. The image holds steady. An inspection, a cold recording, not a fan video – those always jerk and sway with excitement. Michael sits still, focused on his phone. Playing a game? Texting a friend? His face blank. Then, slowly, his eyes move from the phone's screen. He is looking directly at the camera, directly at you. He's found you. No, you realize, he's known the whole time. You expect the autopilot bright-light smile but there is none. His stare is level and static. You want to stop watching but you can't. Looking at you, Michael stops chewing. He takes his gum from his mouth and says a word. The security guard sitting beside him puts out his hand. Michael puts the gum in the guard's hand who then walks off the screen, returns. Michael continues to look at you. *Stop it*, Michael mouths. The video continues for thirteen minutes. *Stop it,* he mouths again. Michael does not look away from you.

A morning show interview someone has uploaded: a video of the TV screen. The hazy darkness of someone's living room around the image. Kitchen sounds from offscreen. First a cartoon of a sunny-side egg and the host's face floating in the yolk. *Hi Philadelphia*. The jingle.

Then Michael in white jeans, a heavy silver belt-buckle pushed to the right of centre, a form fitting sweater unzipped over a v-neck shirt, his hair molded to his narrow head. The interviewer in a pencil skirt, sitting at thirty-degree angles to Michael and the camera. Michael in a fashionable classroom slouch. He straightens up.

So you were discovered on your YouTube channel. Did you expect this kind of success?

Uh yeah, no, on YouTube, no, this has been really crazy, you know, coming from a small town in Canada, I'm just really glad, just really honoured by all the fans and, the attention, you know.

It's an amazing story.

Yeah the producer found my videos cuz I sang a cover of one of his singer's songs and flew us down to LA.

Michael smiles through the questions. Teeth bared, eyes ready. Doe-eyed, the columnists call him; deer in the headlights, sometimes. Michael blinks. His blink is his trademark now, has been the subject of essays in national newspapers and fold-out posters in all the teen heartthrob glossies. From his first YouTube videos, that shimmer, part hesitation, part flash, they write.

The host is a woman a decade younger than his mother and Michael fits his smiles to her questions until she is motherly, encouraging, suggests words to fill out his choppy answers. *So it's been a year since you posted those first videos, how does it feel to not be able to walk down the street without being recognized?*

Michael looks at you, holds up a hand, flips a peace sign, lets his hand crumple like a leaf in a small sudden fire. *I owe it all to my fans.*

How have you dealt with all the attention? Michael talks about his crew that is his new family, his mother who always travels with him, the R&B artist who signed him and is like a *father, I mean like a mentor to me, he's just always reminding me to stay humble. And my swagger coach, that helps too.*

The host laughs. *Swagger coach?*

Michael laughs. You look closer, see his embarrassment start.

Yeah, you know, he, you know, shows me how to be smooth and stuff.

You mean a stylist.

Yeah yeah, a stylist.

Michael slides down the leather studio couch, crosses his hi-tops – silver and plum to match his sweater. He observes the camera angle travelling, twists his knees to reciprocate and to show you his new shoes, the patterns on their sides like lacquered feathers. *It's cool, it's all good, just appreciating, just appreciating.*

The interviewer smiles and Michael smiles. He is perfect in that picturelock moment, and she is another adult in front of whom he has melted and slipped by.

So tell me about starting your YouTube channel.

A shot of a girl in the audience, wearing sunglasses. The right lens reads MICH in white-out. The left lens reads AEL.

Well singing was just something I always did, brushing my teeth, in church, at family picnics and stuff you know and in my bedroom and I started my YouTube channel just for fun, you know, just something to do, most of my friends did like weblog stuff like talking about movies and their classes so I thought I'd just sing.

Teeth. Timing.

He blinks. Not a blink to mask the water-surface of eyes, you notice, but a long blink. Staged short-circuiting of his famous eyes. Michael believes that he is sending messages with his eyes. You are watching Michael's eyes, all of these videos, for messages.

Please come by again Michael, good luck with the tour. Thank you.

No thank you, thank you.

Michael's new single fades in. Heavy bass and his autotuned voice singing an arpeggio over the liquid guitars.

As the music cranks up, the camera pans the studio audience, rows of silent watching girls who now, released, finally, can begin to scream.

+

The choppy thrash of a minicam's mic battling wind. You squint at the bleached picture until the light separates into forms and Michael becomes clear. A cricket Michael, legs reaching bent from a tall stool, the guitar gigantic in his arms, the outdoor stage showing its metal braces. *Um, this is a song by Sarah McLachlan, yeah, um, here it is.* Aluminum sky. Bleachers scattered with people picnicking.

The comment below the video: *Michael before he was famous... sorry about the video quality... you can hear his voice pretty great though... ignore my kids screaming in the background they wanted hot dogs as you can probably tell* LOL.

The wind rises and drops sheets of static.

Michael's arms cradle and struggle against the guitar. His head bent. He studies his fingers on the strings, preparing for the combination of sounds he will make. His huge white sneakers dangle like sunspots on the fuzzy image.

A backward baseball cap too big for his head – blown off by the wind, sent tumbling across the stage. Michael watches its panicked dance.

The minicam's long shaky zoom, the squarish pixels of Michael's pink cheeks, an abstract mosaic. The audio persists purely. White-blond hair. Michael at ten, eleven? His voice slices the distortion of the picture. The guitar dwarfs him, a hollow pine-bright buoy he is grasping.

He repeats the intro, begins the song on an off-beat, recovers. His voice staggers through the first verse.

He starts the chorus, then startles at the cry that splits the soft grey air an inch from the minicam's mic: *Moooooooom hot dooog hot dog hot dog.*

The image zooms out.

You catch a glimpse of the heavy plastic watch on his wrist, the kind a kid could win from an arcade machine at a movie theatre. You are looking at the watch because Michael is watching it carefully. He is using the watch to keep time. *Mom mom mom hot dog.*

The picture plunges. A child's eye. Accusing you. Four black finger-stripes across the screen. You are pulled downward, against the words blasted by her huge lips. Michael's voice now just an electric background whisper. *Mom. Hot dog. Now.*

✚

A slideshow of photos of Michael compiled by his mother after his disappearance. Uploaded to his music label's YouTube channel – then it goes viral across all the fan channels.

The line of text running along the bottom of the photos: *Michael if you are watching this I love you. REWARD REWARD REWARD.* Each photo stays on the screen for ten seconds. Things that could be used to identify Michael. Things to identify the most YouTubed person in the world, you think.

The birthmark on the right side of his neck.

The joint of his right pinky, which is crooked.

The small-print tattoo he got on his sixteenth birthday, just over a year ago, on the inside of his right arm, his microphone arm: Perfect Pitch Is A Curse.

Three conjoined photos of him in each of his three favourite hoodies.

A close-up of the silver bracelet he always wears on his left wrist.

+

Michael wet, slipping out of the Australian ocean, the flash of cameras from the beach, the hot flash of the sand, the studio beauty of his after-swim smile, a girl shouting *Oh my god he isn't wearing a shirt!* He steps forward, leg bent flexibly out, so they can catch him in mid-stride. The cameralight shines off the salt on his skin. The light is a shining hood he sheds. This video is thirteen seconds long.

+

The radiant screens of phones held up, recording, a frantic starchart. A stadium venue. This phone recording the shaky, blaring video is one of hundreds. The noise billowing off the crowd. The phone cracked open by the speaker system and thousands of screamers. Struggling to stay on that one moving spot on the stage – Michael in white.

+

Michael's shape burned white in the darkness, streaming rays of motion, Michael leaping onto an amp, leaping off and landing mid-run, the chorus chasing him up the runway built over the audience. Footwork, weavebacks on downbeats. *Oooh you are all I want and want and want.* Darkness.

The image pans the stadium for a moment. A rippling silvery valley lined with bodies. A roar pierced by *I love you Michael* and the siren-cry *Marry me.* How can he sing to each of them.

Small lights.

Everyone holds their phone up like a candle.

The picture skims shoulders and heads back to the stage.

She. Michael's arm reaching down from the stage. One fan, chosen, pulled out of the sea.

You turn the volume down on your computer, the scream is so sheer, so total. One scream.

She – barely standing, holding her head. Michael cradles her elbow in overstated public tenderness, circles her, half a moon-walk and back around her, popping up behind one shoulder, a cute trick from a home video, the microphone held in front of her mouth and she brays the lyrics she has known for months. *You and me for-evah and evah girl.* Her hands up over her mouth and eyes. Michael leads her across the stage and she vanishes – a larger shape, a security guard, is waiting to escort her to an exit.

Michael sprints back to the centre of the stage, arms spread-eagled, head down, and everyone has forgotten the girl by the time he reaches the centre. They want to forget her so he will sing to them, to you, again.

The song ends. The silence is loudest. The thumping space hollowed out by the speakers. Michael raises his arms, gives you two peace signs. The one scream again.

The screen above the stage that shows the close-up of Michael shows his blink, his smile. He crosses his arms and poses at an angle, a child's *Come on impress me* pose. His six-teen year-old face dominates the arena. The one scream – the roof is made of sound and it is breaking.

Michael kneels and unlaces his left shoe. He balls the lace up in his hand and throws it. Radiant string.

The first watcher speeds through the loose line of security. Then ten girls, then thirty. Over the lip of the stage. The screen shows Michael's arms fall, then his hands go up flat, No Stop. His speaking voice, once in the mic: *No don't please.* The hard sound of the live mic hitting the stage when he drops it. Turns to run. As security emerges from the wings, Michael is tackled at the knees by a girl.

He folds.

The guards come up against the girls, pull them off Michael, toss them easily forward. The crowd roars, as if this is wrestling, a part of the show. The guards move forward, eight of them, in formation. Where is Michael? You look. A bright smudge on the stage, pressed to it. A spotlight, a bright hole.

The bass intro for the next song starts. Michael is a white ball of light carried offstage between three guards.

When the phone's eye sweeps back again, the crowd is silenced.

The phone is turned around and you see the person who has recorded this video for you: a boy, twelve or thirteen, wearing a white v-neck T-shirt and two silver wings on a chain. His short bleached hair. *If one of you assholes who rushed the stage watch this I want you know you ruined it for everybody.* The image wavers, his hand trembling. *We all love Michael and you ruined it for everybody.* His smooth lips pinch. His eyes contemptuous. *I love him and you ruined it.* Around him the stadium lights come up. A thunder of disappointment rises. *I love him.*

Michael Michael Michael Michael. The chanting shakes the air.

The video ends.

+

Is that neck or lightcurve. Slide of stomach or a blanket around a limb, a curtain pulling the lens past the shadow's shoulderline.

Breath.

Beginning of arm.

Your low resolution eye. The points of three white knuckles, or toes floating upward, two bodies going under like a burial at sea, slipping under a sheer surface. Polished surface or light-less surface, the two are the same. Breath, hard. A microphone cries. Michael chuckles. And under.

The back of his head, hair sways forward.

Where are you. No there. You can tell from the note in his voice that he does not know that this is being recorded. Strained, weakening. *Oh god.*

A female voice sings a line from Michael's first single, the one he recorded when he was thirteen, the first to hit No. 1. No, he moans. *I hate that fucking song.*

The lens molts shadow, gains ground on skin.

Background grid, high-up window, the faint silver of overcast sky, the roof of a metal world.

You glance at the number: 7,523,418 views since the video was uploaded a week ago.

The rim of the picture drifts. Eyeswitch of angle. *Oh. There.*

The camera drags, a finger at Michael's waist. Retaliation, quiet plunge of laughter, this is Michael's neck, white open shoulders. This is before a question or the placement of cold glass over his laid-bare chest. Because it is skin that lets.

Part of a forehead, a wide eye. The back of Michael's head bright, blocking the light meant for her chest. Her eye on yours.

+

The first video Michael uploads after his disappearance.

This video isn't for you, he says.

A plain room around him, in a hotel or not, a room that could be anywhere.

I just want my mom to know I'm ok.

He should look emaciated, starved. Kidnapped, as the headlines have said. A millionaire many times over, a few months older than seventeen. He blinks. Calm forehead, white-shirt. He leans forward. The video ends.

+

In this video Michael speaks to you directly. Today is the release date for his second album.

Michael's face fills most of the screen. Behind his shoulders, a white-and-contrast-cream hotel room, a stripe of industrial sky. Michael speaks quickly, his eyes on yours. *I just want to uh thank you guys for everything, this all happened because of you guys, I owe it all to my fans.*

You notice the bluish semi-circle below each of Michael's eyes. The fine net of light tethered to his skin. The near translucence of his eyelids and core-white of his teeth. The ticking silence of the hotel room.

Wow the millions of uh hits I just couldn't have imagined this could have ever, like, happened to me, just a regular guy you know. When I started this channel like just over two years ago. His voice has broken. His voice is deeper. Since recording the songs on this album, most of which have been leaked to YouTube, his voice has changed into another version of itself. He got two albums in before his voice broke.

Michael leans back for a moment. Nostrils and eyelids so smooth, android from this angle.

The click-hush of a door opening and closing. A link appears across Michael's chest: BUY MY ALBUM ON ITUNES NOW!!!!!! A shadow moves behind Michael. The door opens and closes again. You wonder: his mother? a routine security sweep? Silence again.

Michael blinks. *Anyway I just wanted to say thankyou thankyou thankyou guys you're all amazing.* He reaches forward. The screen goes black and fades to an ad for the album. You click on the iTunes link.

+

Michael standing in the glow of a large hotel bathroom. He looks into the mirror. *Hey MuchMusic this is my tour diary thanks for watching! This going to be so much fun!* He brushes his teeth and spits into the marble sink.

+

Wide cement steps leading to a theatre. Michael sits on the top step. The video is clear and steady. A day without wind. Blue light, evening. His guitar case is open on the sidewalk. He is singing. Snaps his shoulders side-to-side. His sneakers add dull-edged syncopation. A Coke can on the step below him. A gospel song.

He plays to the camera, without looking at it. The obliviousness and bravado of an experienced busker. The person holding the camera speaks to someone nearby, her voice rasping on the mic: *This child is my hero he's here like every day. You're my hero little genius child!*

Michael switches tempo into an R&B song. He sings: *Oh I gotta stop thinking about having my first chile.* Laughter. *Chile you planning on having a chile?* Michael tilts his face, mouth and eyes clenched with emotion: *ooooooh girl can't stop thinking of you.* He bears down on the downbeat.

A small audience gathers on the steps around Michael. A woman in her thirties sits next to him, arms looped around her knees. Her face blank at she watches him. She takes large bites from her hotdog. She chews slowly.

A shout from offscreen: *Kid hey how about some Joni Mitchell.*

No Jay-z. Jay-z kid.

Isn't it past your bedtime kid.

Michael sings a verse of Joni. He yells *Switch.* Then screams out Jay-z.

Oh kid's got game.

Laughter. Taunting, admiring.

Coins and bills fill his guitar case.

In profile, Michael's jaw works and flexes. Chewing the words.

The song-pulse prodding his neck from the inside.

He presses one finger into the centre of his audience. Belts a slowjam chorus over their heads. Coins thrown.

Light wind tosses Michael's hair across his eyes.

Switch, a man yells, *Hallelujah.*

The Rufus Wainwright version or the Leonard Cohen one, Michael says.

Throttle-sound of laughter flooding the mic.

You choose kid.

He sings Leonard Cohen's version. A hoot from the crowd. The crying of wheels. *Hallelujah*

Halle

lujaaaaaah.

It begins to rain softly and the crowd moves onto the steps, which are protected by an overhang offscreen. The camera now films Michael from the side. A man crosses his legs, lights a cigarette, sits with his head dangling. His head moves back and forth, a long shadow moving like a minute hand over Michael's sneakers. *How'd you get to be so old kid.* A seagull lands on the top step. Michael must be from a town near the ocean. You've never thought before about where Michael might be from. Dark now, Michael and his audience ghosts sketched in the night, touches of streetlight from beyond the edges of the steps. *Shit my battery's dying shit shit shit.* The image streaked with white regions that flow, the audio fluxing, Michael's final *hallelujah* an interrupted moan. The sound of a can opener turning, working. Chords turn their soft-sided wheels. The video cuts out as Michael begins the Rufus Wainwright version.

+

Michael stepping through the open sliding glass door of a hotel room onto a balcony. A blast of screams that the camera moves towards. A city square below, crowded with women, a black perimeter of cops, visors pulled up and glinting, riot gear, a reflective sunset of plastic shields. Someone speaks rapid German in the background – a reporter, you assume. Two security guards, one for each of Michael's eyes, feet, arms, knees, as he moves towards the edge of the balcony. His red-and-yellow checkered boots tie into the amber and cherry tones of his smoker's jacket, ironic and loose-fitting over a black v-neck shirt. Another guard is already standing at the balcony railing. Michael reaches out and takes the megaphone out of his hand. The guard looks surprised, then nods, moves quickly around Michael and into position with the two other guards and the small crowd that has emerged from the hotel room: Michael's mother, his manager, a few others you imagine are producers or assistants. They hang back as Michael paces the balcony railing, holding the megaphone. He puts a finger to his lips, looking down at the crowd, its shrieking. *Shhhhhhhhhhhh*. He moves the finger out and then softly replaces it to his lips.

The crowd stills.

Oh I need you, Michael sings. A capella for the first time in years. The first time you've seen since those first videos.

His voice blurts harshly through the megaphone. *Oh yeah. I need you girl.*

The crowd screams. Stills. The boundary of police take one step in as the crowd moves closer to the balcony. Michael doesn't move.

Marry me Michael.

He's fourteen or fifteen in this video. His shoulders have filled out a bit.

Come and get me, he speaks back – the megaphone thundering his voice.

One scream.

A security guard moves forward and stands at the railing, scans the crowd for snipers. He taps Michael's shoulder and Michael grins at him, shouts lyrics into the megaphone again. The security guard extends one hand and wraps his fingers around Michael's wrist. Michael begins to struggle – sudden, fish-like movements, a full-body snap from his stomach to his knees. His mother rushes forward and leads him back into the hotel. He goes. The guard who held him follows. Michael turns suddenly and blasts painfully into the guard's face: *Baby.* The guard staggers back, steps forward. Michael runs into the hotel, waving the megaphone like a small flag, laughing. Sprints into the building. Retaliation saved until he reaches open space.

The guard follows.

Then turns, holds a hand over the camera. The broad palm cancels all light as it draws closer, before covering everything.

+

Dim gold light of a recording booth. Michael in a white T-shirt and the thin gold necklace from his first uploads. Beyond the booth's window, the figures of men. Michael's head clenched between the oversized ears of his headphones. The bassline leaking out, his voice naked as he sings his lines over the playback into the mic. One of the men raises his hand. Michael nods. Brief silence and he begins nodding to the beat. *You and me,* he sings. The man raises his hand again and Michael stops. Silence, again, then the music starts and Michael starts. This is repeated twelve times. Michael continues the thirteenth time, his body inside the song's lockstep harmonies. *One more time,* a piped voice states. *A third higher. Yeah sure,* Michael says. This is recorded once, approved with a wave from beyond the glass. Syncopation in Michael's finger joints, played against his waist. *No I didn't get that at the end,* Michael says. *What Mike?* Michael shakes his head: *It wasn't right. Ok one more time then.* After this repetition Michael slides his headphones off, drops them, lets them dangle. *Perfect,* Michael says. His voice cracks. A jump in the middle of perfect. A break. Michael shakes his head violently. The men behind the glass laugh. *Per-fect,* the mimic. *Per-yeee-fect.* Michael turns and you see his face for the first time. Eyes nakedly red from the session's focus. He blinks, stunned, at you, surprised to find you here, too.

The last video Michael uploads after his disappearance. He has been gone for nine months.

His hands. The police confirm that those are in fact his hands. His hands opening and closing. Occasionally, breathing can be heard in the background.

You watch his hands. Where they would grasp the microphone.

His hands opening, closing. Because it is the last video, it is watched by everyone. Twenty-two million views, then more, more, the most viewed video on YouTube.

His hands open and close. You watch this video again, again. For the same reason that you watched every other video of Michael; because you love him.

The opening and closing of his hands, a steady rhythm, cupping and revealing something you cannot quite see, you think, looking closer.

Shadows in the creases at his knuckles, but that is all.

This video is eighteen minutes long.

Acknowledgments

Thanks to Maurice Mierau for believing in this project, and to Mel Marginet and everyone at Great Plains for their support. Special thanks to all of the contributors to the book.

Friend. Follow. Text. would not exist if not for conversations, via Facebook and e-mail, with Megan Stielstra and Brian Joseph Davis; thank you both. Thanks too to Kathleen Rooney and Abigail Beckel of Rose Metal Press for early support and encouragement. Thank you, Emily Schultz, for your support of my own first efforts to blend literary fiction with the conventions of social media.

Thanks to the publishers who have previously published earlier versions of some of the stories in this collection: Coach House Books, Cormorant Books, Exile Editions, Freehand Books, *juice,* Knopf Canada, *Metazen,* Oolichan Books, *Plenitude, This Magazine* and *Xenith.*

Thank you to my literary mentors, Kathryn Kuitenbrouwer and Marnie Woodrow. And to all my peeps who have nurtured me in literary efforts and life more generally, including Jeffrey Keith Briggs, Paul Schofield, Wes Doherty, Don Pyle, Jason Winkler and one of my earliest and most exacting editors, Claude Mercure.

For their support of my own writing in this book, I gratefully acknowledge funding by the Toronto Arts Council and Ontario Arts Council.

About the Contributors

Kate Baggott recently returned to Canada after a decade in Europe. Her work has ranged from technology journalism to creative non-fiction and from experimental fiction to chick lit. She is the author of the collection of short stories *Love from Planet Wine Cooler*. Using Facebook, while full of risks and problems, remains her primary way of staying in contact with friends and family accross oceans and continents.

Heather Birrell is the author of two short fiction collections, *Mad Hope* and *I know you are but what am I?* Birrell's writing has won the Journey Prize for short fiction, the Edna Staebler Award for creative non-fiction, and been shortlisted for the National and Western Magazine Awards. Her work has appeared in many North American journals and is forthcoming in the anthology *Truth, Dare, Doubledare: Stories of Motherhood*. A high school teacher and creative writing instructor, Birrell lives in Toronto with her husband and two daughters.

Sonal Champsee is a fiction writer from Toronto. Sonal is studying for an MFA in Creative Writing through the University of British Columbia's optional residency program. Sonal can be found on Facebook and Twitter, and blogs at sonalchampsee.com.

Trevor Corkum's fiction and non-fiction have been published widely across Canada, most recently in *The Malahat Review, Prairie Fire, Little Fiction* and *The Journey Prize Stories 24*. He's a graduate of UBC's optional-residency MFA program and is currently completing both his first manuscript of short fiction and a novel. "5'9, 135, 6 c, br bl" was originally published in *Plenitude*, was a finalist for the 2011 *Matrix* Litpop fiction contest and was adapted for stage reading by Workshop West Theatre in Edmonton as part of the Exposure Festival. You can find him online at trevorcorkum.com.

Judy Darley is a fiction writer and journalist who specializes in writing about travel, the arts and anything that catches her eye and fires her imagination. Judy's short stories, flash fiction and poems have been published by literary magazines and anthologies including *Fiction 365*, *Riptide* volume 7, *Litro Magazine*, *The View from Here* and *The Love of Looking*. Judy's debut short story collection, *Remember Me to the Bees*, is due out in 2013. Find out more at skylightrain.com or http://twitter.com/ EssentialWriter.

Dorianne Emmerton reviews plays in Toronto for *Mooney On Theatre*, and is a host on the University of Toronto's radio station (CIUT) Sex City show, as well writing strange little fictions. You can read her work online in a couple of places, all of which are linked to on her website at dorianneemmerton.com. She's in the ebook *Little Bird Stories Volume II*, a collection of stories that won the second annual Little Bird contest run by Sarah Selecky. She's in a couple of anthologies printed on paper too, like *Zhush Redux* and *TOK 6: Writing the New Toronto*. Dorianne gets excited about science, cheese, cats and summertime. She spends far too much time on Twitter as @headonist and has thus far managed to restrain herself from joining Reddit. She sometimes writes erotica and does so under her real name, hoping the world is sufficiently advanced enough not to hold that against her.

Steven Heighton's most recent books are the Trillium Award finalist *The Dead Are More Visible* (stories), *Workbook*, a collection of memos and fragmentary essays, and *Every Lost Country* (a novel). His 2005 novel, *Afterlands*, appeared in six countries, was a *New York Times Book Review* editors' choice, and was a best-of-year choice in ten publications in Canada, the US and the UK. His short fiction and poetry have received four gold and one silver National Magazine Awards and have appeared in *London Review of Books, Best English Stories, Best American Poetry, Zoetrope: All-Story, Tin House, Poetry, Brick, TLR, The Walrus* and five editions of *Best Canadian Stories.* Heighton has been nominated for the Governor General's Award and Britain's w.h. Smith Award, and he is a fiction reviewer for the *New York Times Book Review.*

Robert J. Holt is a freelance writer living in downtown Winnipeg. Deeply interested in the ways social media reshape our interactions with one another, Rob has written on the subject for newspapers, blogs, magazines and academic journals. He can often be found sitting in a pub, muttering to himself and scribbling on cocktail napkins. "Deletion" marks his first appearance in a literary anthology. A collection of his writings – from his awkward, lanky high-school years up to his less-awkward, still-lanky twenties – can be found at resultsshownnottypical. wordpress.com.

K. Tait Jarboe is a new media artist based out of Boston. Their other work can be found in the Lambda Award–winning anthology, *The Collection: Short Fiction from the Transgender Vanguard* (Topside Press, 2012), and on their website, toomany-feelings.com. Their current projects include a novel and a radio play.

Steve Karas lives in Chicago with his wife and daughter. His short stories have appeared in *Necessary Fiction, Bluestem, Little Fiction, Whiskeypaper* and elsewhere. He's not on Facebook, but feel free to visit him at steve-karas.com.

Greg Kearney is the author of the story collections *Mommy Daddy Baby* and *Pretty,* and the novel *The Desperates.* He lives in Toronto.

Alex Leslie has published a book of short stories, *People Who Disappear* (Freehand, 2012), shortlisted for a 2012 Lambda Award for LGBT debut fiction, and a chapbook of microfictions, *20 Objects For The New World* (Nomados, 2011). Her writing has won a Gold National Magazine Award for personal journalism and a CBC Literary Award for short fiction. She edited the Queer issue of *Poetry Is Dead* magazine. She is working on a second collection of stories. Website: alexleslie.wordpress.com.

Clayton Littlewood was born in Skegness, England, in 1963 and grew up in Weston-super-Mare. He writes the "Soho Stories" column for *The London Paper* and contributes regularly to BBC radio. His first book, *Dirty White Boy: Tales of Soho*, was published in 2008 and named the *Gay Times* book of the year. He turned the book into a play the following year. *Goodbye to Soho* (2012) is his follow-up. His website is at www.clayton littlewood.com.

Charles Lowe's writing has appeared or is forthcoming in *Guernica, Essays & Fictions,* the *Pacific Review, Midway* and elsewhere. His fiction has been nominated for the Pushcart Prize. He lives with his wife and daughter in Zhuhai, China, where he is an Associate Professor and the Director of the Contemporary English Language and Literature Program at United International College. He is at work on a series of interconnected stories entitled *Eating Out at Goubuli.* "Our Warm Peach" is from that collection.

A winner of the 9th Glass Woman Prize for Fiction (2011), **Beverly C. Lucey** moved back to western Massachusetts after dallying in the South for a decade. While in Georgia, she learned that "bless your heart" is not necessarily meant to comfort; while in Arkansas she learned that every politician must make an appearance at the January Gillett Coon Supper, where deep-fried raccoon is indeed on the menu. She has an extensive fiction presence online in e-zines

About the Contributors

(*Zoetrope, All Story Extra, LitPot, Feathered Flounder, Absinthe Review* and others), and her short fiction has been published in *Flint River Review, Moxie, Quality Women's Fiction* (UK), *Wild Strawberries* and, most recently, in *Twisted Tales*. Four of her stories are anthologized in *We Teach Them All* (Stenhouse).

Lisa Mrock is a writer from Chicago. She has had fiction and non-fiction pieces published in *The Toucan Literary Magazine*, the *Flash Fiction World Volume* 3 print anthology and *Chicago Literati*, and has had interviews published in *Chicago Innerview Magazine*. When she's not plotting for world domination, she is reading, writing, supporting her local literary and storytelling scene, and working toward a BA in Fiction Writing at Columbia College Chicago.

Sara Press is a recent graduate of the University of Guelph, where she studied English and French Literature. Born in Toronto, she is currently enjoying the nomadic life and finding new stories to write in her travels. This is her first publication.

Marcy Rogers is a Dora-nominated playwright who always wanted to write books. Her website is fairytalesforthedisenchanted.com.

Angelique Stevens teaches Writing and Literature of the Holocaust and Genocide at Monroe Community College in Rochester, NY. She is also an activist and her travels have taken her across the globe. She lived in Chiapas, Mexico, to be a witness for peace with the Zapatista rebels, volunteered in an elephant refuge in Thailand and drilled a water well in South Sudan. Her essay "Exposure" about travelling in Cambodia won the Silver in the Best Women's Travel Writing 2013 Solas Award. She is one of the founders of A Straw Mat, a women's writers group in upstate New York.

Megan Stielstra (meganstielstra.com) is the author of *Everyone Remain Calm*, a *Chicago Tribune* Favourite of 2011, and the Literary Director of the 2nd Story storytelling series (2ndstory. com). She's told stories for The Goodman, The Steppenwolf, The Museum of Contemporary Art, The Chicago Poetry Center, The Neo-Futurarium, Theater on the Lake and Chicago Public Radio, among others, and she's a staff writer for The Paper Machete live news magazine at The Green Mill. Her writing has appeared in *The Rumpus, The Nervous Breakdown*, PANK, *Other Voices, Make Magazine, Fresh Yarn* and elsewhere, and was recently selected by Cheryl Strayed for *The Best American Essays 2013*. She teaches creative writing at Columbia College and the University of Chicago.

Ben Tanzer is the author of the books *My Father's House, You Can Make Him Like You, So Different Now* and the forthcoming *Orphans* and *Lost in Space*, among others. Ben also oversees day to day operations of This Zine Will Change Your Life and serves as Director of Publicity and Content Strategy at Curbside Splendor Publishing. He can be found online at This Blog Will Change Your Life, the center of his growing lifestyle empire.

Sarah Yi-Mei Tsiang is the author of *Sweet Devilry* (Oolichan Books), which won the Gerald Lampert Award and was long-listed for the ReLit award. She is also the author of four children's books, including picture books and non-fiction, all with Annick Press. She is the editor of the anthology *Desperately Seeking Susans* and the forthcoming anthology *Tag: Canadian Poets at Play*. Her current poetry project *Status Update* was published by Oolichan in September 2013, and her new YA novel is forthcoming with Orca Books in 2014.

Wyl Villacres is from the north side of Chicago. He graduated from Columbia College with a degree in Fiction Writing and too much debt. His work has been featured in *Time Out Chicago, Hypertext, The Good Men Project, Thought Catalog, Bartleby Snopes* and elsewhere. Currently, he works in public relations and drains the ink from pens too fast. He loves to talk in 140 characters or less, so hit him up on Twitter: @wyllinois.

Jessica Westhead's novel *Pulpy & Midge* (Coach House Books, 2007) was nominated for the ReLit Award. She was shortlisted for the 2009 CBC Literary Awards, and selected for the 2011 Journey Prize anthology. Her short story collection *And Also Sharks* (Cormorant Books, 2011) was a *Globe and Mail* Top 100 Book and a finalist for the Danuta Gleed Short Fiction Prize.

Zoe Whittall is the author of two literary novels: the Lambda Award–winning *Holding Still for as Long as Possible* (House of Anansi) and *Bottle Rocket Hearts* (Cormorant Books), which was named a *Globe and Mail* Best Book of the Year, made the CBC Canada Reads Top Ten Essential Novels of the decade, translated into French and optioned for film. *Holding Still for as Long as Possible* was shortlisted for the Relit Award and named an American Library Association Stonewall honour book. She has published one short novel for adults with low literacy skills called *The Middle Ground* (Orca Books). She won the Writers' Trust of Canada's Dayne Ogilvie Award in 2008. Her poetry books include *The Best Ten Minutes of Your Life* (McGilligan Books), *The Emily Valentine Poems* (Snare Books) and *Precordial Thump* (Exile Editions). She edited the anthology *Geeks, Misfits & Outlaws* in 2003. She lives in Toronto.

Christopher Woods is a writer, teacher and photographer who lives in Texas. His books include a prose collection, *Under a Riverbed Sky*, and a book of stage monologues for actors, *Heart Speak*. His photography can be seen in his gallery, http://christopherwoods.zenfolio.com.

About the Editor

Shawn Syms has written about sexuality, culture, gender and politics for twenty-five years. His fiction, essays, poetry, journalism, political analysis, book reviews and other writing have appeared in more than fifty publications, including the *Globe and Mail, National Post, the Rumpus, the Collagist, Lambda Literary Review, subTerrain,* NOW, *This Magazine, Spacing, Xtra* and anthologies including the award-winning *First Person Queer, Love Christopher Street: Reflections of New York* and *The Journey Prize Stories 21*.

He has found it an unqualified delight to work with all of the absolutely fantastic contributors to *Friend. Follow. Text.* and would do it again in a heartbeat. Shawn has completed a collection of short fiction and is at work on a novel.

Permissions

Friend. Follow. Text.